A CONVENTIONAL BOY

ALSO BY CHARLES STROSS

CHARLES STROSS

▶◀▶◀▶◀▶◀▶◀▶◀▶◀▶◀▶◀

A CONVENTIONAL BOY

TOR PUBLISHING GROUP

NEW YORK

A CONVENTIONAL BOY

A Tordotcom Book
Published by Tom Doherty Associates / Tor Publishing Group
120 Broadway
New York, NY 10271

www.torpublishinggroup.com

Tor® is a registered trademark of Macmillan Publishing Group, LLC.

The Library of Congress Cataloging-in-Publication Data is available upon request.

ISBN 978-1-250-35784-7 (hardcover)
ISBN 978-1-250-35787-8 (ebook)

Our books may be purchased in bulk for promotional, educational, or business use. Please contact your local bookseller or the Macmillan Corporate and Premium Sales Department at 1-800-221-7945, extension 5442, or by email at MacmillanSpecialMarkets@macmillan.com.

First Edition: 2025

Printed in the United States of America

0 9 8 7 6 5 4 3 2 1

For old gamers everywhere

A CONVENTIONAL BOY

I

►◄►◄►◄►◄►◄

There was only one kind of weather in Camp Sunshine, and the wind threw rain by the rattling bucketload against the office window as Derek leaned myopically close to the typewriter's platen. He dabbed a blob of correction fluid onto the stencil, biting his upper lip with concentration:

CANP NEWSLETTER, MAT 15th

Derek sighed. "I need new glasses," he muttered, flipping them up onto his forehead so that he could squint the page into focus. A second blob followed the first, along with a sigh of exasperation. *Am I turning long-sighted as well?* He'd heard that happened with age. But the traveling optician wasn't due to visit again for another couple of months. *I'll just have to wait.* The correcting fluid stubbornly refused to dry:

CAMP NEWSLETTER, MAY 15th

Greetings to our new readers! This is the Camp Sunshine newsletter, brought to you by the Arts and Entertainments Office and edited by Derek Reilly.

WHAT'S NEW IN ARTS AND ENTS

We're in for a rainy May, so this month we're bringing you a shimmering schedule of indoor arts and pursuits. Jenny Morgan will again be teaching her extremely popular course in basket-weaving in Crafts Block 'C' on Tuesday afternoons, and Ryan O'Neill will be facilitating a workshop on Mayan poetry—

Derek lost himself in concentration, and laboriously typed another ten whole lines without needing any more of the precious correction fluid—it was fiendishly hard to get management to sign off on the stuff. The keys of the manual typewriter thwacked into the stencil, gouging letter-shaped indentations as he stolidly hammered out the news, referring occasionally to handwritten notes that he took from an in-tray. After transcribing each item he speared the notes on a rusting six-inch nail, where they fluttered in the draft from the window. Another jugful of water splashed off the glass and gurgled down the side of the Portakabin: Derek grunted and typed on and on, marching down the front page in disciplined single-spaced silence.

"Derek? Coo-ee!"

The door burst open, admitting a howling gust of rain and an unwelcome interloper.

"Hello, Marge."

Marge—Margaret Nash, plump and busily forty-ish—unzipped her bright yellow kagoule and hung it atop Derek's on the coat hook behind the door. "I brought you the *Gazette*," she said brightly. "It's Baltic out there! Is the kettle on?"

"It just boiled." Derek peered at his nearly completed front page. He had a vague recollection of switching on the electric kettle awhile ago. Time really flew by when you were cutting a stencil. Marge sidled over to the chipped Formica worktop at the far side of the cabin and readied two tea mugs, with a prodigious clanking and clattering of crockery. "Any news?"

"Oh, you!" She chuckled as she switched the kettle on again. It began to rattle and hiss: the solitary filament bulb dangling from the ceiling flickered, a victim of the ancient camp wiring. "Iris was saying something about the *public private partnership* that's just come in"—she emphasized the unfamiliar phrase—"about us all having to move out for six months while they rebuild everything."

"*What?*" Derek finally looked up: "What did you just say?"

"The reconstruction! The budget's come through." Marge looked uncertain. "She says we'll all have to move out. All of us lifers."

"All of . . ." Derek trailed off uncertainly. He shook his head. "She can't mean it. There must be some mistake?"

"Of course there's a mistake!" She sniffed, pointedly. "We wouldn't *be* here if there wasn't *some mistake*. But this rumor's true, for sure. The camp's closing while they rebuild the accommodation blocks, and Iris says they're going to rehouse us for the duration."

"But what about the, the regular in-inmates?" Derek stared at his almost-finished front page, totally perplexed. "Are *they* going to be moved?"

"Oh, you! Of course they're going to be moved!" The kettle gurgled to a crescendo and clicked off; Marge slopped near-boiling water into the two mugs, then put it down. "I heard they've got another camp all ready," she said confidingly. "Somewhere in the Welsh borders, or maybe South Georgia. It's going to be announced tomorrow morning at roll call."

"But, but—" The nearly finished stencil mocked him from behind the platen. "—what about my newsletter? It's going to the duplicator before then."

"You'll just have to do a special edition!" she said, showing no sign of awareness of the extra day's work she was prescribing: "Think of it as an exclusive! Isn't it exciting?"

►◄►◄►◄

Marge and Derek were both lifers: long-term inhabitants of Camp Sunshine who had arrived there through an unhappy chain of circumstances many years ago, and who had failed, for their own peculiar reasons, to reintegrate into civil society.

Most of Camp Sunshine's population were transients, consigned to the camp therapists for reprogramming and rehabilitation prior to release back into the community. In most cases mere months separated their arrival (raving and straitjacketed in the back of a fake ambulance at midnight, their imprecations stifled by the containment grids built into the walls of the prisoner transport vehicles) from their departure (with friendly if slightly uncomprehending goodbyes, clutching a cheap overnight bag as they waited for the minibus to the railway station). If someone was still there after a year, it meant one of two things: either they were a member of staff, or the Laundry had fucked up.

The Laundry—not its real name, but it had been established during wartime in offices above a Chinese laundry in Soho, and the name had stuck—was the department of the Secret State charged with defending Great Britain against occult threats. Mathematics is more than an abstract intellectual pursuit; when we solve certain theorems we set up disturbances in the Platonic realm of Theory, creating echoes which beings in parts of the multiverse far stranger than our own can tap into. Theoretical computer science is a branch of formal logic—itself a branch of mathematics—which encompasses some very disturbing phenomena, including applications of computational demonology. And where you get demons, you get worshipful cultists.

The government had eventually learned—the hard way—that killing dissidents—or cultists—was counterproductive. It was better by far to monitor the harmless ones and only arrest the violent cases, then deradicalize or deprogram them at suitably secluded sites before releasing them back into society. Temporary disappearances could be explained with a variety of cover stories, but mass graves increasingly tended to leak ghosts these days. Furthermore, like armed political radicals, followers of the Elder Gods were less likely to fight to the bitter end if they knew they would not be killed if they surrendered. For these and other reasons, the Public Control Department of the Laundry pursued a tedious course of containment and harm reduction—and Camp Sunshine was a key component of the war against the cults.

Camp Sunshine was not exactly a prison, although an inmate who tried to walk to the gray-green fells of the Lake District visible in the distance would inevitably find their feet leading them back to the huddle of buildings at the foot of the isolated valley. (And the less said about the fenced-off driveway leading to the nearest road, the better.)

The facility had been built by Pontins Holiday Camps in the 1950s. Pontins marketed their holiday camps on the basis of sun, sand, and fun—a cheap all-included package holiday experience suitable for all the family, a short coach ride from the factory gate for those enlightened workplaces who ran annual summer clubs.[1] Camp Sunshine was an experimental attempt to break out of their seaside niche and cash in on the hill-walking market. But it was doomed to failure from the very start by the whimsical microclimate of the Cumbrian valley it was situated in. The Lake District is one of the most beautiful, if hilly, areas of North West England, but it's also notorious for its rain and Camp Sunshine sat on the lee side of a low mountain, downwind of a semipermanent hairball of dank, gray cloud.

Alternately freezing cold and raining, and cursed in the rare intervals of sunshine by midges that had apparently evolved from stealth-equipped horse flies, the package holiday entrepreneur finally gave up and traded Camp Sunshine to the government in settlement of a tax bill after three disastrous summer seasons in a row.

The Laundry had not been at the top of the list of organizations on whose behalf the Ministry of Defense bid for the land. But the Adjutant General's Corps rejected it for a military prison (hardship pay for the guards had been an issue), then the Air Force passed on it for a radar site (not much use in a valley), and the Fleet Air Arm didn't want it for a bomb range. At which point it defaulted to the lowest priority user: and so it was that Camp Sunshine was taken over by the Laundry and run on a shoestring budget, paint peeling, weary, and unmodernized since the early 1950s.

Camp Sunshine had never delivered on Pontins's promise of sun, sand, and fun. Instead it rained sideways eight days a week, the local mice had evolved webbed toes and were working on gills, and such recreational necessities as paper and crayons were strictly rationed lest the inmates amuse themselves by sketching elder signs in their cell blocks after lights-out.

Derek was admitted to Camp Sunshine in 1984. Like everyone else he arrived in the back of an ambulance, straitjacketed and sedated. He was admitted as part of a batch, along with his friends

---

1. By the twenty-first century they were in decline, market cannibalized by cheap flights to the Costa del Sol and Ibiza, and a victim of rising expectations for those British adventure parks that had installed high-g roller coasters and go-kart tracks.

Ian, Tony, and Nigel. Ian's usual character was a level-eight halfling thief, Tony had a sixth-level dual-class half-elven fighter/mage, and Nigel a seventh-level human cleric. Derek, of course, was their Dungeon Master—or, as it said on the charge sheet, "suspected cult leader."

What had happened was this: a concerned teacher, sensitized to the possibility of the occult dangers inherent in D&D by a Chick Publications comic someone had left in the staff break room, called an anti-terrorist tip line. "Last night I cast my *first* spell! This is *real* power!" boasted one of the children in the comic, and the teacher (being of an earnest, not to say religious, bent) desperately wanted to talk to someone about the problem pupils in Class 4B. He'd overheard them talking Demogorgon and Asmodeus behind the bike sheds, and the world of tabletop role-playing games was sufficiently unheard-of in southeast England at the time that the duty officer in Dansey House thought it better to be safe than sorry, and sent a snatch squad.

The snatch squad did their usual thing: they secured the ritual paraphernalia in accordance with their standard secure containment protocol, then detained the suspects before delivering them to Camp Sunshine for investigation and deprogramming. The family members were left memories of the disappeared going on a boating holiday in the lakes and a profound conviction that everything would be all right. Reports were written, memos sent, a case file created for Operation MIDNIGHT DUNGEON. Then the snatch squad went home—done and dusted.

But for Derek, the best years of his life were already over—and he was just fourteen years old.

▶◀▶◀▶◀

The Arts and Ents Portakabin sat at one side of the fenced-off administration block. It was separated from the inmate barracks by two more fences: one of them conventional, the other featuring sacrifice poles bearing the oddly misshapen skulls of eldritch ungulates and a series of wards fit to curdle the blood of any necromancer who clapped eyes on them. The rain was still bucketing down as Derek shrugged into his kagoule, zipped it all the way up to his chin, and dashed across the gravel-strewn mud to the permanent site office.

As a trusty—an inmate who had been deemed useful and co-opted by the short-staffed management to fill a zero-risk job, in exchange for pocket money and access to the staff break room and its flickering tube television—Derek was legitimately allowed to wander freely inside the perimeter fence. (A freedom he mainly used in order to stay as far away as possible from the more deranged short-termers cluttering up the high-security zone.) Now he opened the outer door to the site office, turned left along a narrow, paint-peeling corridor, walked to the end, and knocked on a door.

"Enter."

Derek opened the office door—sorcerously constrained to only allow entry with the permission of the occupant—and walked inside. Iris was working, or at least appeared to be working, so he sat in the least creaky visitor's chair and waited patiently for Mrs. Carpenter to finish whatever she was reading. *Admissions file,* he thought absently. (Blessed with a photographic memory, he'd long since learned to recognize all the different admin documents at a glance by their table layout. He'd created some of them himself. Knowing how to design a character sheet turned out to be a useful life skill after all, despite his mum's admonitions.) *Probably another of the Golden Promise people.* He tried to remember which bunch Mrs. Carpenter had been with when she was pulled in: Red Skull Cult, maybe? Or was she one of the Crawling Chaos crowd?

Like most of the other camp administrators, Mrs. Carpenter was an inmate—one who had come from the Laundry itself. She had done something unspeakable for which she was now paying the price: not so much one of the Slow Horses as a Slow Equoid. But because she'd been management level in her old job, she already had the necessary security clearances to work in camp admin. It was safe enough: she was watched and bound by *geas* to prevent her falling back into old bad patterns of behavior, and she could no more leave without permission than any other prisoner.

Mrs. Carpenter finally sat up and gave him a look that scattered his woolgathering thoughts like a blast of birdshot through a murmuration of starlings. It wasn't a *hostile* look, exactly, but it had more than a faint whiff of *what, now?*

Derek cleared his throat. "I, er, heard a rumor," he said experimentally, then his brain crashed and his lips froze and the world came to a screeching halt outside his head. "A-a-a-a—"

Mrs. Carpenter held up a hand, his cue for a time-out. "Sneeze or stutter?" she asked.

"Stutter." Simple binary questions were easily answered. Derek took a deep breath while he got his thoughts back in order, then tried again. "Marge said the reconstruction budget's been approved and I was w-wondering if I could ask you a few questions for the newslet-letter?" His stutter got a lot better—almost went away, in fact—if he got the words out fast enough. It was like rushing over a rope bridge, pointedly not looking d-d-d-*down*. Thought was the speech-killer.

"Of course. Let me just put this away." Iris stood, character sheet in hand. She walked to the wall of filing cabinets, muttering something as she passed her fingers over the front of a drawer. It opened just far enough to suck the pages right out of her hand before it slammed shut again. There were no writing implements on her desk: she wasn't so slack that she'd leave a *pen* in full view of the window, however many fences there might be between her office and the high-security zone. She walked back to her chair, dusted her hands on her jeans, then dropped her formality like a wet cloak. "How about we go to the break room for a cup of tea while I fill you in? You'll want to take notes." She gestured at the stationery cupboard he'd been wistfully looking at, unsealing it with a flicker of *mana*.

Oops, Derek thought guiltily. She'd somehow seen right through him. But—"It wasn't a pretext," he said defensively, "I really d-*do* want to write it up! Special issue, even."

"Teatime," she repeated firmly. Derek surrendered: he was at least a decade older than Iris but she clearly wore a +3 invisible cloak of authority, the same kind that head teachers, mothers, and policemen were all issued. She led him helplessly through to the break room, where somebody had already boiled the kettle.

Over the next half hour she gave him a quick rundown of the plans. "There is projected to be a four hundred percent increase in prisoner numbers over the next four years, due to circumstances you aren't cleared for," she began. *Are the stars coming right?* Derek pondered: there were plenty of rumors about *that,* an historic conjunction that thinned the walls between the worlds and brought the creepy-nasties out to play, making it easier to practice all sorts of mischief and magic. But he didn't dare ask—loose lips didn't sink ships half so much as they led to some energetic jobsworth organizing a fake boating accident, so that some poor fool like Derek ended up spending the next thirty years in pokey.

(Nigel, Tony, and Ian had been bound to silence and released into the wild under false identities pretty much as soon as Psych and Cults realized their mistake, a year after the midnight snatch. But Derek had swallowed too much esoteric lore about gods and demigods, then gone diving for legends and fables in the mythology section of the school library to customize the campaign he was running. It took them too long to work out that he was just a harmless Nerd of Dungeon Mastery with a stutter, some signs of mild autism, and an iffy talent. Once stripped of supportive family and friends, he was effectively institutionalized. Camp Sunshine was worse than a prison: it had become his home.)

"So we're all going to have to move out for at least six months," Iris was explaining. "They've prepared a temporary facility for you—a room in an approved safe house—and apparently there'll be some job-related training. When the Phase One construction is complete and it's time to move the trusties and admin teams back you'll be offered full-time employment on-site. You'll be an official staff member of the Arts and Entertainments department! Isn't that good?" She smiled at him encouragingly, so Derek nodded, even though something inside him wanted to curl up and die. "You'll be paid more, and though security will be tighter you'll be housed in the staff wing—there'll be much fewer restrictions there, you can even play video games and have your own DVD player." Derek nodded. He'd seen adverts for DVD players and video games on the black-and-white TV. They didn't make much sense to him, but he was sure there was a reason why people wanted them.

"When is it starting?" Derek asked.

"What, the phased shutdown?" Mrs. Carpenter side-eyed him. "Have you counted the prisoner intake this month?" Derek shook his head. "We stopped taking in new subjects three weeks ago—they're all going to Camp Tropicana instead." Camp Tropicana was on Mingulay in the Outer Hebrides, which had been vacated by its last residents in 1912. "What's coming next is phased discharge plus care in the community for all the level-four inmates"—the ones within spitting distance of sanity, who could be trusted to refrain from sacrificing the neighbor's children to Dagon—"then the hard cases will be shipped up to Tropicana and those of us who are essential adjuncts get rehoused along with the permanent staff. Don't worry, it's all planned, all you need to do is pack your personal effects when it's time. For now, we just pretend everything is normal so we don't upset the unstable."

"So . . . a few weeks?" Derek asked, slack-jawed.

Mrs. Carpenter nodded. "A few weeks," she agreed, "then all of this will be demolished!" She looked around the shabby room as if seeing it for the first time: the damp patches near the corners of the ceiling, the carpet that had once been the color of boiled Brussels sprouts, the MAGIC CIRCLE OF SAFETY public information posters. "It'll be the end of an era. Can't come soon enough, if you ask me."

"I'd better g-go and write it all up." Derek stood hastily, folding and double-folding his sheet of note paper.

"Do remember to run your draft past Barry in Censorship before you publish." Mrs. Carpenter grinned encouragingly. "I can't wait to see it!"

▸◂▸◂▸◂

That evening, after eating his dinner in the canteen (third sitting, as usual), Derek returned to his bedroom in a state of heightened anxiety, where he considered his options.

As a trusty and a lifer Derek rated various privileges, from post-room access and television viewing rights to a room of his own. It wasn't a cell: the door had a lock, but he had his own key to keep out other inmates. There was a narrow bed he'd never shared with anyone, a washbasin, an overstuffed armchair, and a bookcase. He had a collection of old clothbound notebooks, rule books, games magazines he'd been permitted to subscribe to, and library loans. The bookcase was an office castoff he'd been permitted to repurpose: it locked using a different key, and would sound a *very* loud alarm if he left the room without securing it.

Derek also had a desk with a folding camp chair. He'd spent years at this desk, studying the school curriculum they'd grudgingly permitted him—there'd been no exams, but he'd had plenty of time to study to A-level standard in those subjects that could be completed with pencil and paper. The desk, too, had a lockable stationery drawer, where he kept his writing implements, current notebook, and the papers for the play-by-mail game he ran. At the back of the drawer he kept his dice bag: it was to this that he resorted when he needed to calm his nerves and choose a course of action. And it was in an envelope taped to the underside of this drawer that Derek kept his biggest secret.

When he was eleven Derek had taught himself to type on his mum's battered manual portable typewriter. (It had made DM'ing for his mates easier: he knew how to use carbon papers and produce legible handouts.) Now his skills came in handy for producing the camp newsletter on the antique equipment in the trusty's Portakabin—nothing electronic, electronics were *dangerous,* you could summon nightmares with electronics—but he had the use of a wide-carriage Imperial '66' and a 1950s stencil duplicator. As it fell to him to type up the newsletter, it had gradually also come to him to edit and write most of the contents.

The first rule of Camp Sunshine was: "Don't upset the patients." Too much information about the outside world was held to cause agitation and disruption among the newly committed, who were encouraged to think of their involuntary incarceration as a holiday from the bad influences that had led them to practice twisted rituals and solve dark equations. But something that outwardly resembled a newspaper in form if not content[2] had been deemed to

---

2. Not unlike *USA Today.*

be useful, signaling normality in the minds of the disturbed, and it had to be produced locally.

Derek had been granted newspaper and TV privileges so that he could cull entertaining but essentially meaningless snippets for the *Camp Sunshine Times*. The highlight of his morning was scanning the local newspapers (the *Lancaster Advertiser* and the *Scarfolk Courier* in particular), and every day brought him one or two useful clippings. Every week he typed them up on four sides of A4, cutting the waxed stencil sheets in the process, then (subject to the censor's stamp of approval) ran off fifty copies on the clattering hand-cranked Gestetner mimeograph.

What Barry in Admin (the censor) didn't know was that in addition to the cuttings Derek culled for the *Camp Sunshine Times*—lawnmower road rage in the suburbs, school crossing warden receives medal for fifty years of service—Derek furtively maintained his own morgue of newspaper articles of interest. Any time an article about games showed up, he cut it out (making sure to trim some other random column-inches for plausible deniability) and added it to his secret stash. And the day before yesterday, he'd stumbled across a very interesting piece tucked away on page seventeen of the *Scarfolk Courier*:

Game Players Roll in to Scarfolk Hotel for Annual Conference

DiceCon 16, the North West's annual convention for role-playing nerds and people who like to dress up as elves, is coming to Scarfolk for the first time this year. A fixture of the Blackpool off-season, the convention received a warm welcome from the Scarfolk Council Tourist Board after a massive blaze tore through their regular venue at the Blackpool Grand Hotel. The event has been relocated to the Britannia Hotels Georgia Inn, and attendees may book accommodation with a convention discount. There are also beds available at the Scarfolk Central Youth Hostel. There is going to be a marketplace, various role-playing tournaments, a fancy dress masquerade, and an awards ceremony. Memberships are still available for £30 on the door. Friday 18th to Sunday 20th inclusive . . .

Derek smoothed the clipping on his writing desk, then laboriously copied it by hand into his current notebook. He'd never been to a convention but it sounded like a lot of fun. It also sounded daunting, despite the patronizing tone of the newspaper article. Even leaving aside the challenge of getting there, he'd have to work out how to pay for a room and how to buy a membership. How to talk to people who were *interested* in games. How to talk to people who *didn't* know how to summon a Level Three Manifestation of Inchoate Dread and send it forth to drench the walls in blood and entrails if they got their hands on a stub of pencil for just thirty seconds. How to emulate the appearance of a normality he'd only caught fractured glimpses of out of the corners of his eyes for the past third of a century. How to cross a street again, how to buy a bus ticket, what *beer* tasted like . . .

Agitated, Derek slid the clipping into his envelope. Then he pulled out the black velvet dice bag with the uneven stitches he'd laboriously made for his twentieth birthday, checked that the curtains were shut and the door was locked, and tipped the precious cargo onto his desk.

More than fifteen years ago he'd hatched a foolproof escape plan. Unfortunately by then he had nowhere to go. Less than a month after he and his gaming group had been incarcerated, an overenthusiastic jobsworth in Masking and Concealment had arranged a fake boating accident and four closed-coffin funerals. (Derek had been officially declared dead; when the others were released they'd required new identities—that jobsworth had ended up costing the agency a lot of money.)

But now Derek's home was about to be demolished and he had no reason to stay. Nothing could, or would, be the same again. So why *not* pretend he was Cinderella and her Fairy Godmother rolled into one (albeit rather more male, portly, and middle-aged than Disney dictated)? Why *not* magic up a pumpkin carriage and mouse-footmen, pack up his dice bag, and say goodbye to the ashes and chores of quotidian life? Roll versus Wisdom to run away to the big city and have an adventure unsupervised by the camp administration: roll versus Intelligence to win the tournament: roll versus Charisma to get the girl (Derek had little idea what that involved, but it sounded like something normal adult males aspired to). Derek wanted it all: but above all else he wanted a taste of freedom before his fiftieth birthday.

Derek picked out certain platonic solids among the dice he had carved by hand from the car park gravel and shattered dreams littering Camp Sunshine: then he made a silent wish, and rolled the oracular bones.

▸◂▸◂▸◂

Here is what it is like to awaken one morning, and discover that in your sleep, instead of being transformed into a monstrous verminous bug, you have been mistakenly detained in a camp for dangerous cultists:

It *sucks*.

For the first week, Derek was kept in a windowless prison cell with only his pajamas to wear. The light bulb switched off periodically. Meals—some kind of cereal with milk, some kind of gray stew, and some kind of meat pasty—came through a slot in the door. They were served in cardboard bowls with a disposable wooden spoon, and if he didn't eat fast enough the bowl turned soggy and disintegrated. Once a day (he was pretty sure it was only once a day, going by the lights-out cycle) men came to the door and put a hood on his head and handcuffs on his wrists, then walked him to another room with two chairs, a table, and a man who repeatedly asked him meaningless questions. The first time they did this, Derek cried; the second time, he threw a tantrum—both times, the guards took him back to his cell and left him alone. There were no beatings, and when Derek realized what this might mean it scared him even more.

On the third day he answered the questions. (Have you ever summoned Azathoth? What is the square root of minus one? Can you prove the consistency of Peano arithmetic using only the axioms of Peano arithmetic, rather than a stronger system like Zermelo–Fraenkel set theory?) (His answers were: *Who? I don't know, I don't understand this stuff.*)

On the fourth day, because he was bored, he answered the questions creatively. For some reason his interrogator didn't believe him.

There were still no beatings, but his supper did not arrive before lights-out.

On the fifth day there was no interrogation, but right after he returned his breakfast bowl the slot in the door opened and a book slid through it. It was his very own dog-eared copy of the *Gods, Demigods, and Heroes* supplement—he'd written his name on the third page. Derek sat cross-legged on the bed and rocked back and forth cradling the closed book, too distressed to read. Lunch came. Afterward he felt very tired, and when he awakened the book was gone.

On the sixth day . . .

The interrogations continued until Derek lost track of time. Sometimes they'd change interrogator—blindfolded, he could only tell by their voices—but always the nonsense questions, repeated in various shapes and sizes and flavors until he wanted to throw up. Had he ever tried to summon a succubus? How often did he gather with Ian, Tony, and Nigel for ritual purposes? Did he know of any other congregations (or covens, or cells)? Was there a polyhedron that admits only an anisohedral tiling in three dimensions? What bindings had he and his coreligionists performed? Could he write a computer program to prove whether another arbitrary program would halt in finite time when executed?

Then, after a timeless age of misery, everything changed.

While he slept he had been moved to a different room. He was awakened by light, but it was a more natural illumination than the electric bulb in the recessed niche behind a pane of wired glass. He had a window, and painted walls, and a battered metal locker—like the one he had at school, but without a lock—standing beside a table and chair. Outside the window he saw gray-green hills and gray-white clouds. It was, although he did not know this yet, his first view of Camp Sunshine, and it seemed glorious, so he cried.

►◄►◄►◄

Derek's dice roll told him he should go to the convention, but they didn't tell him how to get there. Not to worry: he would take it one step at a time. The first step—three steps, actually—was to escape from Camp Sunshine without being detected, so that he had a good head start on pursuit.

This was easier said than done. Camp Sunshine was designed to be escape-proof. The only people who came here were prison service officers who had been read into the program by Detention Admin, agents of the Laundry—more formally, Q-Division of the Special Operations Executive, a secret government agency left over from the Second World War and tasked with defense against occult threats—and the sundry cultists, necromancers, and computer scientists-gone-bad who were targeted by the Laundry. Sometimes the categories overlapped, as in Mrs. Carpenter's case. Occasionally someone like Derek wound up in here by mistake. But whichever category you belonged to, you only got in or out inside a vehicle with a steel body, grounding chains, and a very special kind of pass. The side of the camp that didn't curve back on itself through spacetime was fenced off from the outside world by concentric containment grids and the shadows between the fences lay outside this universe—as did the alien predators that lurked in them. Nobody in the camp had seen one of them and lived. So the initial problem confronting Derek consisted of (a) getting into an outbound vehicle, (b) getting out of it at its destination, and (c) not being noticed.

There were no computers in Camp Sunshine, for computers were powerful thaumaturgic tools and giving computers to cultists was like giving assault rifles and sugary drinks to toddlers. Everything ran on paper, and outside the administration block paper and pencils were rationed. Modern electronics were forbidden even in the offices: it was all manual typewriters and carbon paper in triplicate. Which certainly made things tough for any inmate planning to brute-force the perimeter firewall by throwing demons at it—but it also made things hard on the administrators.

Mail came in and mail went out every day, along with paper and typewriter ribbons and other stationery. But they inspected the underside of the mail van with a mirror on a pole before it left every time, just in case there were any fugitives clinging to the underside, and the carbon paper was double-counted. Once or twice a week a secure transport would arrive or depart. Those were usually disguised as an ambulance or a Police Ford Transit, the kind with blue lights on top, two rows of seats, and a window-less, lockable cage in the back for prisoners.

To the best of Derek's knowledge, since he had arrived at the camp a couple of would-be escapees had gotten as far as stage (a). Familiar faces had disappeared from the canteen, only to reappear a few days later—thinner, with bags under their eyes and a perpet-ually haunted expression. When asked what had happened they fell silent or shuffled away, eyes downcast and shoulders hunched. And nobody had succeeded in getting as far as stage (b). One ter-rible day in 1996 a high priest of Azathoth had teamed up with an expert systems theoretician who'd been driven mad by Dempster-Shafer logic: they'd gone full Bonnie and Clyde and hijacked a mail van using hand-carved slide rules and a "sacrificial dagger" looted from the kitchen stores. The camp administration had re-voked the protective ward on the van as soon as it cleared the inner gates, and the following day the moving shadows beyond the fence had been fat, sluggish, and horribly satiated.

But Derek had a resource that none of the other would-be es-capees had: time. The average detainee stayed for three to six months before their ticket of leave came. Derek, in contrast, had lived there for decades. And over the years Derek had become aware of patterns in the cycle of escape and recapture (or escape and digestion) that eluded the transient population. He had no-ticed that people entered the camp all the time—and then *left* the camp. The trick was to do so with permission. Escapees always got caught, but permission was simply a matter of filing the cor-rect paperwork: and Derek had paperwork down cold.

The morning after Mrs. Carpenter explained the redevelop-ment initiative, Derek sat down in the newsletter room and bashed out an article singing the praises of the planned redevelopment. *New furniture! Fresh carpet! Air-conditioning!* There were even rumors about computers with access to the internet coming to the site office, although Derek was inclined to discount such wild fan-tasies as too ridiculous for words. (He wasn't sure what computers were good for, and TV made the internet out to be a dangerous swamp full of sickos and stalkers. He thought it was probably a bit like sex: something people swore was better than sliced bread, but that had passed him by for some reason.)

I suppose I'll find out soon enough, he thought, as he wound a blank form he wasn't supposed to have through the newsroom typewriter and filled out a travel authorization and a counterfoil pass.

Draft newsletter—and forged travel paperwork—went into a file, and Derek headed across to the site office. Mrs. Carpenter wasn't on hand (he'd carefully checked the rota: she was on her lunch break), which meant the outer office was staffed by . . . ah, it was Mr. Berry's turn today. Mr. Berry was sixty-ish, with sallow hair and gray skin (or maybe it was gray hair and sallow skin? In the perpetual Camp Sunshine overcast they were hard to distinguish). His suit fit him like a mummy's windings, and he had a graveyard cough that manifested every winter.

"Derek?" he wheezed. A perpetual miasma of cheap cigarettes clung to his yellowing shirt cuffs. "Where are you going?"

Derek held up the file. "N-newsletter draft for Iris," he announced, pausing at Mrs. Carpenter's door. "Can I drop this off?"

"Go right ahead." Mr. Berry turned back to face the window, which he spent hours staring out of every day. By the time Derek entered Mrs. Carpenter's den Mr. Berry had forgotten him. Derek remembered when George Berry had arrived, a seasoned forty-something veteran of Detention Admin. Derek had already been a trusty back then: as far as Mr. Berry was concerned he was part of the furniture, a walking, cardigan-and-spectacle-wearing piece of equipment for composing the camp newsletter.

Without bothering to close the office door Derek slid the folded travel authorization form into Mrs. Carpenter's out-tray, which would be collected in half an hour, just before the end of the second lunch sitting. Then he left the folder with the draft newsletter in the middle of her blotter, awaiting approval.

The counterfoil pass itself—the ticket which would let him onto the prisoner transport tomorrow morning, tomorrow being Friday—remained in his pocket. When he presented it, the driver and guard would check him off against an approved list. The travel authorization form (assuming nobody noticed it was a ringer) would put him on that list. If his dice had given him the correct serial numbers and approval codes—he'd rolled the oracular bones on a number of less critical form-filling experiments over the years—they'd have no reason to doubt him.

He had only to return to his bedroom that evening, assemble his kit, and present himself at the gate after breakfast and he was as good as free.

So why did freedom feel like standing blindfolded at the top of a cliff, preparing to jump?

▶◀▶◀

Barely an hour after he stepped off the top of the cliff, Derek was feeling distinctly carsick. To be fair, it was the first time he'd been in a moving vehicle in more than a quarter of a century. After crawling for a quarter of a kilometer through the shades and shimmering veils that surrounded Camp Sunshine, the driver reached the exit from the track leading to the camp. He floored the accelerator as if all the eaters out of some arcane hell were after his soul, hurling the Transit along a winding, narrow mountain road with a steep drop-off to one side. The van had a shot shock absorber and lurched horribly as he took the hairpin bends too fast. Derek looked out of one side window at the dry stone wall hurtling past centimeters from his nose, checked the other—nothing but sky and clouds—and forced his eyes shut.

On today's run, the van was empty apart from the driver, Derek, Derek's small tartan suitcase (inherited from a long-departed transient), and a payload of inter-office mail stashed in the safe in the back. A sheep wandered onto the road ahead: the driver gurned horribly, dropped the clutch, and revved the engine until the animal shambled placidly onto the embankment. Then he took off again with a screech of tires, aiming at the edge of the cliff just past the next bend. "Where d'you want dropping, mate?" he asked Derek.

Derek swallowed. "At the next bus stop, please?" Buses were safe: he knew how to buy a ticket with cash, how to read a timetable . . .

"There's a couple in the next town. Where you off to? Maybe I could drop you closer—"

"I'm h-heading for London," Derek said. "I mean, j-j-just catching a bus to the train station." Derek's stutter tended to come out when he was lying, and although he'd rehearsed his cover story repeatedly under the bedding after lights-out, his guilty conscience prevented him from delivering it flawlessly. But the driver accepted his excuse without quibbling. Fifteen minutes later the van slowed and pulled over in a picturesque street lined with tearooms, a pub, and a couple of camping-and-hiking supply stores.

"Penrith! Bus stop's to your right, it's the middle of the week so there should be one along in an hour or so," the driver told Derek as he climbed out, clutching his tartan suitcase to his chest like a life preserver. "See you around!"

"I hope—" Derek began hesitantly, just as the van screeched away from the curb in a cloud of choking diesel fumes. He coughed for a minute, then straightened up. "Oh well."

The clock was ticking, but he'd rolled for surprise and held the initiative: so he marched across the road (there was barely any traffic) and looked around the bus shelter. Fogged Perspex sheets covered an empty white space where there ought to be a timetable. A sign at one end announced service numbers for something called FIRSTBus; another pole staked out territory for StageCoach. "Uh," Derek said to himself, then sat down and shoved his right hand in his trouser pocket, which jingled heavily.

As a trusty, ever since 1989 Derek had been paid a stipend for his work on the camp newsletter. "All prisoners who participate in purposeful activity must be paid," said Prison Service Order 4460, and it applied just as much to Camp Sunshine as to any regular jail. But minimum wage law didn't apply, and Derek's salary had been the princely sum of twenty-five pence an hour.

On the other hand, there hadn't been a lot to spend his pocket money on. Derek didn't gamble, it was impossible to smuggle drugs into Camp Sunshine, and consumer electronics were forbidden. He'd been clocking up a thirty-hour work week for two and a half decades, and over the years it added up to nearly 400 pounds a year. Despite nuisance expenditures—postage and role-playing game rule books (the latter took months to arrive, thanks to the censors)—he'd managed to stash nearly two thousand pounds under the bed, most of it in pound coins. He had thirty of them in his pocket right now, because he wasn't sure quite how much an inter-city bus ticket would cost. He had another ten kilograms of coins in his suitcase, wrapped in rolls stitched from pillowcases to stop them from clanking, and a couple hundred in ten- and twenty-pound notes he'd swapped for cash with members of staff. He'd also packed three changes of underwear, a clean shirt, and his first edition AD&D rule books; his dice bag he kept in his jacket pocket.

It made him feel dangerous and nervous, walking around with a plaid treasure chest pulling painfully on his arm. But however often he swiveled his head, nobody seemed to be watching him: Penrith high street seemed remarkably short on muggers, unless muggers came camouflaged as brightly clad hill walkers.

A lilac-and-purple bus came wheezing along the high street and pulled up at the shelter. From its state of repair it had probably been in service since the end of the last ice age. A door hissed open and Derek stepped aboard. "Where are you going?" he asked the driver, who sat behind a glass screen.

"Morecambe by way of Bowness-on-Windermere and Scarfolk." The driver didn't look at him.

"And, er, how much is a ticket?"

"Five pounds ninety."

Derek peered at the driver and the rather odd machine covered in buttons next to a slot in the plastic shield. "Where do I put the money?" he asked.

Now the driver looked at him, his face eloquent disbelief personified. "In the slot." He pointed. "No change given."

"*Right*. I-I knew that." Derek counted out six pound coins and deposited them in the ticket machine, wincing internally at the extra half hour's labor he was giving the bus company for free. The machine whirred quietly and spat a piece of paper at him while the driver went back to staring out of the windscreen, evidently bored out of his skull.

Derek took his ticket and walked to the back of the almost-empty vehicle, careful to give no sign of his inner excitement. He found a seat, hauled his bag up beside him, and tried to sit still despite everything. Eventually the driver gave up waiting for additional passengers and moved off.

Yes! Derek exulted. He was on his way to DiceCon 16, and nothing could stop him now.

▸◂▸◂

In the event Derek's escape went according to plan, and his prediction of how long it would take for his absence to be noticed was spot-on.

Camp Sunshine's administration did not insist on a daily morning roll call. This had not always been the case: throughout the 1950s and 1960s the camp had been run by the prison service with advice and oversight from PCD and the Security Section. But as the years went by with no sign of a successful escape attempt, fashions in cult deprogramming changed, the original management team retired, and their replacements were earnest young men in tweed jackets with patched elbows who read books by R. D. Laing and Ivan Illich. They emphasized deinstitutionalization and rehabilitation, tried to turn the prison camp into a therapeutic environment, and abolished the most overt reminders of regimentation and incarceration. And when they, too, retired, their successors carried on the now established traditions of camp governance.

Derek had taken the time to eat a full cooked breakfast before he boarded the van because he was unsure when he'd next get a hot meal. So his presence had been subconsciously—if not formally—noticed that morning.

If his luck was *really* good, nobody would have noticed his escape until the following Monday. But Mrs. Carpenter had found his draft feature for the camp newsletter waiting on her desk, and Mrs. Carpenter was energetic and efficient. She was a former SOE subdepartment manager as well as an inmate. They'd put her in a position of responsibility for Arts and Entertainments to keep her busy. A&E didn't need much managing, but an idle Iris Carpenter was a dangerous thing, and she even worked weekends when the urge took her: so Iris read Derek's draft article and red-lined it.

And in midafternoon, annoyed by his persistent invisibility, she picked up the draft, walked to the site office to see Mr. Berry, and asked, "Have you seen Derek today? I've got some edits . . ."

►◄►◄►◄

"I'd, er, like to buy a membership pass for the conference." Derek sweated nervously as he stood in front of a table beneath the Dice-Con banner in the drab hotel lobby area.

It was midafternoon and Derek was hungry and footsore. The bus had carried him to Scarfolk—then out to an industrial estate in the middle of nowhere, because he hadn't known how to signal the driver to stop. Eventually he managed to get off, then walked a couple of kilometers back into town. And hadn't *that* been a strange experience? Just being able to walk in a straight line without having to stop and turn round after two hundred paces had left him jittery, hyper, and weak-kneed with a sudden apprehension of freedom. Then he'd had to ask around for directions to the convention hotel.

The first few people he approached had ignored him, until he worked out that the odd white plugs in their ears weren't hearing aids and the glowing things in their hands were phones. Then he'd had to explain that he'd lost his phone, and wasn't *that* odd. But he'd finally arrived, despite being shocky from the realization that he'd managed to escape and being battered on all sides by the unfamiliar. (It turned out that black-and-white TV was a *terrible* medium through which to keep up with the twenty-first century.) Now he was confronted by a desk covered in brutally futuristic-looking computers, behind which sat a girl and two boys—or students, Derek was out of touch with youth culture these days—trying very hard to ignore him.

"Excuse me?" he said again.

The bearded bloke in the Munchkin tee-shirt was busy explaining something tediously obvious to the spectacled girl—no, woman: she was at least in her midthirties, Derek realized—who had crossed her arms defensively and was leaning as far back in her chair as a Red Skull initiate cornered by a Mute Poet evangelist.

Beyond her, the skinny guy was rocking back and forth, repeatedly mouthing *yeah, yeah,* and rotating his wrist around some kind of gadget. His ears were plugged: no help from that quarter.

"Excuse me?" he repeated.

"—You can't multiclass as shadowdancer if you started out as a vanilla rogue and then picked assassin, it doesn't work that way—"

Wrong, patently wrong, but Derek wasn't going to correct him. "This-this *is* the registration desk for DiceCon sixteen?" he asked, raising his voice uncomfortably (meaning, to something approaching emphasis).

"Registration's closed," said Yeah-Yeah Man, just as the woman looked at Derek and sat up straight.

"Not for another three minutes!" Spectacle Woman said brightly, giving Yeah-Yeah Man an *I told you so* look. Leaning forward: "So you want to buy a day pass for tomorrow?"

"Y-yes—no! I mean, I want a full membership, for the entire conference?"

"Oh, right," Bearded Multiclass Guy looked annoyed. "That'll be thirty pounds. You need to fill this out." He shoved a character sheet at Derek.

"Y-yes, I can do that." Derek eagerly accepted the sheet, then his stomach sank. "I haven't got a pen."

Bearded Multiclass Guy smirked. "Riiight. What kind of gamer doesn't have a pen?"

Spectacle Woman rolled her eyes at Multiclass Guy and produced a cheap biro from the backpack beside her chair, which was bright blue and looked formidably technical to Derek. "Keep it," she told him, "I have plenty more where this one escaped from."

"R-right." Derek bent over the character sheet to conceal his confusion at being spoken to by a pretty woman—he was fairly sure she was pretty—who wasn't an initiate of some alarmingly sanguinary human sacrifice cult, and thus a lethal existential threat to any adult male virgin within a ten-kilometer radius. "Thank you." He hastily scribbled the bare minimum of details, including the address he'd grown up at and the home phone number, leaving the space for email blank.

"That'll be thirty pounds, please," she said, smiling at him from behind her thick-lensed glasses. Her brown eyes showed no sign of harboring a bottomless well of deep craziness, even though she was being inexplicably kind to a complete stranger.

"Just a minute." Derek reached into his pocket and began counting out a fistful of brassy coins, constructing a tower on the table in front of her. ". . . Twenty-six, twenty-eight, thirty. There!"

Bearded Multiclass Guy glowered, then looked at his companion. "You got the strong box, Linda?"

"I—" She froze for a moment. "Keith?"

Yeah-Yeah Man twitched guiltily. "Yeah?"

"Strong box, Keith." She waited patiently for him to snap out of whatever fugue state he'd lapsed into. "Where is it?"

"It's in Ops."

"Well *fetch it,* then." Her voice acquired an edge of steel. The penny dropped: Perhaps she was being nice to Derek to prove a point, to demonstrate how fed up she was with Keith and Bearded Multiclass Guy? "We don't want to keep this nice"—she glanced at the character sheet—"Derek waiting." Keith grumbled but shuffled off to fetch the cash tin obligingly. Meanwhile Linda looked up at Derek. "You're new, right?" He nodded. "Your first convention?" He nodded again.

"Do you even game, bro?" Bearded Multiclass Guy asked skeptically.

Derek's cheek twitched. "Yes, actually I do." He hefted his suitcase. "I've been running a play-by-mail campaign for the past twenty-eight years—"

"Well, *good,*" Linda said emphatically, cutting him off: "There's a dealer room through there, and on the other side there are breakout areas for sessions, there are talks and panels running in the main function space, they're serving refreshments from a table there, and—" She rattled through a list of attractions as she reached down into a cardboard box and pulled out a canvas tote full of papers and, judging from its weight, a hardcover manual—"a freebie from our sponsors, Omphalos Corporation, who are giving away a copy of their game *Bones and Nightmares* to all attendees."

"*Bones and Nightmares*?" Derek echoed: "What's the setting? What are the mechanics like?"

"You don't wanna play *that*," Bearded Multiclass Guy said dismissively. "It's really clichéd and there's a strong pay-to-play grift with the accessories, I mean real games start with the d20 core ruleset then—"

Keith returned, bearing a cash tin which he ceremoniously placed on the table. "Here," he grunted, and sat down.

Linda's hackles rose. "Hey, just because *you* don't get it—"

Derek cleared his throat. "I need somewhere to stay?" he said gently.

"Hotel front desk is behind you, I think they still have rooms. The Youth Hostel is first left when you go out the door, cross at the lights, second right, you can't miss it. Omphalos's games are all pyramid schemes—"

"—*Eye* in a pyramid, maybe—"

Linda scooped Derek's thirty pieces into the tin and passed him a slip of paper. "Ignore them and they'll go away," she told him, glowering at Keith and Bearded Multiclass Guy as they went at each other over the relative merits of different rule systems. "I'm off-shift in ten minutes. See you around later?"

"Okay," Derek said amiably: then he tiptoed away with bag in hand to book himself a room.

►◄►◄►◄

Buying—renting?—a hotel room was nothing like as easy as Derek had expected. Admittedly his expectations were based on endless *Fawlty Towers* reruns. Apparently they expected him to have a credit card or a driving license or other arcane certificates of participation that weren't so easy to forge with the facilities at Camp Sunshine. In the end he paid for three nights in advance, which wiped out almost his entire stash of twenty-pound notes. To add insult to injury, they called the manager out of her office to inspect the cash under a glowing purple light. But in the end money was money and a room was a room, and Derek got what his pre-rolled dice told him to ask for. There was a television with a very flat screen that looked like it had been squashed, and no channel buttons. There was a cramped but luxuriously equipped bathroom with an electric shower as well as a toilet, sink, and bathtub. The window opened over the car park, and there was a desk in front of it with a pile of brightly colored tourist leaflets and a gadget covered in buttons that he thought might be a modern telephone.

Derek shoved the leaflets in the bin and spread the contents of his goodie bag on the desk. There was a stapled pamphlet titled PROGRAM that turned out to contain the convention's Arts and Ents schedule for the weekend. Another couple of pamphlets turned out to be adverts for games. And the biggest thing in the bag was an A4 box, its lid depicting a queue of worshippers approaching an altar in a shadowy temple. It was titled *Bones and Nightmares*:

Build your congregation! Recruit missionaries! Infiltrate the Inquisition! Be the first to Immanentize YOUR Eschaton!

"Hmm," said Derek, unenthusiastically running a blunt thumbnail around the plastic caul the box was encased in. He shook the box and it disgorged a thick hardback manual, several printed sheets, a cardboard GM's screen, and a set of boringly mundane d20s. He rolled them on the tabletop but there was no buzz of magic, no softly glowing aura of possibility: they were as dead as the set of d6 from the staff room Monopoly set (which could only be signed out of the safe in Mrs. Carpenter's office with a permission slip from the warden himself).

The dice were dull, but the manual might be worth reading later: Maybe after curfew? Derek's stomach rumbled. The digital clock on the squished television said it was nearly four thirty. Time to look around the dealer room, then find something to eat.

The hotel might have struck a more critical eye than Derek's as shabby and run-down, but after Camp Sunshine it felt luxurious and well-maintained. The carpeted corridors soundlessly absorbed his footsteps. The doors neither slammed nor creaked, and it took him a little while to puzzle out how the lift buttons worked. But he mastered them like a pro, feeling a triumphant upwelling of XP as the doors slid open on the ground floor. He sauntered out trying to look bored, as if he did this sort of thing every year. Someone had helpfully put up printed signs directing attendees to the game rooms and program area, but the dealer room was closer. The door was propped open, and a bored, bearded guy was going through the motions of guarding it. Derek hovered for a few seconds before he realized he didn't need permission to enter, that he had *bought* permission in the shape of his membership badge. So in he went.

Half the room was lined with white-draped tables bearing displays of game boxes, miniatures, and accessories, and the other half was occupied by a passable replica of the temple from the cover of *Bones and Nightmares*. Derek barely had time to boggle at it before a pair of well-endowed young ladies in tight blue jeans and even tighter tee-shirts simultaneously aimed arc-light smiles at him and closed in. "Why, hello there!" purred the brunette cheerleader, while her blonde companion made an elaborate gesture with both hands. It was clearly some sort of sorcerous pass designed to take control of his limbic system: "Hi, cute guy! What's your name?"

"D-D-D-D—" Derek zoned out briefly. The name tag he'd carefully sewn a ward inside on the back of his shirt collar stung him back into sapience: "Derek," he finished, caught like a deer in the headlights. *Wandering Monster encounter,* he realized. *Don't show fear.* "Who are you?" he asked.

"She's Sister Selene!" said the brunette, pointing at her companion.

"And she's Sister Celeste!" said Sister Selene, before they succumbed to a fit of giggling which perplexed Derek.

"Out of *Bones and Nightmares*?" Celeste informed him, ending on an upward intonation that made it sound as if she was asking a question, which she clearly wasn't. "Our company's new game! We're launching it here and at other gaming conventions around the world this week! It doesn't go on sale until next month!"

Oh, realized Derek. "You work for Omphalos Corporation," he deduced.

"See? I told you he looked smart!" Selene beamed at Celeste, obviously lying through her teeth because Derek was certain she'd never seen him before in her life and therefore lacked any evidence on the basis of which to pass judgment on his cognitive functioning (or lack thereof). She focussed on Derek, targeting him with both her chest and a bright smile: "There's a tournament running tomorrow and Sunday, would you like to join?" she squeaked.

Derek did his best to pay her breasts exactly as much attention as they deserved, which was to say no more than any other magic weapon of +1 bamboozlement: "I'd love to," he forced out, trying not to choke on his traitorous tongue, "but I'm looking for people I run a play-by-mail game with and can't commit until we've arranged a face-to-face session."

It's a love bombing, he told himself. *They don't actually* like *you, they just want to* use *you.* Derek had come of age in a deprogramming camp for cultists. Cultists could love bomb like a B-52, and left their target in much the same state. He'd been a virgin when he arrived in Camp Sunshine, and he was still a virgin because he'd seen what happened to a desperate, unfortunate—desperately unfortunate—teenage inmate who had confessed his state in an attempt to get his ashes hauled. Cultists could extract *mana*—magical energy—from ritual sex, but even more *mana* could be obtained from human sacrifice. Derek knew exactly what they could do with the aid of a couple of crayons, a tablecloth, and a cleaver stolen from the kitchen: and he wanted none of it.

Something of this must have shown in his expression because Selene's smile dimmed. "Well, I hope to see you around!" she trilled with a goodbye wave, as Celeste took her arm and led her toward the polystyrene altar (which glowed an eerie indigo beneath the overhead ultraviolet spotlights). "It's not you, honey, he's just a fag," the brunette headhunter consoled her companion as she led her away: "or another bloody aspie, they must have a fucking vaccine factory here or something."

Derek ignored the rude dismissal and instead turned to inspect the rest of the dealer room. *That was very odd,* he mused as he bent over a table decked with typecases full of glittering dice. *Are cult recruiters common at conventions?* Never having been to one before he had no basis for comparison, *but,* he told himself, *if they* were *common, the Laundry would be onto them and I'd have a gaming group in my cell block instead of having to play by mail: Right?*

"Oof": someone grabbed Derek's shoulders. He jolted to a stop and tried not to topple over. They continued: "Why don't you watch—oh, it's you."

"I'm sorry," he said automatically. "Linda?"

"Yes, it is I." They blinked at each other through their respective glasses, then Linda seemed to realize she was holding on to him and let go. Details began to inflict themselves on Derek's overstimulated senses. The cuffs of her jeans had frayed where they covered the tops of her slightly grubby Docs, her breath smelt of strawberries, and she'd had her nose buried in a pamphlet when they collided. She appeared to have no designs on him, unlike the arc-light smiles of the Omphalos Corporation love-bombers: Linda might actually be safe to socialize with. "What?"

"N-nothing—" Derek mentally kicked himself—"I'm starving: is there somewhere to eat here?"

"Of course, your first convention?" Her lips quirked in a reflexive half smile. "Food and drinks aren't allowed in the dealer room, but there are snacks next door in the bar. I was just heading there myself."

"Mind if I j-join you?"

Linda paused momentarily, but her smile slipped as she followed his gaze and saw Celeste and Selene standing in a conspiratorial huddle with a pair of sleekly turned-out male counterparts. "Not at all. We'd better hurry. Don't make eye contact," she warned as she hurried toward the door.

"What happens if you make eye contact?" Derek asked as they reached the safety of the corridor.

Linda slowed. "They try and *recruit* you."

Her suppressed shudder told Derek everything he needed to know.

▶◀▶◀

An avalanche starts with a single snowflake, which triggers a cascading chain reaction. In the case of the Great Escape of 2010, the snowflake was a scribbled red note in the margin of Derek's article explaining the forthcoming closure and refurbishment of Camp

Sunshine. The note was simple enough, and familiar to secondary school students everywhere: *See me,* it said, the teacher's shorthand for "I have concerns (too many to enumerate in one squiggle)."

"Have you seen Derek today?" asked Iris: "I've got some edits for the next issue. I want him to get final copy to me before five o'clock—can you give this to him?"

"Haven't seen 'im since breakfast time." Mr. Berry coughed glutinously, then frowned up at her. "Is it urgent?"

"Well, if he doesn't get this before lunchtime it *could* be," Iris smiled toothily. "Do you think you could find him?"

Mr. Berry braced himself on the edge of his desk and grimaced as he forced himself to his feet. (His knees hated him and wanted him to suffer, and he believed in sharing their misery freely with those around him.) "I'll get me running shoes on," he promised, then shuffled painfully toward the door.

Time passed.

Iris was rechecking the monthly expenses spreadsheet with the Kurta mechanical hand-calculator chained to her desk—the figures in the paper ledger didn't recalculate themselves—when Mr. Berry creaked back into her purview. "He ain't there," he said, in a tone of gloomy satisfaction.

"Where is the *there* you are referring to, precisely?" Iris asked, putting down the peppermill-shaped calculator and focussing her attention on him.

Mr. Berry wilted. "I checked the newsletter office. Then I checked the canteen, and—" he cringed—"knocked on his bedroom door. Can't find 'im, Missus Carpenter, can't find 'im anywhere."

Iris sighed, then closed the cover on her ledger and padlocked the Kurta back in its cubbyhole. "I'll go and talk to Security," she said. "Don't you worry about it, I'll deal with him. He's probably just found a new hidey-hole." She was lying, of course: All her built-in alarm bells were ringing. Derek was nothing if not predictable. At this time of late afternoon he'd be in the newsletter office, the break room, or the bathroom. Mr. Berry was so slow that he'd certainly have run into Derek either coming or going as he made his rounds. The time to worry about predictable people was when they broke their routine: and so Iris worried.

Half an hour later, Iris, Mr. Berry, and David Turnbull, the Head of Security, agreed that Derek couldn't be located in any of his usual locations. It was not yet an emergency, but it was close enough to send the camp administration into a frantic flurry of checking seldom-used closets and making notes on numerous clipboards: the organizational equivalent of searching every pocket in all the jackets on the coatrack to locate the missing keys. And after an hour of *that,* as they were approaching a mandatory camp roll call, someone else (a clerk in Human Resources) spotted something out of place on a vehicle movement form, and the shit hit the fan.

"Duty Officer, please," Turnbull spoke into the mouthpiece of the antiquated telephone handset that usually gathered dust beneath a padlocked cover in the Security Office. Portly, methodical, slowly working his way towards retirement, David was not prone to displays of emotion. Even so, one eyebrow twitched as he spoke: "This is the Security Office at Camp Sunshine. Yes, and I'm sorry to interrupt your supper, but I have a Code Yellow notification for all stations. We have a—yes, that's Code Yellow—we have an escapee. Successful, I'm afraid. Six to eight hours. You need to locate the driver on today's daily supply run, serial 4622, a Don Pratt; he should be able to confirm and give you an exact time and location for the—yes, it's a trusty, subject number 1523, he forged a prisoner transfer order with a valid authorization number and waltzed right out. Yes, only one confirmed, we're now on lockdown and about to perform a full evening roll call to make sure he's on his own. No, I can't confirm that. You'll need to page the Duty Auditor and get him to activate the contingency plan. Call me back when he's available."

He hung up, then slowly turned to regard Mrs. Carpenter, who was leaning against the door frame, wearing an expression midway between nostalgia and resentment. "Yes?" he asked.

"Roll call." She rolled her eyes. "*I* can't do that, as you know."

"Right, well, you can wait here and call me when *he* phones, can't you?" Turnbull's mood was clearly turning foul. He stood, flipped up the bright yellow cover concealing a red button on the wall labelled DO NOT TOUCH, and pressed it. Lights and sirens ensued, followed by the sound of army boots running. "Call me," he warned Iris, then disappeared in the direction of the ready room to muster his troops.

►◄►◄►◄

Linda unwound slightly once they made their escape. Derek sympathized: he'd come to the convention expecting some respite from cultists, and it had set him right back on his heels to recognize their ilk in the dealer room. Times had obviously changed, but surely not that much?

His stomach rumbled. "That sounds urgent," Linda remarked. "The bar is this way, there are some casual games going on but it's mostly a social space. Do you know anyone here? Were you meeting friends?"

"I, uh, I—" Derek mentally kicked himself—"it was a last-minute dec-decision," he managed. More fluidly: "I run a play-by-mail game but I don't know anyone here. It's m-my first convention, you know—"

"Yes, you already said that." Linda led him into an over-furnished canteen with a bar along one side, fronting an array of brightly labelled bottles and some hand pumps. A few of the tables and booths were already occupied, by people who were reading, drinking, or reading and drinking simultaneously, which struck Derek as dangerously intrepid. "What would you like?"

"I think I'd better stick to the Cola," he said, warily eyeing the beer dispensers. "And a sandwich. Let's see what they've got." He paused, and a long-rusted cognitive gearwheel creaked into life, shedding fragments: "I'm buy-buying?"

"You don't have to—"

"You saved me back there," he told her, hoping he didn't sound deranged. (Midnight altars, obsidian blades, saving throw versus human sacrifice: Derek not only knew the drill, he'd ghostwritten the rule book for *Rituals and Rosicrucians* back in the day. Or, rather, he'd run it as a side-quest in his PBM, then discovered a couple of years later that the proprietor of Bloody Giblet Games was one of his players and had *creatively recycled* the scenario.

Which, as an inmate, Derek was unable to do for himself.) "I'd like to."

"Okay." Linda looked at him doubtfully but let him pay nevertheless, then retreated to a corner booth with a cramped table. Derek followed her, carrying their slightly wilted sandwiches and two pints of Pepsi that came out of a weird tap-on-a-hose gadget. It tasted almost but not quite right, but Derek was too tired to care. Besides, he hadn't had a ploughman's pickle sandwich in nearly a third of a century. "How long have you been running PBMs?"

"About thirty years! It's the same game, although it changed a bit—I originally called it *Cult of the Black Pharaoh* but I changed it to *Eater of Souls* because, uh . . ." His face fell as he grappled with the impossibility of saying *because Mrs. Carpenter threatened to withdraw my stencil duplicator privileges if I didn't:*[3] to do so would lead to Questions, these Questions would inevitably prompt Linda to query his sanity, and then he'd be all on his own again (at best).

"Really?" Linda was looking at him strangely.

"R-really?" His brain froze again. Desperately, he rolled a mental six: "There was a movie? And they sent me a threatening letter s-s-so I changed the name."

Linda was still staring at him, but now her expression morphed into sympathy. "Play by mail?" she asked: "How do you get new players? Is it on the internet?"

"No, I'm really old-school, I run it a bit like an APA, sending out mailshots on paper. I started with the original AD&D rules, then wrote my own supplements, which go in the mailing package, and the players copy them, add their moves, and it circulates."

"APA—" She clicked her fingers. "You really aren't kidding when you say old school, are you? Do you know a guy called Greg Larsson? He was into PBM about—"

---

3. In reality, he'd discovered that (a) the Cult of the Black Pharaoh was real, and (b) Mrs. Carpenter was an ordained priestess: she took a *very* dim view of blasphemy.

"—Greg plays a pyromaniacal gnome with a halfling foot fetish, doesn't he?"

"Yes! He's—" Linda did a double take. "You're *that* Derek! He went on and on about your game when I first met him! What are the odds?"

"They're—" Derek clenched his lucky dice bag through his jacket. "Roll for surprise?"

"*You're* Derek—the DM." She stared at him in disbelief. "Greg and I were together until ten years ago. We met twelve years before that."

"Oh. Is-is he here? Wait! You're Greg's wife?"

"I fucking hope not," she said under her breath, then cleared her throat: "I divorced him. He cheated."

"He *cheated*?" Derek couldn't keep the indignation out of his voice. *At what?*

Linda smiled. "You're sweet: don't change." She finished her Cola. "I think Raven and Sam are supposed to be here, and maybe Phil the Ferret as well. Were they in *Black Pharaoh,* too?" Derek nodded, surprised. "If I run into them I'll introduce you. They're going to be wowed! I had no idea you were in the area."

"I—" Derek took a drink to cover his confusion. "—I k-keep to myself a lot." He took another drink lest his traitor tongue give him away. The truth—*I've just spent thirty years in prison for playing D&D unwisely*—seemed like a good way to kill the conversation. "I don't get out much," he admitted.

"Well you're out *now,*" she said, and stood up: "Don't go anywhere, I need another drink and I think I see—*hey, Phil!* Over here! You'll never guess who I found!" She waved vigorously and Derek was about to plead with her to stop drawing attention to him, then realized he'd left it too late when the person she was calling stopped and turned to face them.

"Phil! Phil! It's Derek!" She bounced up and down on her feet. "Derek who runs *Cult of the Black Pharaoh*!"

"What?"

"Derek, meet Phil: Phil, Derek. I'll be back in a minute, play nice." Linda disappeared, leaving Derek face-to-face with a skinny, long-haired bloke in double denim whose face vaguely resembled a mustelid with constipation.

Phil approached Derek with something like awe in his expression. "You're the DM," he said. "*The* DM."

Derek cringed inwardly. It seemed he was famous, for a certain hyperspecific value of fame. "I . . . may be," he admitted.

"Are you planning on running an in-person session this weekend?" Phil slithered into the booth opposite Derek. "Because that would be amazing!"

"I—" Derek blinked. It had been so long since he'd played face-to-face, other than a sandbox campaign for a constantly rotating group picked from among the saner rehab cases, that he'd almost forgotten what it felt like to game with people he *knew,* even if only through the medium of ink on paper. "How would I go about setting that up? I mean, do I just claim a table here, or . . . ?"

"There's a sign-up form on the front desk," Phil explained. "There are a limited number of tables but I think I can get you something for tomorrow, if I kick some shins?" Derek nodded. "Great, *don't move,* I'll be right back." Phil undulated away rapidly, just as Linda returned from the bar carrying two glasses filled with something that looked suspiciously as if it might be beer.

"Is that why they call him the Ferret?" Derek asked.

"Um, maybe?" Linda slid a glass under his nose. "Assuming you're not on the wagon, may I propose a toast? To the Black Pharaoh!"

Derek took a big mouthful of the amber liquid with a foamy head, then abruptly choked, trying not to spray it everywhere. It wasn't that he was totally new to alcohol: he'd sneaked a couple of furtive cans of Double Diamond with his gaming friends in the BC era—Before Camp. But once inside Camp Sunshine, alcohol was only available to trusties and staff, and controlled through scarcity pricing. When one earned the princely sum of two pounds a day, beer at three pounds a pint (from the Staff Rec Room bar, which closed at 9 p.m. and didn't open at all on Mondays) wasn't terribly appealing. In fact, this was Derek's first experience of a modern, free-range, artisanal, cask-conditioned IPA, and his first beer in more than twenty-five years, so it took him completely by surprise. It tasted of stale, sweaty socks and freedom, and it was so lip-curlingly sour that he had to take a second gulp to wash his mouth out.

"I'm not sure I'd want to praise him in public," Derek cautioned once he stopped spluttering: "there was a reason I renamed my campaign." (He'd thought the Black Pharaoh was just a myth until a couple of new inmates arrived and he rolled the bones to check whether to offer them seats at the sandbox. He'd rolled triple-ones eight times in a row, then an unscheduled storm blew in over the mountain and sent three lightning strikes in quick succession through the admin block's switchboard. Which he'd taken as a sign.)

"But you brought your books, right? And your lucky dice?"

Derek nodded as Linda waved at a couple of thirtysomethings who were standing at the bar, clearly mouthing something like *he's here!* in their direction.

"Well then! Let's see if Phil can get you a slot. Here come Raven and Sam! They may know if any other players are here. Listen, this is going to be *really great . . .*"

►◄►◄►◄

It was ten o'clock on a Friday night. One roll call and an extensive search later, Camp Sunshine confirmed to the Duty Office in London that an escapee was on the loose. They'd found Derek's forged prisoner transfer form. They'd checked his room and discovered that some of his personal effects were missing, although there was no written inventory anywhere—an oversight on someone's part.

London requested the escapee's personnel file. It took a couple of hours to come up from the archives (the Laundry never slept, but it tended to lapse into a fitful understaffed doze on summer weekend evenings). On arrival it was found to be fat but unrewarding. Derek was a long-hauler, but he'd never actually done anything to deserve incarceration. Worse, he'd kept his nose clean for more than a quarter of a century. He was a trusty inmate, an embarrassment to the Laundry, like the random goatherds who ended up in Guantanamo Bay because someone had sold them to a credulous CIA agent in return for the bounty on Al Qaida members. All the other teenage gamers who'd been rounded up in the same sweep had long since been released because they were magically inactive. But Derek had shown signs of untrained talent and was flagged as "weird/uncooperative" by a 1970s Assessment Officer who hadn't been trained to spot the signs of high-functioning autism in teenagers because kids weren't routinely screened for it until the 1990s. As they didn't know what to do with him, successive rehab officers kicked the can down the road; meanwhile nobody took Derek aside and explained how to go through channels to appeal his assessment.

Then, after a quarter of a century he just *vanished,* executing an escape plan that was both fiendishly simple and clearly impossible. At least it was impossible without correctly guessing a couple of eight-digit serial numbers on a piece of internal paperwork he didn't have access to. So pointed questions were now being asked by senior officers who'd been called in around midnight on a Friday night: *Why* had he been left to rot for a quarter of a century, *how* had he gotten those numbers, *where* had he gone, *why* had he chosen to leave *right now*—

("I think it might be my fault: I told him about the upcoming refurbishment plans," Iris Carpenter had confessed to Mr. Turnbull. "I thought he was taking the news a bit too calmly, to be honest, but he's always struck me as quite placid so I wasn't terribly surprised. He can seem a little simple to strangers but he has hidden depths. He doesn't let a lot out, except through his role-playing game sessions." Mr. Turnbull had scowled in thought, then said, "Tell me about these sessions . . .")

The details and the forensic analysis could wait. As of the small hours on Saturday morning, the Laundry had a problem. And as with most problems, there was a plan on file for dealing with an escape (category: single inmate, risk category: unknown, security state: confidential/agency-only). Because the plan existed, the plan would be executed. Unclassifiable risks justified a recapture-or-kill response. And because SOE did not have unlimited personnel to draw on, the cooperation of other national agencies would be obtained by judiciously withholding the full details of the situation from those agencies who were not officially aware of the Laundry's existence.

Before six o'clock in the morning email notifications went out to every Police force in the North West of England. Derek Reilly, aged forty-one, serving a twenty-five-year sentence for child abuse, had absented himself from HM Prison Altcourse in Liverpool. Nearing the end of his sentence, he was supposedly on supervised day release for work purposes. (HMP Altcourse itself would receive a special visit from a security officer who would explain enough of the facts of the matter to prison management for them to back up the story—and to bind their tongues to silence.) Notices also went out to social services, hospitals, ambulance/paramedic services, mountain rescue services (just in case), and bus and taxi firms.

Inconveniently, the notifications were accompanied by a poor-quality black-and-white scan of the most recent photograph of Derek in his file at HQ. The film from his last mug shot had been fogged due to an unexpectedly high thaum flux, and the request for a replacement had been unaccountably ignored. Policy only mandated updates once a decade, so the one that went out showed him aged twenty-four with long hair, a beard, and no glasses or double chin. Two-decades-younger Derek resembled, to a reasonable first approximation, a tabloid journalist's stereotype of a beardy-weirdy child molester; present-day Derek resembled the Prime Minister on Casual Friday with a worse haircut.

To make matters murkier there was a complete dearth of the supplementary data that normally accompanied an escape alert. Derek had no known mobile phone number, email address, or social media accounts. (He'd been taken into custody a decade before public internet access was a thing.) So there was no phone to track, no email to read, and nothing to monitor.

His parents had moved away from his last known address so there was obvious stakeout potential. The Reilly house was more than four hundred kilometers away from Camp Sunshine and it seemed likely that Derek would be picked up long before he got there—if indeed that was his destination.

As a trusty he had mail privileges, and his correspondence was read and logged. But it appeared there was rather a *lot* of it. Every

month a fat envelope arrived, and a week or two later a fat envelope departed, addressed to an ever-changing rotation of boringly
ordinary people who somehow decoded the hundred-plus pages
of single-spaced gibberish with references to the first edition Advanced Dungeons and Dragons rules—which had lapsed from print
in 1989, and did the Archive Stacks have a copy? Did they *fuck*—as
amended by Derek himself. Once a year Derek's mailshot incorpo-
rated his own samizdat rule book, building on top of the original
AD&D and supplements. To the perplexed officers trying to make
sense of it in London, it was like reading Hansard in Sanskrit (with
zero familiarity with the rules of parliamentary procedure). Also,
the scans were blurred and a couple of the mailings had been fed to
the machine upside-down so that only the blank reverse sides were
retained, because Derek had been sending them out for *decades* and
nobody other than the Camp Sunshine censor had bothered to read
them before, at least not since the late 1980s . . . and the censor had
mostly given up years ago.

Around six o'clock in the morning, one of the officers working
the situation desk had a sudden flash of insight and began to col-
late the names and addresses of all Derek's mail contacts. Derek
had no social media presence, but *they* did: If he surfaced and
made contact, surely someone would say something on Facebook?

But it wasn't until late the next morning, after Iris Carpenter's
third debriefing with Mr. Turnbull, that she remembered to check
the papers he'd left in the newsletter office.

▶◀▶◀▶◀

The first thing Derek noticed the next morning was that his bladder was full; the second was that his head was pounding; and the
third was that all his joints had been filled with ground glass and
his muscles hammered with a meat tenderizer until they ached.

Derek had heard of hangovers, but this was his first experience of one. It was not improved by encountering it in his very
late forties. He managed a pitiful moan as he crawled out of bed
and shuffled to the bathroom, where he was sick. Then he drank
some water and crawled back into bed and spent the next hour

wishing he was dead. *But I only had four pints!* he pleaded with his personal demon: *Why are you punishing me like this?* Four pints on an empty stomach was apparently sufficient to turn a nondrinker into a lifetime teetotaler, and he promised himself that he wouldn't repeat the mistake.

Once he felt marginally less deathly, Derek filled the electric kettle and brewed himself a mug of tea. He even figured out how to open the tiny plastic milk cartons without spilling the contents: thus fortified, he retreated back to the bed—this time with his copy of the *Bones and Nightmares* rule book.

Build your congregation! Recruit missionaries! Infiltrate the Inquisitors! Be the first to Immanentize YOUR Eschaton! screamed the cover: *a role-playing game for 2 to many players! Tabletop AND live-action friendly—*

"Huh?" Derek realized he'd spoken aloud as he did a double take. Temple-building TTRPGs weren't so unusual—it emphasized a skills matrix based approach rather than character classes: the goal seemed to be to recruit followers, tithe them, fly under the authorities' radar, and build your temple without being witch-hunted to your doom or eaten by Shoggoths—but the live action element was . . . "Daring, very daring," he mused, a smile of incredulity tugging at his cheeks.

Now he threw himself into reading the rule book, first skimming the table of contents, then chomping down the quick introduction, then dipping into the more interesting corners. Superficially it looked like a straight rip-off of D&D 3.5e, extensively customized for a specific setting but following the same basic logic of alignments, classes, feats and skills, levels . . . The format was familiar but some aspects of the game were anything but. Opportunities for LARPing—live-action role-playing—were minimal in Camp Sunshine for obvious reasons, camp management having good and sufficient reason to ban hiding in dark corners and leaping out at people brandishing papier-mâché weapons. So Derek hadn't bothered with that so far. But there were also fascinatingly alien aspects to the game: Something to do with content "downloadable" from the internet? A thing called an app for your smartphone that was useful for something called Artificial Reality

Gaming? (Did that mean you needed one of the iPhones he'd seen in the news? Or something else?) And what on earth did "register with Omphalos Online for free premium content" mean?

It was beginning to look as if you couldn't really get into *Bones and Nightmares* without a lot of commitment—a computer's worth (not forgetting the internet thing, of course), plus appropriate regalia for joining in a LARP in which you had to play a cult member or clueless civilian (synonymous with sacrifice), *and* the tabletop game and the smartphone Artificial Reality Game as well: it was actually four or five games in one, and the TTRPG box set he'd been given was just a taster.

Back in his spotty teens Derek had thought that AD&D was a bit much, a suffocatingly vast realm of rule books, dice, and miniatures in which he could lose entire weekends and evenings. But if AD&D was a biplane-era canvas and guy-wire vehicle for fantasy, this was a giant jet airliner come to whisk you away to uncharted vistas of sorcerous invocation. So he contented himself for now with a deep dive into the TTRPG materials, including the sample scenarios and the Abstract Syntax Notation diagrams for the summoning metagrammar, the *mana* acquisition scores of various sacrificial/sacramental preparations—

"Hey, wait a minute—" Derek vocalized, pausing with one finger raised above a paragraph extolling the virtues of summoning your familiar by co-opting your pet cat or dog for a peculiar ritual at midnight during a full moon. "I *know* this!"

Despite not himself being an acolyte of eldritch horrors from beyond spacetime, Derek had been unable to avoid learning a little bit about the invocation, binding to service, and unholy rituals surrounding Elder Things—if only so that when he had occasion to run screaming to the Security hut he could tell them what was happening in the detention block. Three decades spent as a trusty inmate in Camp Sunshine had much the same effect as a PhD in the social anthropology of necromancers or the necrotic sociology of anthropophagists, or maybe both: whichever way you cut the sacrifice it still bled and the invocation remained the same, and this aspect of *Bones and Nightmares* rang true for good reason (even leaving aside the core rules, which looked like a straight mod of d20).

"Holy crap," Derek mumbled to himself, "holy *holy* crap." He closed the rule book and placed it in its box as carefully as if it were some variety of explosive—which, in a manner of speaking, it was. Did he really want to spend two more nights in a hotel full of people playing a simulation of a sanguinary mystery cult? But he'd already paid up front using much of his available cash and didn't have anywhere else to go. Besides, Linda, Phil, Raven-and-Sam (who were in a hyphenated relationship), and any other fans they had rounded up would be expecting him to GM a session today or tomorrow. So he couldn't duck out now, not if he wanted to keep *Cult of the Black Pharaoh* alive when he— He shied away from the thought of going back to the camp.

"I should go for breakfast before they stop serving," he told himself. He'd paid an amount of money that made the tip of his nose itch with indignation for the hotel breakfast, but he needed to eat, and it was far more attractive than thinking about the Omphalos game . . . "I should eat," he told himself. Emphasis drove it in: "I *should* eat."

Derek pulled his clothes on (changing his pants and socks but not his trousers and shirt, for he only had one spare shirt), hastily ran a comb through his hair, then went in search of the hotel dining room. Eventually he found it, down a corridor from hotel reception. There was a big room full of small dining tables with a buffet at one end—quite similar to the Camp Sunshine canteen, only more expensively furnished and with a wider range of food. It featured the exact same oil-slimed fried eggs and tinned mushrooms, similar half-cooked tomatoes, and highly suspicious sausages. The black pudding was unspeakable but the bacon was better. He found the belt-fed toaster perplexing, but worked out how to use it by copying a slump-shouldered zombie. (Clearly he was not the only person the worse for wear this morning.)

Piling his plate high with questionably edible food that he'd paid for, dammit, Derek went in search of a seat. The dining room appeared to be segregated, like the transient/long-hauler distinction at Camp Sunshine—if you were a long-hauler you avoided the tables full of neatly groomed people with distant stares because they wouldn't be around long. Here the population seemed to fall into defensive-looking family groups, who performed a burlesque threat-display of normalcy to keep the less conventional population at bay: *students* (Derek thought uncertainly), and a sprinkling of older individuals who had an indefinable look to them. Derek squinted: the sparkling probability dust of dice clung to their fingertips even as they shoveled sausage, baked beans, and bacon onto their forks.

The nearest table of gamers had a couple of empty seats. Derek ambled toward it: "Is this taken?" he asked diffidently.

"Go ahead," said the man in the next chair. He was somewhere in indefinable post-university adulthood: beard, glasses, ginger hair, and a plate loaded with carbs and fat. Breakfast of championship tournament winners, evidently.

Derek plonked his plate down and sat. His neighbor made no attempt at conversation, which was fine by him. Looking around the room between mouthfuls, Derek finally spotted the table populated entirely by happy shiny people—cheerleaders and rugby stars—surrounded by a numinous haze of eaters: parasites attracted by the stench of magic. He cringed and dropped his gaze. Out of the corner of one eye he saw that they were all wearing *Bones and Nightmares* promo tee-shirts. "Oh crap," he mumbled.

"What? Oh." His neighbor followed his gaze. "Just ignore them. You should be glad they're here, anyway." Ginger Beard took a bite of stone-cold toast and chewed methodically.

"What? Why?"

"Without them DiceCon wouldn't be happening this year. After the fire at the Grand, our second-choice hotel got taken over and hiked their event space prices so we had to go looking for a third at short notice. Normally a Britannia would be out of our price range but the happy-clappy crowd over there paid up front for exhibit space and their own accommodation, which swung it with the hotel management."

"Happy-clappy." Derek thought for a minute. "Why d'you call them that?"

"They're tech evangelist types. Not real gamers, I mean they've got no heart." Ginger Beard had a definite grognard attitude. "The RPG they're pushing is just one corner of a franchise property along with the MMO, the LARP, the cosplay, and a bunch of tie-in novels. They're very corporate, deep-pocket stuff—there's some serious venture capital bankrolling them. It's like, imagine Games Workshop suddenly turned up twenty years ago with the entire 40K franchise fully developed, all the way to the movies and animated TV series? The free copies for congoers are a loss leader—they're counting on us to spread it by word of mouth. They probably plan to ride a commercial breakout into the mass market, IPO, then cash out."

"They tried to love bomb me yesterday," Derek admitted. "It was really creepy."

"Yeah, that kind of behavior doesn't go down well in the community, you know? But they've got lots of money and they're splashing it around, so—get them to buy you a drink in the bar next time. Better still, get them to buy everyone a round."

"They—" Derek stopped. Ginger Beard had cleaned his plate and was clearly impatient to be somewhere else, somewhere that involved rolling dice rather than enlightening the newbie. "How do you know this stuff?" Derek asked. "About the business side?"

"I see it at work. I was in a dot-com back in the day, before I took an arrow to the knee." Ginger Beard stood. "See you around," he said dismissively and wandered off. Derek blinked: There was no sign of a limp. *Is the arrow a lie?* he wondered: If so, what else had he been misinformed about?

Having eaten himself halfway into a food coma, Derek picked himself up and shambled to the session sign-up desk. Here he found that Phil had indeed booked a table and a time for a defiantly retro-titled *Cult of the Black Pharaoh* session with **Derek!!!** Heavily inked in the DM's slot. There were eight players, all taken, and he recognized at least half the names, Linda and Phil among them. "Well," Derek said, "well, well."

At least they didn't expect him to start until after lunchtime: there was time to pull his notes from the sandbox session he ran in the camp and tweak them a bit for more experienced players. Maybe throw in a surprise or two? And if Omphalos Corporation were maliciously handing out copies of *Bones and Nightmares* to gain converts, who was he to turn down the free source material?

> ▸◂▸◂◂

Derek was standing in front of the sign-up table, trying to work out where he was supposed to be, when Linda found him.

"Oh, hi," he said awkwardly.

"Hi!" Linda beamed at him. "Are you ready for the game?"

"I think so." He hefted his box file nervously. "Do you know where I can set up?"

"It says here we're in room 103." She pulled out a copy of the pamphlet titled READ.ME that had been in his membership kit. "Let's see." There was a map of the hotel, of all things. *Of course* there was a map: but Derek had mistaken it for a pocket dungeon and left it behind when he couldn't work out which ruleset it was designed for. "Along here."

Derek drifted along in Linda's wake as she made her way past a portal leading to a row of cells (disappointingly labelled with a TOILET sign), then along a tunnel that debouched into a cavern— well, a conference room wallpapered in pastel landscape print that didn't quite line up, with a couple of tables surrounded by dining room chairs. The window provided a picturesque view of the car park and loading bays behind the supermarket next door, full of melted-looking, twenty-first-century trucks. While he was gaping at the hydraulic lift on the back of a delivery truck—nothing like *that* had ever visited Camp Sunshine—Linda settled at a table where someone had placed a neatly printed piece of paper saying CULT OF THE BLACK PHARAOH.

Derek sat at the end of the table and examined the A4 label. The print was amazingly crisp and clear, in a typeface that was so restful it brought tears to his eyes. *Laser printed,* he realized, feeling something like awe: he'd seen them on TV but never in the flesh.

"Coffee?" asked Linda. "It's pretty crap but it's free, thanks to our 'friends' from Omphalos." She handed him an empty paper cup to hold.

"Um, yes?" Derek was taken aback. She lifted a silver carafe and poured, then offered him a bowl full of strange plastic capsules the size of d20s. Derek was learning: he took two, then waited and watched while she helped herself. (The capsules proved to be full of strange-smelling milk. He dribbled one into his coffee and left the other for later.)

Over the next ten minutes a handful of players showed up. Raven, Sam, and Phil the Ferret were all sometime regulars of his play-by-mail campaign. They seemed to be friends in real life, a midthirties countercultural couple—Raven bearded and long-haired, Sam blonde and hippyish—Phil narrow-faced and dark-stubbled—and they approached Derek, a total stranger, with something like awe. *He's the DM,* Phil had announced the evening before, as if he were the star of a soap opera or a footballer or someone important. Derek sipped his coffee and listened as they exchanged greetings, then cleared his throat. "Now then, this is a one-off based on a sandbox I've been running in person for a few years. I've got some standard pre-rolled characters to hand out—names and backstories are free, though, so if you each pick one you can customize them and we can get started faster. Here—"

Someone cleared their throat behind him. "Excuse me, but is this the Cult of the Black Pharaoh session?" It was one of the Omphalos employees—the twittery one from the booth the night before. "Are we too late to join? I'm Selene, this is Ivar, nice to meet you."

They were both blond twentysomethings—chipper cookie-cutter salespeople from the Planet Stepford—but today they had dressed down: Sister Selene wore a baggy hooded sweatshirt over her cleavage-enhancing top, and her male companion wore a polo shirt. Derek gave them a quick inspection, but seeing no sign of robes, razors, or books bound in human skin, he nodded reluctantly. "Please take your seats."

"Thank you!" gushed Selene as Ivar (who seemed to be the strong silent type) pulled out a chair for her. "I'm so happy! We thought we were too late, and we've got a quota to meet—"

"What kind of quota?" Phil demanded suspiciously. Derek glanced at Linda, caught her warning tic, and nodded minutely.

"We're supposed to play all the games! For research purposes, you understand—"

"Competitive analysis," interrupted Ginger Beard, who had paused by their table. "That's what you're doing, isn't it?"

Ivar bristled. "Why don't you mind your own business?"

"Competitive analysis." Derek suppressed a smile. "Cult of the Black Pharaoh isn't a commercial game," he told the Omphaloids. "It's not competing with anything: it just *is*."

"But it's very good." Sam smiled tentatively. "It's kind of famous in the right circles, if you know what I mean," she added.

"What's it about?" Sister Selene asked as Ginger Beard drifted toward the table at the far end of the room, which appeared to be set up for a game of original Black Box *Traveller*.

Linda picked up the challenge. "Oh, it . . . it runs on its own rules? Like, it started out D&D-like, but then—" She paused helplessly. "Derek? Your game?"

"All right. I'm going to abbreviate this introduction because most of you have played it before, although this scenario is set further in the future of the game-world." Derek closed his eyes and intoned: "The time: August of 1943. Britain is at war. Alan Turing has just codified the formal rules of magic in terms of the Lambda Calculus while working at GCHQ, cracking the Enigma codes. His work comes to the attention of the government. Fast-forward forty or so years. Microcomputers are everywhere and turn out to be *really powerful* tools for doing magic, summoning extradimensional critters that can be bound to do the sorcerer's bidding: they become a significant weapon in the Cold War. But the computer revolution is still gathering pace. Fast-forward forty more years and the consequences are horrifyingly clear.

"The year is 2017"—seven years in the future—"and Britain languishes under the jackboot of the New Management, a government (some would say dictatorship) led by Nyarlathotep, the Black Pharaoh, a nightmarish alien god. He rose from his cosmic tomb as the stars came right, a grand cosmic conjunction foretold by H. P. Lovecraft. In the grim future of the New Management, magic is ubiquitous: there are sorcerers and supervillains on every street corner, and *you* are employees of a secret government agency battling to defend the British Isles from the scum of the multiverse. Special twist: you reluctantly find yourselves working for the Black Pharaoh, because there are *much worse* gods out there—"

Strong-but-silent Ivar bolted to his feet. "No!" he insisted. "There *is* no greater evil! How can you say such—"

Selene grabbed his arm: "It's a *game,*" she hissed, "a game we're supposed to play. Stop making a scene!" She stood and whispered something in his ear that sounded suspiciously like *we're gathering intelligence,* then continued, "If you don't want to play you can report to Brother Taë—"

Ivar sobered abruptly, but remained standing. "I do not think I will enjoy this game," he pronounced grimly. "I am sorry, sister." He squared his shoulders. "Pray continue. I will make my report." He stalked off as Sister Selene sat down again, quietly fuming.

"Are you sure you want to participate?" Derek smirked.

She gave him a saccharine smile. "Why wouldn't I?" She giggled, but it was a pale shadow of the previous night's trill. "It sounds as if it might even be compatible with *Bones and Nightmares!*"

"So, about the current scenario. Which I procedurally generated"—Derek shook his dice bag—"a couple of weeks ago. Like I said, you all work for the Department of Existential Anthropic Threats, and you've been called in by your boss, Baroness Howard, a former civil servant. She's an assassin and musical virtuoso who runs a deniable specops team working for the Black Pharaoh. It has been discovered that a hostile cult who worship a quasi-Aztec god, the Mute Poet, have been taking over small evangelical churches across England. Your mission is to find out where they're headquartered, go there, and capture or kill their leader. Which may prove difficult because they're extremely secretive, their bishop has been missing for three months, and the lesser priests are now fighting it out to see who takes over . . ."

►◄►◄►◄

Iris was back in David Turnbull's office by midmorning on Saturday. "It's not good," she said, without preamble: "I think Derek has been hoarding clippings from the local newspapers. He had reading privileges for the newsletter and I found a copy of the *Scarfolk Courier* in the newsletter office bin—luckily nobody had emptied it—from three days ago. I think he was removing them from the staff break room before they went out in the bagged waste and looking through them for some reason. This one is missing half of page seventeen and page eighteen. Find out what was on it and we might learn something useful about his state of mind."

Turnbull nodded, then wordlessly raised a finger. He reached for the phone: "Camp Sunshine Security Office here, I have a request. We need back issues of the *Scarfolk Courier* for the past week—no, make that the past *month*—to review in light of the ongoing Code Yellow. Subject 1523's manager has reason to believe this may shed light on the escapee's objective."

He hung up. "Well, ball's in their park now," he said. "Any thoughts?"

"Scarfolk." Iris looked pensive. "He was also tracking the *Lancaster Advertiser* and a couple of other newspapers, so it might be a deliberate decoy."

"But you don't think so," Turnbull opined.

She nodded. "Problem is, we don't know what *else* he kept clippings from. The bagged waste doesn't hang around and he might have been gathering intel for mo—no, for *years*."

"But this is the most recent one," Turnbull pointed out. "Was he, in your opinion, devious enough to leave us multiple false trails?"

Iris thought hard. "He's a gamer." She thought some more. "No, he's a game *master*. He runs a regular game session for the transients—creates the scenarios, the shared reality, himself. It's guided storytelling, and he puts most of the work into it. The other participants are along for the ride."

"Like us," Turnbull snarled quietly.

"Quite possibly." Iris refused to give in to optimistic self-deception. Reality—not to mention her fellow field operations staff—had kicked her in the face once too often for that. "He may very well be gaslighting us. But on the other hand . . ."

You could know your enemy like yourself and build your plans around their weaknesses, and they would still surprise you, if only by making mistakes that led them away from your traps, or tricked them into misinterpreting your clues. (That was why Iris was here, after all: *she'd* done everything right, but her enemies had screwed up.)

"Here's what I think," Iris said, sitting up. "He's an obsessive gamer and a bit of a nerd, which is a given. But he's been thoroughly institutionalized. He went straight from being a teenager living at home to being a lifer, and he's been on the inside since the 1980s. So there are plenty of escape routes that aren't open to him. He never learned to drive, never had a job—I don't count a paper round or mowing the neighbor's lawn—he doesn't know how to cook, never rented a flat or opened a bank account. He's never lived independently and *all* his life skills are decades out of date. If he tried to go to ground the way you or I would—head for London, get a cash in hand job, and crash in a hostel while building a new identity—he'd fail miserably. So he's going to look for a familiar niche, one where he *can* survive because the stuff he can't do is all provided for him. Meals, bed, laundry service, work."

Turnbull snorted. "You make it sound like he's going to check into a boarding school. Shame he's thirty years too old. Or maybe an all-included resort hotel?"

"Hold that thought." Iris grinned humorlessly. "Now we have something to look for, don't we? There must have been something in the *Scarfolk Courier* that gave Derek a reason to go over the wall *right now*, rather than waiting for the relocation order to come through. He knows it's only a few weeks away. I'll grant you it might be a psych-out but I think the timing is significant. And it'll be something, some event or incident or place, that he feels reasonably confident in dealing with."

Turnbull picked up the phone again. As he dialled, he caught her eye: "Time to light a fire under some feet," he said grimly. "I'll get you those papers. Then we'll see."

▸◂▸◂▸◂

Derek had been running his play-by-mail *Cult* campaign for years—decades, if he was honest with himself—and his regulars were all veterans, as comfortable with the rules as a pair of broken-in army boots. They were house-trained grognards, happy just to be here, playing face-to-face and able to cross-examine him on arcana in a way that simply didn't work via mail. And he'd been running sandbox campaigns for the transients at Camp Sunshine for nearly as long, as part of his make-work in the Arts and Ents department. In his experience, the transient inmates were casual gamers at best, bewildered by pencil-and-paper rules but mostly good-natured and happy to escape the boredom (as long as he avoided contradicting their creed).

But he'd never run a game that crossed the streams, with a mixed-ability party of grognards and frighteningly literal-minded true believers, and he'd barely guided the latter through completing their 80 percent pre-filled character sheets when the wheels began to come off (or at least to emit the sort of ominous squeal that was usually a harbinger of wallet-lightening maintenance bills to come).

"I *insist* we start by visiting the Church in Chickentown," says Linda, getting into character as Eve—a high-powered, brittle, blonde executive with an entire warehouse full of skeleton-stuffed closets. "We need to observe and orient first, before we act, and the best way to get started is to observe one of their services."

"Then burgle the vestry," Raven adds enthusiastically. (He's playing Eve's younger brother, a supervillain called Imp who seems to be mostly obsessed with filmmaking.) "There might be"—he smacks his lips theatrically—"*clues.*"

Per the backstory, the team has assembled in her corporate HQ, in accordance with Baroness Howard's orders. Apparently they're some sort of Mission: Impossible/Dirty Dozen mashup, disposable minions who can be thrown at a problem without risk of blow-back spraying brown matter over the New Management (who-ever they are). Besides Eve and Imp—a power-suited Boardroom Barbie with a penchant for backstabbing, and a superpowered hippie channeling the spirit of Withnail—the grogs were playing a mathematician called Alex (secretly a vampire: played by Phil the Ferret), and Officer Friendly (a superpowered policeman played by Sam).

But then Derek had a problem. Or rather, two problems. Sister Selene seemed to be mostly at ease playing Sybil Cunningham, a middle-aged vicar's wife who *just happened* to be married to a priest in the target cult—at least, she was staying almost in character—but Brother Ivar—

"Chickentown is in London," Ivar announced. "How are we going to get there from here? Without leaving our posts?"

"We're already in London," pointed out Linda. "Eve's headquarters is in—"

"But this is the Britannia Hotels George Inn Scarfolk," Brother Ivar pointed out. "We would be deserting our posts, sister."

(A five-minute time-out ensued, during which Sister Selene patiently explained that they were not *actually* going to London, but *make-believe* going to London.)

The game resumed. "I phone the ops room and tell Sergeant Gunderson to organize my transport and an escort of bodyguards," announced Linda.

"That will . . ." (Derek rolled his dice, under cover of a makeshift GM screen) "cost you eight thousand pounds in salaries, wages, and ammunition. Not counting the London congestion charge."

"I pay." Linda sniffed. Breaking character: "Can I just say, it's *really neat* playing an evil billionaire executive with a heavily armed mercenary corporation behind her? It's, like, unlimited gold."

"Wait 'til you need an executive jet," Derek warned her. (He'd never actually been on (or seen) an executive jet, but he'd heard they were stupendously expensive.)

The party assembled, and with a minimum of supplementary dice-rolling and grumbling about the lawfulness of carrying heavy weaponry into a Church service in London—Officer Friendly appeared to be a stickler for the letter of the law, no surprise there—they set off in a convoy of SUVs with tinted windows driven by men (and a few women) in black.

"You arrive at the Church!" Derek announced. Flourish of dice: "It's six fifteen and the service doesn't start until seven. The front doors are closed and the building, which appears to be an old masonic hall, is deserted."

"It's after sunset in winter, isn't it? So I go and inspect the sign-board out front," said Phil, who was extremely daylight-averse because as a creature of the night his character, Alex, was susceptible to third-degree radiation burns when the daystar was above the horizon.

"You go, you inspect, roll versus Perception, plus eight advantage, please."

Phil rolled his dice. As expected, he successfully read the Church circulars pinned to the notice board, including the warded one concealed by magic from anyone who didn't know what to look for.

"You succeed in reading the true Notice of Ceremonies, not just the fake Christian one," Derek explains. "This is the Chickentown Branch of the Church of Saint Ppilimtec, the Mute Poet, Prince of Song and Verse, he who sits at the feet of Smoking Mirror—"

Ivar lunged to his feet, scattering dice and paper in all direction. "Heretics!" he snarled. "We can't go in there, our very souls are at risk!"

Sister Selene grabbed his elbow and yanked. "Sit *down,* Ivar, you're making a scene," she hissed. "It's just make believe, okay? I'm so sorry," she simpered at Derek, "he means well, but—"

Ivar lowered himself into his chair again, but rocked back and forth as if stimming. He muttered quietly in a language Derek had learned a bit of during his time in the camp. His skin crawled at the cadence of Old Enochian verse, and the grognards were all leaning away from Ivar as if he might explode. "L-listen," Derek told Sister Selene when his twitching subsided enough to make communication possible again, "your friend s-seems to have a real problem distinguishing in-game narratives from real life. D-d-do you think he should be playing?"

Sister Selene was clearly off-balance. "He's not like this in *Bones and Nightmares,*" she said defensively.

"Have you played any other games with him?" asked Linda.

"Well, no . . ."

"Take fifteen! Refreshment break," Linda announced, acknowledging Derek's discomfort. To Sister Selene and Derek, she said, "Selene, can you take over his character if he needs a lie-down?"

Derek nodded. "Y-yes, you should absolutely do that, otherwise I-I'm going to have to stop the game."

"But I—" Sister Selene was momentarily torn. "—I'm in charge of him? I have to supervise! But I'm supposed to be, uh, playing to, to—"

"Competitive analysis, yes, I heard you," Linda soothed as the other players headed in the direction of the bar. "You don't need Brother Idi—Ivar for that, though. Find someone else to take care of him and come back here?"

"I can't c-continue the game with him present," Derek warned. "I know he doesn't mean to be disruptive, but—"

"Oh all right," Sister Selene surrendered grumpily. She stood, then delicately pinched Ivar's ear. "Come with me," she hissed at him. Ivar whimpered and lurched away from the table. "You have brought shame upon the Order: it's time for Brother Taë to purify your soul . . ."

►◄►◄◄

The sandbox game resumed after a beer break, with Brother Ivar's character now being run by Sister Selene (with advice from Linda). The game ran slightly more smoothly: but then it lurched drunkenly off the rails Derek had mapped out for it and went on a detour to an ancient asylum full of steam-powered robots in Grantham for no obvious reason. Through it all, Derek's dice remained stubbornly cold, rolling only plausible-sounding integers and not glowing or balancing on edge, which was a relief: Ivar's outburst had shattered Derek's nerves. Luckily Sister Selene seemed to understand the concept of "it's just a game," and although she had some odd misconceptions they could be ascribed to her lack of experience with TTRPGs other than *Bones and Nightmares*.

Things progressed nicely, if more slowly than Derek had planned for—the party got hung up dealing with a haunted mainframe in the asylum basement, before making a cross-country dash to Portmeirion in Wales and then up the coast to Blackpool in search of a family of kidnapped children and their villainous superpowered nanny—but sooner than he liked it was time to break for lunch.

Derek drifted toward the bar in Linda's wake. He'd already had one beer so he'd resolved to stick to soft drinks until dinner time, but he was acutely aware that his stash of coins wasn't getting any bigger and the food in the hotel restaurant was eye-wateringly expensive. Linda seemed to be having similar thoughts. "We could go into town," she suggested.

"Why? What's there?" he asked.

"Plenty of fast food joints, if nothing else," she said briskly. "It's the weekend so Greggs and the office worker cafes will be shut, but there ought to be at least a Subway. Coming?"

"O-of course." Derek marched alongside her, his head spinning. They left the hotel and she took his arm as she turned right toward the town center. The sheer impossibility of the situation hit Derek like a sledgehammer: here he was, walking along a pavement in a perfectly ordinary town, *not* a prison camp, a pretty girl on his arm (or vice versa), and they were stepping out for a meal together— *Is this a date?* he wondered confusedly. If so, it was his first, ever. Baffled, uncertain, but definitely happy, Derek allowed her to guide him. "H-have you been to Scarfolk b-before?"

Linda snickered softly. "People don't visit Scarfolk, they escape from it."

"Sounds like home."

She looked at him as they waited for the lights to change on a Pelican crossing: "Where do you come from again?" she asked.

"It's a, a holiday camp in the Lake District," he said vaguely. "I've lived and worked there for the past twentysomething years." It wasn't entirely true and it wasn't entirely a lie either. For some reason not lying to Linda seemed to be important to him. "I do office work, run the newsletter, and so on."

"Do you do any online gaming?" She raised an eyebrow at his lack of response: "Internet stuff?"

"There's no internet in the camp. Not many computers, even." He extemporized fast when she looked baffled: "Way I heard it we're in some kind of black spot for, uh, wireless signals."

"But surely there's a cable . . . ? Telephones?"

What does the internet have to do with phones? he puzzled. "It's very tranquil. People go there to get away from all that stuff," he said. *Kicking and screaming, straitjacketed in the back of a prisoner transport.* "Going without is calming, apparently. We get a lot of people recovering from nervous breakdowns brought on by the pressure of—" *human sacrifice* "—work."

"Yikes. I think I'd go mad within a week," she said, tucking his arm inside the crook of her elbow assertively. "I do web design for a living and going without would be like being deaf or cut off from civilization or something . . ."

Derek nodded along, although secretly he was befuddled. He'd heard of web design—something to do with the internet, and computers?—but it wasn't something you saw explained in the *Blackpool Gazette* or on the "News at Ten." Linda clearly wanted an audience and Derek was happy to listen as she talked, occasionally prompting her to expand on something or asking her to explain this and that.

They drifted along the pavement together, passing a Poundland, then a row of newsagents, charity shop outlets, and an ever-mysterious off-license (Derek had never been inside one). Eventually they turned a corner. "This looks promising," Linda noted as they passed a couple of shuttered bakeries, a McDonald's, and some kind of cafe that sold only tiny, overpriced chocolate cakes. "Are you okay with curry?" she asked, pausing in front of a deserted-looking restaurant.

"Uh, I—I don't know," Derek admitted. The canteen served something called "curry" on Thursdays: it was a bit like peppery gravy on white rice with lumps of mystery meat embedded in it. "I think so? The camp kitchen isn't very adventurous."

"Well, are you willing to find out?" Linda asked: "I'll save you from accidentally ordering anything dangerous."

It was Derek's first ever experience of a hole-in-the-wall north Indian diner—red velvet flock wallpaper, age-darkened carpet of questionable origin, starched tablecloths, metal beakers and water jugs—and his first experience of a curry that didn't come out of an industrial catering keg. They were offering an all-you-can-eat lunch buffet, so he wolfed down a pile of chicken korma, lamb bhuna, and bhajis on rice. He enjoyed it so much that he went back for more: Linda gently steered him away from the lamb phaal. He ate until he was bursting. It was so much better than the hotel breakfast, never mind the camp canteen, that he nearly wept.

Finally they were done. "Back to the campaign?" he asked.

"Of course!" Linda sounded positively cheerful. She took his arm again. "Let's just circle the block first? I need a walk after all that food."

They rounded the corner and passed a fire station, then a faceless concrete eyesore that turned out to be the town police HQ. There was a notice board out front, and Linda slowed. "Huh. That's odd," she said.

Derek peered at the fogged Perspex covering the notices: his glasses didn't quite bring them into focus. "What is it?"

"Oh look." Her grip tightened. "Derek Reilly."

"What?"

"Nothing, let's go." She tugged him away from the notice board before he could read past the headline in screaming Comic Sans. DANGEROUS—WANTED. Her stride shortened but she sped up until Derek had to hustle to keep up.

"*What?*" he said again.

"Derek Reilly. What are the odds?"

"Odds on what?" *Roll for surprise,* Derek thought, his dice hand clenching instinctively.

Linda stopped dead in her tracks, still holding his arm. "Prisoners in high-security jails don't get to run play-by-mail games," she said aloud, "and if they escape, they don't do it so they can attend DiceCon." She gave him a hard stare. "*Are* you an escaped pedophile and child-killer, Derek?"

"Er . . . I—I—I don't *think* so?"

Linda glanced away after a couple of seconds. "So why was there a poster with your name on it outside the cop shop?" She snorted faintly. "Terrible mug shot by the way, nobody'll recognize you."

"I—I—I—" Derek gasped for breath, then tried again. "It's true that I escaped but I'm not a murderer! Or a pedia—pedo—podo—thingy. Whatsit."

"What were you locked up for, then?" Linda asked.

"Running a D&D campaign." Derek stared at his toes as he

spoke, too ashamed to make eye contact. "It was a long time ago. They released the other players, but not me. I run the camp newsletter now."

"For heaven's—*when*? How long ago was this?" She sounded outraged. "*Who* arrested you?"

"Uh, it was 1982? Or was in 1983? I'm not—" He began counting years on his fingers. "Oh, it was 1984. I think. The—the government, I mean, the security services? They thought I was summoning demons. I mean, they—they were very upset by the notes I doodled in the margins of *Gods, Demigods, and Heroes*."

He raised his gaze. Linda was staring at him again—in wide-eyed horror this time. "We've got to get back to the hotel!" she told him. "You can't go out again, not until we work out what to do next. It's a terrible photo but you can't be seen out here, it's too dangerous." She tightened her grip again—his arm was in danger of going numb—and began to walk, casting around nervously. "Jesus. How old were you, fifteen, sixteen? And held in some kind of adult prison for nearly thirty years without a trial, just for playing an RPG? Shit, they must be bricking themselves: if word gets out there'll be a huge scandal, this is as bad as the Birmingham Six—"

"Word won't get out," Derek reassured her. "The people who run the camp don't make many mistakes. Besides, it's their job to protect us from nightmares from beyond spacetime and the cultists who worship them. Most of the time they get it right: if you'd ever met an initiate of the Church of the Mute Poet you'd agree, those people *need* to be locked up."

Unaccountably, Linda did not find this particularly reassuring. Her head continued to swivel in all directions until they were back in the hotel lobby, and even then her grip didn't relax until she'd scanned the front desk for signs of WANTED posters. Finally she eased up: Derek winced and rubbed his elbow as circulation resumed. "Oh god, I'm sorry!" she said, finally noticing. Without any warning she hugged him. "I'm so sorry!"

Had Derek's brain been a computer—had the brain/computer metaphor made any sense—it would probably have crashed at this point. *A girl*—no, a woman—*is hugging me. Of her own free will.*

Not a cultist. Help! What do I do now? He froze. Being hugged by Linda felt very nice indeed, and he was suddenly terrified that if he blinked she might stop. So he didn't blink.

After a couple of seconds, Linda let go of him and stepped backward. Her expression was mortified: "Oh hell, and now I'm *really* sorry, I didn't mean to—"

"—It's all right," he heard himself saying, "I enjoyed it."

"Good! I mean, um, good?" Her smile was tentative, and for the second time in a matter of seconds Derek froze, scared to do anything in case he got it wrong. "We're all good, then?"

"Yes, we are." A chorus of angels was circling his head, singing hosannas.

She touched his arm lightly. "Back to the game . . . ?"

"Y-yes?" He turned toward the corridor past the hotel bar, toward the room they'd been playing in.

Their table was littered with papers and dice and empty soda cans, abandoned by the other players. Derek pulled out a chair for Linda, then seated himself behind his GM screen (which had toppled over), and began to shuffle his papers back into sequence.

"It should be a crime," Linda said grimly.

"Wha—?"

"What they did to you. They didn't give you a trial, did they? Or a lawyer?"

"Uh. I don't think so?"

"Well then." She seemed to have made up her mind. "What was it like in prison?"

"It-it wasn't a, a pri-prison exactly? It's a camp. Where they hold cultists for de-de-deprogramming."

"Cultists like—" Linda tilted her head to indicate the dealer room—"them?"

"Yes? No! Maybe?" Certainly there was something very off-color about the Omphalos Corporation salespeople swarming around this DiceCon, like a swarm of flies drawn to a bloating corpse in search of somewhere to lay their eggs. But they didn't resemble any of the secret congregations or underground sects Derek was familiar with: they were much too *open* about it for one thing, much too in-your-face, like the Silicon Valley start-up version of a cult.

He reached into his dice bag and felt a familiar prickling in his fingertips, a noumenon of uncertainty itching to be rolled into reality. A pair of d12s sidled up against his palm and demanded to be set free, so he let them out and rolled, then rolled again, three, then four, then five—

"Why are they glowing?" Linda whispered.

"Oh, they do that sometimes. When I have an important decision to make." He covered them hastily.

"In theory, if you wanted to get in touch with the, the people who locked you away—I'm just asking, mind—do you have any way to do that? A telephone hotline, for instance?"

Derek thought for a long few seconds as he stroked the top of his 2d12s, reassuring them that he'd noticed their fall and taken note: "No," he said. "I don't know their phone number. Or where their office is. Or much of anything about them, really. They're the government. Why?"

Linda glanced at the doorway. "There's never a cop around when you need one, and they're always in your business when you don't—" Phil the Ferret walked in—"hi, Phil!"

"We can s-start again when everyone arrives," Derek told him, welcoming the distraction. Things with Linda had spiraled with unaccustomed intensity and now he was off-balance, unsure what it meant. *Does she like me?* he wondered warily. There'd been times over the years when he'd gotten inadvisably close to another inmate, only to have a lucky escape when she turned out to be quietly homicidal (*the technical term is a sundew, not a honey trap,* Iris Carpenter had explained once: *honey traps are passive, but sundews are covered in sweet nectar which glues you in place while they digest you*), or a less lucky escape when the woman in question was reclassified as low risk and released—

"Derek?" Linda interrupted his woolgathering. "Are you all right?"

"Sorry!" He jolted upright. Raven and Sister Selene had returned. Of Brother Ivar there was no sign, for which Derek was appropriately thankful. "Let's see, where were we—"

"Excuse me?" Sister Selene simpered briefly. "Can I make a brief announcement?" Derek sat back. "I'd just like to say, it's been great playing with you! But we, I mean Omphalos, are running a *Bones and Nightmares* tournament tomorrow and everyone at DiceCon is invited! We hope to get everyone involved—you'll make a *great* team—and there are cash prizes for the teams that make it through the semifinals and finals! Please say you'll come?" She clasped her hands before her and beamed winningly at everyone in turn, although her smile wilted slightly when it bounced off Linda's implacable exterior.

"I don't think—" Linda began.

"—We'll have to close the function space early if we don't get eighty percent participation," Sister Selene added. "We've very generously sponsored DiceCon so far, but next year's funding depends on the success of our outreach efforts tomorrow. Won't you join in and help make DiceCon 17 happen? It'd be so terrible if we didn't make our targets!"

"This is an MLM thing, isn't it?" Linda glowered. "A pyramid scheme to sell more of your—"

"Of course not! Nothing bad can possibly happen to you if you play. Oh, please say you'll join us?" Sister Selene radiated goodwill and happiness across the table like an uncontained meltdown in a joy reactor. "Please?" she repeated. They'd reached an impasse, or the end of her scripted interaction, or both.

Derek felt a familiar itch. Dice bag upended, he picked and rolled a pair of hand-carved stone d20s that scintillated and speckled with laser-like birefringence. He rolled 20s on both. Then rolled again, just in case the gods of probability were lying to him: same result. "The dice say yes," he announced, then frantically semaphored *please just play along* with his eyebrows until Linda reluctantly nodded.

"How big are the prizes—" Phil began, but then Raven interrupted: "Are we done?" he asked. "Because I wanna get back to our session! Where are we looking for those kids anyway?"

Derek cleared his throat: it was time to kill this discussion before it sucked all the air out of the *Cult of the Black Pharaoh* game. "Back to Blackpool, people!"

Everyone looked at him. When there was silence he continued.

"You have followed the wicked witch of the east to the golden mile on the seafront, and then to a new feature: the Chariots of the Gods experience, an alien-abduction-themed indoor amusement park. As you stand in the lobby, where there are ticket machines and a food court, you hear faint screams and then a monstrous animal's roar from beyond the entrance . . ."

▶◀▶◀▶◀

Derek DM'd until his voice was hoarse.

There were no further interruptions, and just one toilet/beer break in midafternoon as his table were too enthralled to stop playing. His palms prickled and his luck-kissed dice were glowing happily once more, actively guiding the future course of play. (The stones they were carved from had spent decades exposed to the eldritch thaum flux around Camp Sunshine. Neutron bombardment of materials in the heart of a nuclear reactor could be used to create rare isotopes by a process known as secondary activation: the sorcerous irradiation was not dissimilar.)

His players merrily slaughtered a tyrannosaur that had wandered into the Blackpool alien abduction experience from a parallel universe when one of the superpowered kids "thinned the walls between the worlds" a little too enthusiastically. They nearly got into a firefight with the evil nanny (who was much more heavily armed than anyone expected), but then got themselves arrested by the police. And the players were still talking their way out of the custody suite at four o'clock that afternoon when a pair of hotel workers came round to announce they were closing the game room. The hotel was double-booked for a wedding reception that evening, and they needed this space for an overflow cloakroom *right now.*

Derek and the GM at the other table protested, but to no avail: "Soz, bookings are bookings," said the youth in an ill-fitting suit, and then insisted on them clearing out immediately. So at four fifteen Derek found himself standing in the hotel bar, at a loose end as he gloomily contemplated the tariff (lager at £4 a pint, IPA at £4.50).

"We're not going to be able to finish, are we?"

Linda nudged him: "Never say never. Anyway, that was great. Want anything from the bar?"

"I—" he coughed embarrassedly—"I'm running short on money," he admitted.

"Listen, don't worry about it, I'm buying, it's the least I can do for you for running that game. Bartender? Mine's a snakebite and black, he's having—you okay with the IPA?—an IPA—"

A few minutes later Derek found himself sitting in a booth elbow to elbow with Linda, a pint glass in front of him. His beer was bitter and tasted weirdly like grapefruit; whatever her glass contained was ruby red and smelled of apples. Raven, Phil, and the others had wandered off in search of entertainment elsewhere. "I don't know what to do," he admitted to his beer, too bashful to make eye contact with her. "The Omphalos people worry me. I ought to call the, the agency, but I don't know how to contact them."

"You don't want to bring them down on your head." Linda raised an eyebrow.

"No. I can't exactly call the police, can I?" Not after seeing that poster.

"Yeah, you don't want to do that." She raised her glass and drank. "Where were you planning to go after DiceCon, anyway?"

"I hadn't really thought that far . . ." He frowned. "I was going to get the bus back to the camp. Or as close as I could get." But Penrith was some kilometers from Camp Sunshine, and he had no idea how to get there from the bus stop. He picked up his glass, took a mouthful, and winced at the lip-curling astringency. "Why do people drink this stuff?"

Linda gave him a very odd look: "It's an acquired taste, I'm told. Here, try this." She pushed her own glass in front of him.

Derek took a sip. "That's a lot nicer," he admitted. "What is it?"

"Strongbow cider and blackcurrant cordial. Traditional drink of goths."

"Of who?"

"Goths—" She narrowed her eyes. "You didn't know any goths before you were—*How* long have you been in the system again?" She shook her head. "It totally weirds me out, you're like a time traveler from Thatcher's era. But you know what? It totally explains the weird sense of alienation *Cult of the Black Pharaoh* induces so brilliantly."

Derek snorted. "Everyone's a critic!"

"And the kids are all writing books these days." She chuckled, and he caught himself smiling. "Listen, I think we should enter that tournament tomorrow. It'll give us some more insight into what the Omphalos people are doing—I mean, it *may* be all fun and games, right?—and it'll help ensure there's a DiceCon next year, and there's a cash prize. Or it could be total creepsville. But if it's *really* bad the cop shop is within walking distance. Screaming-fleeing distance. I could go there while you hide, or something. Whatever."

Derek shuddered and took another mouthful of beer.

Linda nudged him with one shoulder: he startled. "Hey, it's not that bad."

"No?"

"The tournament is just a game of *Bones and Nightmares*," she reminded him. "You're an absolute legend. And we've got tonight and tomorrow morning to study the rules and put together a team. How about we see if the others are interested when they get back from dinner?"

"Yes, let's do that."

"Or we could go to your room and study the rules?" She waited for his coughing fit to subside: "Forewarned is forearmed, after all."

▸◂▸◂◂

Getting back issues of the *Scarfolk Courier* into Camp Sunshine posed serious security and logistics problems, no matter how urgent the requirement might be. Unsold copies of local newspapers didn't hang around for long before they were recycled, and the newspaper office wasn't fully staffed at the weekend, and the nearest Laundry regional HQ was over a hundred miles away.

After much inter-office backbiting, an unfortunate Duty Officer from Manchester had to expense a private helicopter—which would cause no *end* of a circular bureaucratic arse-kicking contest over who was going to pay the invoice, measured in thousands of pounds an hour, when the bill came due—then, on arrival, was required to convince a skeptical Police Inspector to bang on an editor's front door at 2 a.m. At which point they learned that the editor in question was blind drunk and had misplaced his office badge, and the night security bod on the front desk wouldn't let them inside the building until someone in London got a very irate publishing executive out of his mistress's bed to make a threatening phone call. And *then* having finally obtained a freshly printed set of page proofs for the past month's papers which (thank *fuck*) hadn't been archived to tape yet, the now-yawning DO had to blag a ride in a police car to Penrith, where she arrived at 4 a.m. and was unceremoniously dumped in a bus shelter by the intensely irritated cops, who drove away just as it began to rain.

And lo, there was no mobile phone signal, so by the time Iris Carpenter and Donald Turnbull realized the DO was out of contact and sent out a search party—which in turn required prepping a ticket of leave and rousting the new delivery driver out of bed in the middle of the night—it was six o'clock on Sunday morning.

With the result that Mr. Turnbull finally got to sign for the back issues Iris had requested a couple of hours after he'd sent her to bed for some much-needed rest.

The lost night wasn't completely wasted, though.

After supper, Iris and two prison officers had searched Derek's room again from top to bottom. They didn't have to search it very hard to find his bookcase and his library loan records; then the officers witnessed and signed attestations of necessity, after which Eric from Facilities attacked the bookcase lock with a Black and Decker, and they logged the contents and moved everything into a hand truck. Finally they escorted Iris and her new reading matter back to the Security Office. Whereupon Iris settled in for some late-night reading.

Iris Carpenter—sometime IT Services manager, proud mother of a twenty-three-year-old daughter whom she hadn't seen for a couple of years, sometime high priestess of the Brotherhood of the Black Pharaoh—spent the quiet hours alternately reading, making notes, rubbing her forehead, muttering imprecations under her breath, and brewing and drinking one pot of tea after another. For the first time she began to apprehend just how badly the organization has mishandled Derek. Not just by misunderstanding him, but by underestimating him. And the implications were absolutely horrific.

Derek was a gamer. Sure, Iris had known that in the abstract, but her understanding had been deficient. Her daughter, Jonquil, was a jolly hockey sticks and outdoor pursuits type, as were her friends: she didn't date nerds. Iris herself was old enough that D&D hadn't been a thing when she was a teenager herself—especially not for girls. Derek was an outlier. So, although she'd vaguely been aware of it zipping through the zeitgeist, she'd never actually *paid attention* to TTRPGs until now.

Luckily Derek had left a ton of material behind. Rule books with lots of doodles and marginalia. *Lots* of rule books. It took her an hour just to figure out where to get started—then she read the introductory notes in each book, trying to understand how they slotted into the whole. It was a game, but a confusingly complicated, open-ended thing, which appeared to have different sets of rules for different participants. (Was the Jailer—*no, Dungeon Master*—even a player at all?) Then she spotted the copyright dates. Derek's AD&D rule books dated to the beginning of the 1980s. Surely he hadn't kept to such an old corpus for thirty years? So she turned to his journals, starting with the oldest, and realized she was hatching a headache when she saw that what she was looking at was an entirely different set of rules for something called—

"Oh fiddlesticks," she said despairingly, deciphering a spidery handwritten title that said ~~CULT OF THE BLACK PHARAOH~~ EATER OF SOULS, beneath a painstakingly drawn Elder Sign. "Where did he get this stuff?"

Obviously something had gone badly adrift with Derek's case file. It made no mention of his interest in the Brotherhood—or that he was no longer actually playing Dungeons and Dragons, but had moved on to something worryingly reality-adjacent. Iris flipped pages and squinted at his terrible handwriting and the painstakingly scratched-out tables and charts, trying to make head or tail of it. Much of it was incomprehensible, relying on implied knowledge of obscure acronyms—what did "2d6+1 to save vs. Initiative" even *mean*?—but other parts were absolutely correct in the most alarming way. "The high priest or priestess leads a conclave who, on rendering appropriate sacrifice before the Altar of the Elect in the undercrypt beneath Brookwood Cemetery, may attempt to bind the Eater of Souls—" (*Been there, did that, got locked up for it.*)

As she flipped through the journals she worked out how Derek's play-by-mail game had operated. He'd send a bunch of notes to a list of participants. The first recipient would write down their own moves, then forward it to the next, who'd add their own: eventually the bundle would get back to Derek, who'd do something—*Roll the dice? Read the chicken entrails?*—and determine the outcome of that turn. Then he'd write up a story line describing the unrolling game, and send it back out to his players. Sometimes he'd write additional notes, updating the rules of the game—referring to the original D&D rules which had by now mutated out of all recognition. (One particularly complex grid was headlined *Replacement alignment system*: she had a handle on character alignments by this point, and the new Bureaucratic/Ad-Hoc axis that replaced Lawful/Chaotic felt like a personal attack.) Then the next page was headlined *List of* CASE NIGHTMARE RAINBOW *contingencies,* which was both very real and very classified: when *that* got back to HQ someone was going to get their arse lit up with MLRS rocket fire, because there was *no* way in hell that Derek was cleared to know about that stuff.

The journals were a weird mishmash of horrifying security leaks written up in the language of a Dungeon Master's scenario guide, along with maps, character sheets, and a time line of the events in an ongoing tournament. Iris had an uneasy feeling that Derek didn't necessarily know what he was doing: he'd somehow dreamed his way into the classified records department and was strip-mining them for a goddamned game.

Worse, some of it *couldn't* be true. Everybody knew vampires didn't exist, so why was there an extended side-quest describing a nest of fang-fuckers (he called them FANGs, a very stupid cutesy acronym in Iris's opinion) embedded in an investment bank in Docklands? Also, for some reason he'd written an entire supplementary rule book about hopelessly crap supervillains and the incompetent superpowered police officers who pursued them. Ah well, at least he'd gotten the unicorns right. Iris yawned, then glanced at the clock again. Two o'clock. Time to brew more tea. It was going to be a long night, and a long, long weekend . . .

Iris's windup alarm went off at ten o'clock the next morning. It clattered self-importantly while she dragged herself out of bed. She had an intimation that something urgent needed her attention but she was barely able to keep her eyes open: she'd had just four hours' sleep. She'd thought she'd seen the last of all-nighter study sessions like that when she graduated a quarter of a century ago. But her sleep had been disturbed, haunted by dreams that evaded recollection. She was almost as tired now as she had been when she closed her eyes. "Breakfast," she mumbled to herself, brushing out her morning bed head. She pulled on clean clothes and shuffled toward the staff canteen, then David Turnbull's office, ready to face the new day's music.

"Morning, Mrs. Carpenter." Sleep deprivation had deepened the bags under Turnbull's eyes and lent his jowls some extra sagginess, but he was still in uniform. His expression was neutral, no trace of reproach at her for having nearly overslept. "Did you learn anything useful from Mr. Reilly's journals?"

"I—" Iris yawned cavernously. "—I'm sorry, I need—" He slid a lukewarm mug of stewed filter coffee straight into her hand, and she drank half of it in one swallow. "—oh, that's better. Yes. Derek kept a thorough journal of his play-by-mail game. I haven't been able to read it all as there's nearly twenty years' worth of material, but what I *have* read is quite disturbing. Are we entirely certain he was never one of ours—employed by the Laundry?"

Turnbull pushed himself upright and blinked, then removed his spectacles and began to polish them with the end of his tie. "Quite certain." For a moment he looked very uncertain indeed. "Unless his entire inmate record is a fabrication, which is an . . ." He shook his head. "Anyway he was here when *I* first arrived, sixt—no, seventeen years ago."

"Oh." Iris drained the dregs of her stewed coffee, shuddered convulsively, and put the mug down. "Dear me. Then he must have picked up a leak."

Turnbull put his glasses back on. "How bad a leak?"

"Multiple top secret codeword territory, I'm afraid. Our boy was running a pencil-and-paper adventure game. It started out innocent enough as a Dungeons and Dragons campaign set in the real world, a present-day adventure narrative. He'd write up a story—a description of a setting, some actions, that sort of stuff—then mail it to a player who'd write down their reactions, and forward it to the next player in turn. Eventually it'd get back to Derek, who'd apply a bunch of rules, roll some dice, and write down what happened next. Rinse, spin, repeat roughly once every two to four weeks for a decade and, well, that's why I barely broke the surface of it last night. He filled more than twenty hardbound journals. Anyway . . . he began to customize the rules to his game, which was originally called *Cult of the Black Pharaoh.*" She grimaced: Turnbull flinched briefly. As camp security officer he was familiar with her history and had been cleared for BLACK PHARAOH. "Shortly after I took over Ents he renamed it to *Eater of Souls,* can't think why, only that's not much better." She muttered something under her breath that might have been, *fuck Angleton.* Turnbull diplomatically ignored it.

After collecting herself, Iris continued: "I found references to at least three different codeword operations that I was briefed on back in the day." Before she was arrested, tried by the Black Assizes, and remanded in custody. "You need to loop the Auditors in on this whether or not we get him back. I'm not sure I should continue reading, I may have unknowingly exceeded my . . ." She licked her lips. "More coffee?" she asked abruptly, rising to her feet.

"Sit down." Turnbull pushed a button: a buzzer sounded in the next room. "The coffee will be here shortly." He attempted a smile but it came out wrong. "After you went to bed I went through the papers. Found this."

He slid a sheet across the desk toward her. Iris took it, the touch of laser-printed paper fresh and exotic beneath her fingertips. "Wait, this is . . ."

"Page seventeen of the *Scarfolk Courier* from two weeks ago, yes."

Game Players Roll in to Scarfolk Hotel for Annual Conference

"Oh *crap*." The door opened and one of the canteen staff backed in, pulling a battered metal trolley with a tea urn, a jug of coffee, milk, and a sugar bowl. By tacit agreement the conversation paused until the tea lady withdrew.

"Looks like our lad has not only gone AWOL, he's dumped a major incident in our lap. If you're right, it's a multiple codeword-associated leak potentially in view of dozens to hundreds of witnesses."

"What are we—" Iris leaned back. "Ignore me, I'm still half-asleep: What are *the Plumbers* going to do? And when?" She nerved herself for the coming unpleasantness.

"The Plumbers will do what they always do: a full OCCULUS team set off up the M6 sometime before you went to bed, so I'd say they'll arrive on-site in a couple of hours. First order of the day is containment and capture, I am told they're holding off on a termination order until we have more information. They'll want you to brief them when—" The ancient landline chose just that moment to ring. "Hello, who is this? Yes, Donald Turnbull speaking, Camp Sunshine Security Office. I have Iris Carpenter in attendance." He paused. "Ah. Yes sir, she's been reading Mr. Reilly's notes. She was his line manager—yes sir."

He covered the mouthpiece as he stood up. "He wants to talk to you," he told Iris.

"He . . . ?" She felt a sick sense of dread in the pit of her stomach, an apprehension that one of her worst days had returned to mock her.

"The Senior Auditor." She accepted the receiver with nerveless fingers. "I don't need to hear this," he added from the doorway. "Call me when you're done."

Then he left Iris alone with her very own judge and jury on the line.

▸◂▸◂

The next morning a tired Derek made his way down to the hotel breakfast buffet shortly before it closed, only to discover that they'd run out of sausages and black pudding and the scrambled eggs were the consistency of rubber. There was plentiful coffee, at least. Phil and Linda were still holding down a table, although they had finished eating some time ago. Derek collected his plate and mug and joined them.

"Good morning!" Linda said cheerfully. "Are we all ready for our big day?"

"*Morning,*" Phil echoed mournfully.

"I—" Derek shook his head, then sat down carefully. "I su-suppose so?"

Linda had accompanied him upstairs the previous evening, and they had sat up for a couple of hours reading and snarking over the *Bones and Nightmares* rule books. (Linda had taken the players' manual; Derek had gulped down the GM's guide like a ludic python, then resigned himself to a night of bad dreams.) Afterward they chatted and bounced ideas back and forth, leaning close. At one point Linda had smiled at him and said, "You're sweet," but—not knowing what to do—Derek had pretended not to hear and changed the subject. She wasn't a cultist so kissing her might actually be *safe,* but he had no idea what would happen if he tried so he hesitated, paralyzed, until the moment had passed. And now it was a new day and he didn't know what was between them, or if he'd simply imagined it.

"I checked at the front desk on my way down," Linda announced, sounding altogether too cheerful for this early hour. "There's a sign-up form for *Bones and Nightmares,* so I put us down as Team Grognard. They wanted a list of names so I wrote in us three plus

Sam-and-Raven, who were here earlier. Is that okay with you? Party of five?"

It was too early for conscious thought, so Derek nodded as he shoveled a forkful of baked beans onto his toast, hoping that would be sufficient. The coffee was disgusting, and the food was worse: mushrooms that came in a can labelled *Produce of Yuggoth*, a fried egg that was an aborted cockatrice. On the other hand, it was just game fuel. It'd suffice to keep him going until lunch—assuming the Omphalos people broke for lunch, of course.

Half an hour later Derek (accompanied by his party of adventurers) convened at the front desk. "It sa-says we're to start in room 104," he read, "where we'll be briefed. Wh-where's that?"

"There's a bunch of rooms round the back of reception," Samantha—Sam—offered. She'd gothed her look up today, subconsciously reacting to the town (which seemed to be stuck a long way behind the times, record-scratching its way through a dead and dismal decade).

"Are we ready?" Raven drifted in from the front, smelling suspiciously of clove cigarettes.

"Let's go!" Sam bounced on her toes.

They're morning people, Derek realized to his dismay. *Why am I adventuring with morning people?* But he didn't have time for self-doubt and ennui: Linda sidled up behind him, took hold of his hand, and headed for a shadowy archway close to the toilets. "Adventure time!" she squeed.

Room 104 waited with door ajar. It looked to be a dual-purpose hotel room, one that could accommodate overnight guests with the addition of a bed. Right now it contained a row of folding tables draped in white cloth, some stacking plastic crates, and a floor-standing conference poster. The poster displayed the now-familiar Omphalos Corporation logo—a worryingly pink brain and spinal cord superimposed over an Elder Sign—hovering above a nighttime landscape featuring a step pyramid.

"What now?" asked Derek. "Aren't there supposed to be instruc—"

"Good morning and blessed be all those who seek the starry wisdom!" Sisters Celeste, Selene, and Unidentified Omphalos

Corporation Booth Babe Number Three (who Derek vaguely remembered from his arrival) pranced through the doorway. They'd swapped the tight tee-shirts and push-up bras for long white dresses and wildflower circlets: they formed a long-haired limbo line, beaming glassy-eyed love in all directions. "We are your guides today, and we are here to start you on your voyage of self-discovery!" They curtseyed simultaneously, then each opened a plastic tub and held up a white gown or robe. "Please remove your unconsecrated garments and deck yourself in holy raiment!" Sister Celeste huffed, then hastily unfolded a screen: "Men on this side, ladies over here—"

"—Put your clothes in these bags, we'll look after them during the tournament," Number Three interrupted.

"Blessed be!" trilled Sister Selene, and the other two chimed in with barely any hesitation.

Derek found himself on the same side of the screen as Raven and Phil, who were already stripping off their clothes. Worse: Derek's traitor hands seemed to be unbuttoning his shirt and pushing down his trousers without any conscious volition. He felt oddly passive in the face of a situation which should by rights have filled him with alarm. Decades in Camp Sunshine had done nothing to file off the rough edges of his teenage modesty, and a little voice in the back of his head was screaming in panicky embarrassment—but he stepped out of his shoes and pushed his underpants down regardless, as if on autopilot. *Put your clothes in the bag,* a half-imagined voice rang in his head like the tolling of an iron bell. *Deck yourself in holy raiment.* The holy raiment on the men's side consisted of a pair of incongruously blue Crocs and a hooded white robe, cut for a male torso, with a coarse rope for a belt at the waist; the women got gowns similar to the Sisterhood's. As it slid into place and puddled around his feet (Derek was slightly shorter than his companions), a tension not born of his own anxiety seemed to relax. He pulled the belt in and tied a loose knot just as Raven sidled past him, back into the center of the room.

This is wrong, Derek thought fuzzily, as he slid his clothing into a laundry bag. *I'll lose my dice.* They were still in their pouch, nestling in his trouser pocket. With a titanic effort of will he reached inside—

"Blessed be!" the Omphalos chorus trilled just as he straightened up. Number Three slid the dressing screen aside to reveal the bags of discarded clothing and the five companions, now robed or gowned for the tournament. Derek fumbled with his belt rope, surreptitiously knotting the dice-bag's cord onto it. "Welcome to the world of *Bones and Nightmares*!" They chanted in unison as if it was a hymn rather than a game intro. "We stand before you seekers after starry wisdom as your guides and shepherds, here to lead you into the grace of He Who Shines. Prepare to leave all your earthly woes and ills behind as you take your first steps along the road to enlightenment! You will learn mysteries and undergo great trials as you progress from station to station during your voyage! But today you start as novices in the Holy Order of the Five-Flowered Prince, Saint Xōchipilli! Who we shall meet at the climax of this tournament."

Derek rocked on his heels. Somewhere inside his head the magically muffled screaming intensified. Linda stood by his side, her face slack with concentration: Raven-and-Sam had coupled up on the other side of Phil, who Derek could not see without turning his head (which was oddly difficult to imagine).

The three sisters undulated along the corridor, confused grognards trailing in their wake. Sister Celeste had acquired a wicker basket from somewhere and scattered flower petals as she walked, grinding them into the carpet underfoot. Derek was distantly worried: Surely the hotel cleaners would not be amused? Sister Three led the way, humming an off-key melody that slithered and crawled through Derek's ears. Linda, walking at his side, tried to say something, but all he could make out was "I don't like . . ." before she trailed off, evidently as confused as he was. *This isn't*, he thought, then lost the thread. Something beginning with *g*? *Good? Groot?*

The procession wound around a corner and through a fire door. The carpet disappeared, replaced by paving stones. The walls opened up around them, wallpaper giving way to giant waist-high blocks of stone that appeared to have been carved by hand and fitted together without mortar or cement. Derek tried to look round at the entrance they'd come through but his neck was too stiff to turn. The air-conditioning and lights were out in this part of the hotel, but openings high up in the walls admitted daylight and air that was hot and dry, as if it had been desiccated by its passage across a desert plateau on an alien world. It didn't occur to him—he couldn't quite remember his name, for some reason—to look outside, but he intuitively knew that if he did he wouldn't see cars or traffic or anything familiar. It felt a bit like the passage through the wards around Camp Sunshine, as if they no longer stood within the bounds of their own world.

The adventure had begun.

►◄►◄►◄

"Good afternoon, Iris." The receiver in her hand buzzed and crackled as the sound of his voice stripped her of a couple of years of emotional distance.

"And good mor—afternoon to you, too, Michael." Her cheeks tightened in a grimace. "Been a long time."

"I wish it could be otherwise." He sounded almost regretful, the bastard—he'd consigned her to this place, after all.

Her indignation rose like the sap of a poisonous vine. "You never visited," she bit out. Or called, or wrote.

But Dr. Michael Armstrong, the Senior Auditor, hadn't phoned her to make small talk. "Brief me," he ordered. And Iris did so without complaint. The SA could compel her to spill her guts with a simple coded phrase: she wasn't sure he hadn't implanted other, more fatal commands in case of direst emergency. Staying on his good side—or as good as possible in view of the circumstances of her detention—was merely prudent. And in any case, the current situation was too dire for prevarication.

It took awhile to explain what had happened. Dr. Armstrong was a good listener, and didn't interrupt, although his incomprehension was almost palpable at times. But finally she finished.

"So, to summarize. Our escapee has spent close to thirty years in Camp Sunshine after being hauled in for no good reason during a media-driven 1980s witch hunt. His file notes state he was diagnosed with mild Asperger's syndrome in 1985 but no personality disorders, very good disciplinary record, and no *actual* history of sorcerous activity or nonstandard worship. But in aptitude tests he scored very highly so a decision was made not to release . . . resulting in him becoming completely institutionalized as a result of a chain of case management failures. Now he's chosen to take matters into his own hands, very elegantly forged a transfer authorization, and dropped off the map like an old pro. We don't know where he is, but you speculate that he wanted to go to a *gaming convention,* whatever that is, in Scarfolk of all places. And now I hear *for the first time* that he has postal privileges and corresponded with outsiders for *nearly twenty years* without coming to the attention of Camp Security? Can you explain the oversight?"

Iris tried not to sigh. "Oversight is in place. *All* inmate correspondence in and out is opened and routinely read by the duty censor. It's held and referred to the head of security if there's anything remotely questionable. Ordinary inmates have no postal privileges at all, so he was incommunicado for the first five years. After that, he was in a position—via the Ents Committee—to subscribe to a couple of periodicals, which were read and approved by the censor. Sometime later he wrote a letter and applied for membership of an, ah, play-by-mail game. I looked up the censor's notes— where we still have them, this goes back decades—and his correspondence was signed off on at every stage. Can't ask the censor in question, he retired more than a decade ago—"

"—Died three years later, either from Krantzberg syndrome or early onset Alzheimer's."

"—As you say." She breathed deeply. "This had been going on for nearly twenty years when I arrived, Michael. You can call it normalization of deviance if you like but *obviously* I did a full correspondence review in my first six months: Derek's stuff was deathly dull and didn't raise any flags. I mean, it was basically guided storytelling with dice rolling, for N—N—god's sake! Why can't we just tell the local cops to round him up? We already activated the escape protocol."

It was the SA's turn to groan. "Games aren't harmless, Iris. Like

films and TV shows and books, they create in the audience a willingness to suspend their disbelief—they create plausible entertaining lies that we accept uncritically for the duration of a session."

"Yes?" A nagging hint of insight dragged at the edge of her
attention, like a loose thread in an unraveling knitted jumper. "So
people believe in them?"

"Yes. Now remind me, what exactly happens during a religious
ceremony?" asked the SA.

"People who share a common belief gather together and . . ."
Her tongue juddered to a stop. "Oh *dear*."

"Here's another leading question for fifty experience points,"
Dr. Armstrong continued: "We know what deities and demiurges
we explicitly do or do *not* believe in. But how many potential deities are out there, waiting to be discovered beyond the walls of the
world? How many alien minds who nobody is yet aware of is it
possible to believe in? Possible to invoke?"

"Yes, yes, I see where you're going here," she said, absently doo-
dling skulls and a—totally forbidden—summoning diagram—
deliberately missing out the critical closed path that would activate
it—on her notepad. "Derek's taken his game book and he's going
to a party to hang out with a bunch of believers without adult
supervision. How bad can it be?"

"Funny you should ask," Dr. Armstrong replied briskly. "This
morning I had a very exciting phone call with Forecasting Ops.
They're irate, not to say frightened. Kept saying something about
Omphalos the Five-Flowered Prince, whose followers are apparently about to descend in force on the Scarfolk Britannia Hotel.
Or have *already* descended, they weren't entirely clear—you know
how it is with Forecasting Ops? Anyway, they say it's going to be a
major incident and you are personally required on-site and above
all else, to *bring Derek home*. They were very emphatic about that
last part. They said, and I quote, 'Tell her that if the DM is lost,
her god won't save her.'"

A clanging and banging filtered through the doorway. Iris
looked up. "Excuse me a minute," she said, placing the receiver
very precisely in the middle of the circle on her notepad. She stood

up and opened the door. "Can you keep it down—" she began to say, just as she realized that David Turnbull was not alone.

"Mrs. Carpenter?" asked the army captain standing in the entrance. He wore a police service uniform, an approved disguise for OCCULUS team members. (The public were less likely to panic if they mistook the Special Forces squad for something else.) "The Senior Auditor sends his compliments, and you're to wear this." He handed her a heavy steel locking collar. "You know what it is?"

"I've worn one before." She glared at him as he closed the collar around her neck. The lock clicked into place like a harbinger of death. "You don't need to read me the manual—"

"—explosive charge is to deter prisoners with exotic capabilities or codeword classified knowledge from trying to, eh, you know what? Don't worry, it won't go off by accident." A red LED blinked from the bulge under her chin, its reflection visible in the grubby window glass. "It's strictly an alternative to fate-worse-than-death outcomes, so you don't need to worry unless you were planning to turn coat and murder us all. Come along, your ride's waiting."

Turnbull cleared his throat. "You'll need these," he said, passing her a heavy-duty warding bracelet. He handed her a battered satchel once she'd snapped the shackle around her wrist. The satchel seemed to weigh half a ton: "That's a complete set of AD&D rule books, same version our man uses. There will be a library fine if they are returned late." Next he handed her an envelope. She looked inside it, irritated by the delay. *Ambushed.* It contained a travel authorization counterfoil in her name, and an exit token that would see her safely past the eldritch abominations guarding the approaches to the camp. It was an actual ticket-of-leave, except (thanks to the collar) it merely let her enter a bigger, more dangerous cell. Clearly David had been busy.

"I left the phone off the hook," she said: "Tell Dr. Armstrong I'm on my way." She shouldered the bag of books and followed the officer out to the vehicle enclosure, where something that looked like a Fire Incident Command Unit sat waiting—a big red lorry with CHESHIRE FIRE SERVICE painted on the side. (Iris took note of the discreet thaum field sensors and banishment grenade launchers mounted on the roof: definitely *not* standard for a fire truck.) "Let's get moving."

▸◂▸◂▸◂

"The adventure has begun!" chanted the sisters of Omphalos, followers of the Five-Flowered Prince, as they led Team Grognard toward a stone table. "Choose your weapons wisely! Then having chosen, proceed across yonder threshold!" Sister Three gestured toward an archway limned in shadow. *Should have played a half-elf,* Derek thought fuzzily: *ultravision would really help right now.*

The stone table bore a variety of objects which could, conceivably, be viewed as weapons if one was of an occult inclination. There was a bone flute, polished to an off-white sheen and drilled with finger holes; a black volcanic glass axe-blade bound to a wooden handle; a scroll of parchment, brightly painted with stylized cartoon warriors guarding an alien text; spears with knapped flint heads; and a black rubber sling mounted on a wooden handle.

"I—iro—meta—" Raven cleared his throat and tried again. "Are metal weapons not permitted?"

"Metal—" Sam screwed up her face. "What met-ul?" Her normally animated expression was dull.

It's an enchantment, Derek realized. *We're be-glamoured.* Compelled to comply with the rules the game imposed on them. This was live role play, after all. Not his thing, he vastly preferred tabletop—

Then the rubber slingshot somehow *spoke* to him. He picked it up, blindly accepting the anachronism. Was rubber permitted? Their footwear suggested as much. *But no met—meta—shiny stuff,* he realized.

"Choose your weapons." Sister Celeste's smile was strained, hinting at impatience. "Once you enter the pyramid you may not turn back. You will find food and drink along the way, but beware of rival tribes who seek to attain the flowery knowledge before you." Linda reached for the flute and the scroll, sliding the one inside the other. Phil took the obsidian axe; Sam and Raven were each left with their choice of spear. "Do not attempt to venture outside the pyramid complex, much less approach the fence beyond: that way is death."

The three sisters sang out in unison: "Walk the flowery path! Seek the five-petalled wisdom! Walk the path to summon Xōchipilli! Farewell! Farewell! *Fare*—"

They shimmered and faded out like a bad '60s special effect, leaving Derek and his teammates alone in the room.

"What the ever-loving *fuck*?" cried Samantha, shaking herself.

Derek blinked as everything around him slammed into focus: the hot, dry air, the lack of traffic noise and birdsong, combined with a palpable sense of age.

"Oh fucksickles," said Linda, "I think we're actually inside—"

"—*Bones and Nightmares*," Phil interrupted. He glared at Derek: "Got any suggestions, DM? Because this isn't what I—we—were expecting."

"How did they *do* that to us?" asked Sam. "It was like I couldn't even couldn't even—"

"Think?" Phil asked.

"Hypnosis," Raven said firmly.

"I—" Derek's hand instinctively went to his dice bag. "Oh, oh *yes*."

Linda took hold of his left arm. "Before you have an orgasm all on your lonesome because we've fallen into a bad LitRPG, is there something you need to tell us?"

"A—" The phrase *what's a LitRPG?* died on Derek's lips as the implication sank in. "Yeah, *that*." He took a deep breath, relishing how easily the words were coming now: "You know they held me in a-a special camp for the past thirty or so years? For playing AD&D in my teens? Well, it wasn't *entirely* crazy. Magic is real. You can practice magic by calculation and mathematics or by incantation and belief. There's an entire government department out there devoted to suppressing it, so the first time they came across a D&D session—in the middle of the Satanic Panic of the eighties—they freaked.

"Out of the box, D&D itself isn't magical. At least, I don't think so: with enough rule supplements and lookup tables and the right set of dice you can make *anything* summon a minor demon.

And the D&D core rules are Turing-complete. But anyway, I'm pretty sure the Omphalos people are cultists. *Bones and Nightmares* is designed to recruit true believers in, um, Xō-Xōchipilli. And the other teams in this, uh, tournament, don't know this so they'll be easy meat, soaking it up through their skin. *Bones and Nightmares* actually *is* magic, the kind where you perform rituals that make things that want to be gods in our universe pay too much attention to you. And—" He took another deep breath, then summoned his two lucky d20s into his right hand: they glowed green as he rolled them across the stone tabletop. "—so is *Cult of the Black Pharaoh*."

Everyone tried to speak at once, backed off, then tried again. If looks could kill Derek would have been an instant barbecue wearing a melted pair of Crocs. It took a minute for the grognards to stop banging and fizzling like firecrackers before he could continue. "Let me explain." Derek rolled his dice, then placed the rest of his collection beside them. He had dice for all the platonic solids: tetrahedron, cube, octahedron, dodecahedron, teapotahedron (the latter a manifold that could exhibit symmetry in a non-Euclidean space with a sanity-warping fractional dimensionality).

"I wrote *Cult of the Black Pharaoh* as a set of rules expanding on AD&D 2e that added magical properties, real ones not in-game spells. Magic is a branch of applied mathematics. It relies on alg-algorithms. It's procedural and generative and the laws of sympathy and contagion apply and above all you need a set of rules for it. I made these magical dice for use as an oracle when DM'ing *Cult of the Black Pharaoh* but—" *More* uproar. He really couldn't understand what was so controversial about his approach.

"Listen!" Linda took charge. "We're stuck in this, this *scenario,* but we've read the *Bones and Nightmares* rules—"

"The public version," Raven piped up.

Sam: "Dude, *not* helping!"

"—So we've got some idea what we're up against—" cultists trying to immanentize the eschatological reality of a generative god, one the high priest rolled up from a set of homebrew game tables by means of an oracular process "—and we've got our *own* DM, which has to mean we've got an advantage, right?"

"What?" Derek's voice rose into a squeak. "You want me to roll a *custom* deity?"

Phil looked alarmed: "Let's not get ahead of ourselves here!"

Bones and Nightmares had made it perfectly clear that when the gods squabbled, puny mortals were squished underfoot like bugs. The scenario the Omphalos sisters had sung for them in three-part harmony made it plain that they were already up against a variant Aztec deity. Xōchipilli could well be the cuddliest demi-urge to come out of Tamoanchan, more interested in sex and drugs than mass human sacrifice—his nearest classical western cognate was Eros—but that didn't make him harmless. His rites were associated with board games and games of chance, and it wasn't unheard of for players to gamble their freedom away at his table. If you tried to invite another deity into his sacred space to contest his primacy—

"Look." Linda pointed. "Archway. Unspecified dream-quest in search of starry wisdom about a Nahua god of male prostitutes, fertility, board games, and flowers! Rival teams going full munchkin on the dungeon crawl, getting stabby with obsidian blades! Let's just *go,* all right? Before the floor turns into a pit trap full of giant centipedes or something."

Derek gulped. "Who wants to take point?"

Raven hefted his spear. "After you, fearless leader."

"Check for a portcullis trap," Raven cautioned.

Derek squinted myopically at the capstone of the archway. None of the stones were mortared, but they looked as if they'd stood in place for centuries. Possibly longer, if time in this place stretched the way he suspected it might. He shuddered. "Only one thing for it—"

"Wait!" Linda grabbed his arm. To Raven, "Give me that." She snatched his spear, then poked it ahead as she led Derek across the threshold.

►◄►◄►◄

Death from above—or below—failed to eventuate, despite the threat of portcullis traps and pitfalls. This was a good thing. Derek was acutely worried that his team of inexperienced noobs lacked a healer, not to mention anything resembling armor: in event of an attack by a wandering monster of comparable lethality to a ten-week-old kitten, the likeliest outcome was a wipeout.

As Derek and Linda cautiously explored the stone passage beyond the archway—illuminated by daylight filtering through air shafts high in the walls—his skin crawled. He glanced round just as the others stepped inside. The air behind them began to shimmer: Linda caught his gaze. "Oh great, we're being railroaded." She sounded disgusted. "Tour the dungeon, kill the monsters, detect and evade the traps, steal the treasure, *really*? I thought this was an RPG, not a shopping trip to IKEA."

"They're cultists." A fertile imagination was a bit much to ask of someone whose gray matter was being chewed on by extradimensional parasites, in Derek's opinion. "We can roll with that, can't we? At least we know the general plan."

Phil the Ferret twitched. "Dial clichés to stun," he muttered, hefting his axe. The volcanic glass blade shimmered in the watery light, throwing off a faint glow. Phil startled: "Hey, who knows their geology? Is this stuff radioactive? It feels weird—"

"Probably enchanted," Linda cautioned.

Derek cleared his throat. "The basics were covered in the Congregation Leader's Guide, chapter four, Artefacts and Antiquities. Obviously your axe is a custom piece—this setting doesn't resemble the sample campaign *at all*—but no sane GM would send us into a dungeon crawler unprotected and unarmored unless—"

"—Hey, what's—"

"*That?*"

"—Fuckin 'ell that's a big cockroach!" Phil swung his axe at a dinner-plate-sized black-and-white bug, which hissed like an irate teakettle, waggled its antennae, raised its tail, and unfolded fanlike wing cases that spun and wafted a foul-smelling breeze toward them.

Derek emitted a tiny whimper.

"Oh for fuck's sake." Linda hiked up her hem, stepped smartly forward, and kicked the bug in its mouthparts. "Okay, now we *know* they've got no imagination." She side-eyed Derek. "It's harmless, see?"

"N-*no* it only *looks* like a first edition D&D rust monster, it's got to be a dirty trick—" Derek warned as the bug turned to directly aim its hindquarters toward them. The stench intensified horrifically. "Get back, *no Raven don't poke it you don't know what it'll*—" But he was too late. Raven was unable to redirect his lunge. *"Climb for the air vents!"*

Once they recovered—which involved much choking and coughing, a little projectile vomiting, and unanimous swearing and gasping for breath—Derek inspected the exploded corpse of the definitely-not-a-rust-monster. He didn't bother pinching his nostrils: his olfactory bulb was stunned. Indeed, his sense of smell would probably never be the same again. To be fair, neither would the giant bug.

"Next time," he told Raven, "do *not* stab the—" *gasp* "—skunk bug in the ass."

Raven was still too busy throwing up to reply. Perhaps this was for the best, as none of them were in a good mood right now and they were all armed with implements of carnage that might lend themselves to a really violent barney after pub chucking-out time. Or a tour of an abandoned temple crawling with rust monsters.

"Lessons learned," announced Linda: "Whoever designed this tournament is a devious asshole."

"Turning our expectations against . . ." Samantha trailed off. She turned and glared at Derek.

"What?" he asked.

"This is totally your style, isn't it?" she accused.

"It wasn't me! I'm right here, aren't I? There are no rust monsters in *Cult of the Black Pharaoh*! I clearly remember listing them in the deprecated/obsolete section!"

"No, but you used to play AD&D back in the day. And it'd be just like you to turn our expectation of rust monsters against us, *especially* as none of us are carrying any iron or steel, which ought to be a honking great clue-by-four about the game mechanics, right?" Sam was working up a head of steam.

"Wait a mo." Linda stepped between them. "You're absolutely right but I *know* it can't be Derek, we saw him arrive and he hasn't had time to hole up with the Omphalos crew all weekend so—"

"Collective subconscious," Phil said suddenly. "What if they're feeding our expectations back to us?"

"Procedurally, that would be—" Derek stopped. "Excuse me." He fumbled in his dice bag. "What do you see ahead of us?"

"Uh?" Phil blinked, then sniffed suspiciously. "A corridor—" he trailed off uncertainly.

"I'm going to roll." Years ago, when he'd had a long summer flu and a new round of *Cult of the Black Pharaoh* was looming, he'd cheated and ginned up a set of random dungeon generator tables to keep things moving until he felt well enough to return to a properly designed campaign. Now he blew the dust off it. "1–2, there's a door on the left; 3–4, there's an archway leading to a new area; 5, there's a pit trap; 6, the corridor bends sharply left. Okay?" Derek palmed a single d6 then rolled it along the corridor.

"Two," said Linda. She sidled forward toward the door on the left that hadn't been there a moment ago. "Shit. What happens if someone else calls it? I mean, calls for what's behind the door?" She pointed at the lintel, which resembled a row of grinning stylized skulls, and the doorposts, which were engraved with skeletons. "I am getting a distinct theme here, and it does not fill me with warm fuzzies."

"Sam, would you give me some options?" Derek picked up the die. It was glowing again, the pure sapphire blue of Cerenkov radiation emitted when *mana*—stored magic in its wild indeterminate state—decayed into reality.

"You want me to tell you, or just think of 'em?"

"I, I . . . you know what? You think of something. I'll roll and tell you the number, then when we move you tell me if it matches. Stick to three or four options and map them onto a d6 roll. Is that okay?"

"Sure, roll away . . . now."

Derek rolled. "Three," he announced.

Sam swallowed. "Going to open the door now. Raven? Pointy stick time—"

"—Are we walking into a fight?" Linda demanded.

"I hope not! I mean, not if the dice roll worked properly."

"That's so reassuring," Raven snarked, bringing his spear around and kicking the door open without warning: "*Leeroy*—oh."

"Phew!" Sam dabbed at her forehead in pantomime relief. "*Don't*," she said, grabbing Raven's belt before he could step inside.

"Why? What did you—"

Derek tiptoed forward. The room smelled musty and slightly foul, as if something had died in here long ago. Wan daylight filtered in through a row of air vents high in one wall. Stone shelves filled three walls from floor to ceiling, gray and dusty with age. Wooden boxes a couple of meters long filled the shelves, almost like—

"Coffins," said Sam. "Close enough: roll of three was for a crypt."

"Right." Derek concentrated. There were at least six shelves on each wall, and the coffins were packed tightly enough that there could easily be thirty or forty cadavers in here. Mummies, skeletons, z—"C-crap! Linda, flute, *flute!*"

"What about the flute?" She looked uncertain, even as the lid of one of the coffins behind her slowly began to slide sideways.

"Play something! We've got undead incoming!"

"But what good will—" She held the bone flute in one hand, looking perplexed.

"Start playing now or we're dead!" Derek turned in place, scanning the room. Something was missing, his subconscious screamed: Something was *wrong*. It took him a few seconds to realize that the door had closed while Team Grognard were distracted, *because we're gamers not fucking adventurers*. Suddenly the name of the Omphalos game began to resonate urgently— *Bones and Nightmares*—and he blessed Sam for bringing his attention to the question of game mechanics. "You've got a bone flute and a scroll. That makes you the cleric of the party and you need to figure out how to turn undead *right now* or—"

He fumbled urgently in his dice bag. Dense round objects had somehow gotten mixed in with the dice. He pulled a couple out, feeling the heft of smooth stones in his palm. He raised the slingshot with his other hand. There was a screech of dry wood as a lid clattered to the floor. Bony digits grasped the lip of the open coffin as the bundle of ligaments and parchment, wrapped around still-articulated bones, began to sit up.

"*Fuuuck!*" wailed Phil, waving his axe around—to little effect save to nearly open one of his own arteries. On every side the dead were waking from their slumber, rustling and creaking and in some cases banging their crania on the shelves above. Raven was swearing continuously and turning in place, back-to-back with Sam, both trying to point their spears in all directions at once.

"Blow down the mouth hole!" Derek told Linda, then remembered he had a weapon of his own. He raised his slingshot and let fly at the nearest upright skeleton.

The pebble banged noisily into the side of its coffin and the corpse turned toward him, grinning horribly. For a moment he saw shelves between its open jaws—

Then Linda blew across one of the holes in the flute. She barely made a sound, but the skull that had been leering at him tilted to one side, as if listening to a barely audible call. The flute glowed a pallid green. Derek reached for another pebble, his fingers numb with fright: "Louder!" he called, and somehow shot the mummy that had been creeping up on Phil, hitting it square in the head. *I meant to do that,* he thought, taken aback by his unexpected accuracy.

Linda inhaled and blew properly this time, a flat wavering note like the wind whistling through the rib cage of a long-forgotten sacrifice abandoned to the elements on a desert plateau. Derek drew and let fly again, and each time he did so it went more smoothly than the last, his hands moving nimbly and without any conscious engagement. The game had an imperative of its own, carrying the players along with it. Linda blew a third note, this time covering two of the finger holes, and *now* the mummies that had been rising froze as if in fear: one of them, taking the full force of her trill, clattered noisily back into its box.

"Wait 'til they drop then hit 'em on the head!" Derek told Phil as he selected another target. It seemed the most prudent use for the axe, after all.

▸◂▸◂◂

The Cheshire Fire and Rescue Service command vehicle rumbled through the Peak District with its light bar flashing, using the occasional siren-blast to startle sheep out of the road ahead of it. Iris sat in the middle of a row of chairs in the back of the truck, sandwiched between Captain Anderson and a sergeant called Pete. Their seats faced a desk and a rack of CRT monitors with yellowing plastic surrounds. The OCCULUS vehicles were all a decade overdue for replacement, and this one felt like it was on its last legs: Iris's vision blurred and the teeth rattled in her head as the vehicle bounced up and down on its shot shock absorbers.

Blessedly, Iris thought, this particular team were entirely unfamiliar with her, and presumably unfamiliar with the events leading to her imprisonment: they just knew her as an expert on their target, cooperative (for now) but unreliable. "What extra resources can we call on at the scene?" she asked Captain Anderson. "I mean, is it just us or are there extra teams inbound?"

Anderson, who'd been busy reading an email update, gave her a hard look. "The police have thrown a cordon around the hotel, called in the tactical AFUs, and set up an incident command center, but we're the first responders. First fully equipped, I should say." He glanced at his screen again: "Have you ever heard of an outfit called the Omphalos Corporation?"

"Dr. Armstrong mentioned the name. Can't say I've heard of the company, though."

"He just emailed me an update. London pulled the Britannia Hotel's reservations list for the weekend. Omphalos is a Term of Interest per Forecasting Ops, and these Omphalos Corporation Johnnies have at least a dozen bodies in the hotel. Which is a red flag right there as they're a Silicon Valley start-up and Scarfolk's only IT industry is Bazza the Fence's Refurbished Phones and Chipped PlayStations Emporium. So what are they doing at a pencil-and-paper gaming convention?"

"I—wait." Iris thought for a moment. "Is there *any* chance it's just a coincidence? Or is there a confirmed connection?"

"Their corporate credit card paid for the convention's function rooms. Oh, and nobody's been clocked entering or leaving the hotel in the past fifty minutes. Since roughly ten o'clock this morning."

"Okay, that's definitely not sounding good." She licked dry lips. It was outside her wheelhouse, but she knew who could handle this . . . "Is Dr. Angleton available?"

The sergeant running the comms station next to her visibly flinched. "I can see they kept you out of the loop in Camp Sunshine," said Captain Anderson, his face a closed book. "What you see is what we've got. Dr. Angleton is definitely not available."

"His assistant might—" she shook her head. *It'd be a cold day in hell before Bob would work with me again. Even if he agreed with why I—that.* "Forget him then, let's do this."

Nestled beneath muddy green hillsides patrolled by high-tension grid pylons and diseased sheep, Scarfolk was an indistinct blur of gray housing association estates, bland suburbia, and brutalist concrete shop fronts left over from the early 1970s. When first experienced on a rainy weekend morning it felt like a town where hope went to die. As the OCCULUS truck rumbled along the high street, occasionally balking at crumbling speed bumps so high they posed a very real risk of spinal injuries, Iris speed-read the emails about Omphalos Corporation. They told a very familiar story: she recognized the stench of a front organization for a mystery cult when she sniffed it. After all, once upon a time she'd controlled one.

"Do you have any recommendations for how to proceed?" Anderson asked her. "Other than *Caedite eos: Novit enim Dominus qui sunt eius?*"

Iris shuddered. "I hope it doesn't come to that," she said. "It's just a bunch of nerdy tabletop gamers, after all." But she was whistling past the graveyard, and they both knew it.

The truck pulled up in a desolate car park that had been strewn with police cars by a gigantic, petulant toddler who'd grown bored of their full-sized toy box. Anderson stretched and cracked his knuckles, as the door behind him opened and four soldiers—the door breakers—climbed out. The SAS worked in four-person teams called patrols: this mission had two—the mobility troop who managed the truck, and the door breakers, whose choice of firearms was very nonstandard indeed for a police AFU. For this mission they wore police Armed Firearms Unit uniforms, minus identifying numbers, with cameras on their helmets. "I'll be back in a mo," Anderson said as he stood up and followed the door breakers: "Stick with Pete." Pete, the operator on the signals desk beside her, nodded.

"I hate waiting," Iris muttered.

"Won't be long, I shouldn't think." Pete pushed his chair back and pulled out a Glock with an alarmingly long magazine: "Are you certificated?"

"I was, it expired while I was inside—" Iris blinked. "Wait, you trust me with *that*?"

"There's a *geas* interlock on the grip safety: if you try to shoot any of us it'll tell your collar you're a very naughty girl." He winked horribly as he handed her the weapon. "No, really, it's safe as houses."

"I'd rather not, if it's all the same to you." Not long after arriving at Camp Sunshine, Iris had engaged in some soul-searching and resolved to eschew wet work for the rest of her life. She'd made sufficient sacrifices to prove herself to her Lord: self-inflicted moral injuries never really healed, and she was reluctant to inflict any more on herself. She pushed the gun aside. "Are we expecting to be attacked by corporate marketing drones?"

"Guerilla marketing is the hot new—" Pete stopped speaking, listened to his earpiece intently, then began calmly reciting instructions as his hands flew over a scratched-up video mixing panel. Images sprang into view on the screens in front of them, confusingly jerky B&W shots from moving camera angles. Walls and bodies blurred past. "Red One reports lobby clear, over." Pause. "Red Three office suite clear, over. Gold Commander authorizes you to proceed at will, weapons hot, over." Through the open door, Iris could just make out a group of cops—a real Armed Response Unit, not a fake one—darting through the hotel front doors.

"Red Two function space 103 is clear"—Pete leaned sideways and hastily fumbled in a drawer, pulled out a spare wireless headset, and shoved it at Iris—"sending her out now, Green Two going dark for sixty seconds." He flipped his microphone boom out of the way as he turned to face her: "You put it on like so, there's only one channel on yours, mute toggle is *here,* try not to talk. Skipper wants you over with the Bronze Commander."

"Wait—" Iris pointed at her throat. "—what about this?"

"It's a cervical collar, you were in a car crash. Hey, don't forget your sidearm! Go, go!"

Iris absentmindedly shoved the gun in her book bag and went—the steps were steep and her knees did not welcome a crash landing on tarmac—then hastily scuttled through the cold shower. Captain Anderson was already inside the white incident tent, which was buzzing with cops like bees around the neck of an open jar of sugar syrup. The awning was up, open end pointing at the hotel entrance. Anderson was deep in conversation with a superintendent, evidently the Bronze Commander on-site: a female, with salt-and-pepper hair, who radiated a very strong aura of do-not-get-in-my-way. The super seemed displeased, but at least she was listening to the captain. As Iris approached, Anderson glanced at her.

"This is Mrs. Carpenter, a civil service analyst specializing in this type of incident. Iris, this is Superintendent Kumar, Bronze Commander. Once Red Team have secured the designated materials and our escapee I'll need you to—"

A blast of static from her earpiece made Iris wince. The skin on the nape of her neck wanted to crawl away and hide: somewhere nearby a powerful thaum flux kicked off, magical potential bleeding into entropy. The air in the hotel doorway rippled as if in a heat haze, and she heard, faintly, "Red Four high field encountered, wards holding, moving on, go."

"What—" Kumar began to ask as Iris toggled her mute button. "Sitrep, *right now.*"

"They're in and they've encountered resistance," Iris told Kumar as Captain Anderson ran toward the lobby, then threw himself against the wall beside the front door. Another operator—the driver's mate from the front of the OCCULUS truck—rushed after him, bringing an AA-12 to bear as he, too, took shelter. "Wait, we have hard contact! We should get out of—"

"*Shooter! Take cover! Move it people!*" Kumar shouted, grabbed

Iris's shoulder, and heaved her out of direct line of sight of the doorway. Officers scattered, abandoning the command tent. To her credit Kumar didn't bother swearing: it would have been redundant anyway, as nobody would have been able to hear her over the hammering of automatic weapons inside the hotel. "*What is happening in there—*"

The guns fell silent. Something in the building hissed peevishly, like a snake the size of a tube train or the leaking coolant circuit of a nuclear reactor venting steam. The puddles in the car park potholes vibrated: then the ground-floor windows on the side of the hotel pulsed twice and blew out in a shower of rainbow splinters.

Iris's headset fell silent. Something big—presumably whatever had silenced Red Two—was approaching.

▶◀▶◀▶◀

"So guys, what have we learned so far?" asked Linda.

She was slumped with her back against the wall on one side of the latest passageway, pink-cheeked and panting from the race to outpace the giant swinging axe blade released by Phil dicking around in the room with the clay-and-lapis-encrusted skull racks.

"Cultural appropriation sucks," volunteered Samantha, "especially when the culture in question really desperately wants to sacrifice you so the sun rises tomorrow morning."

"Do not taunt happy fun pendulum blade trap," suggested Phil.

Raven ran shaky fingers through his beard before offering, "Close shaves are best avoided: it's all fun and games until someone loses an eye—or their head."

Derek twitched, his eyes ceaselessly seeking any sign of safety.

Bones and Nightmares relied on a heavily modified version of the D&D character class system—evidently Hasbro's IP lawyers hadn't noticed yet—and the three sisters had departed without handing out character sheets, or indeed anything beyond the advice to "Walk the flowery path! Seek the five-petalled wisdom! And summon Xōchipilli." Which would have been a hell of a lot more useful if any of them could read the local hieroglyphs. But they hadn't even been handed character sheets to play, much less an Olman-English dictionary or anything to fill their spell slots with. Just getting oriented was a grind—and a race against time.

It had become apparent fairly quickly that Linda was some sort of magically augmented god botherer (patron deity: unknown, but probably not JesusVerse™-compatible). Derek was an oracular mage or a recursively embedded dungeon master or something even more ridiculous; Phil the Ferret was clearly a sneak-thief or rogue, albeit a crap one; while Raven and Sam had proven adequate at fending off the walking dead with pointy sticks. They were, in short, a rather bumbling but not entirely atypical dungeon crawler party, which made Derek wish for a torture chamber in which he could chain up the Omphalos Corporation's content creators while he ranted at them about the finer points of running an adventure.

They'd been dice-rolling their way through the passageways, chambers, and pit traps of the ancient temple complex for hours, but the shadows cast by the ventilation shafts had barely lengthened. Without writing implements recording their path had been challenging, but they'd established that the lower level—where they'd entered—was a mausoleum, room after room full of bones. The first chamber had coffins with mostly intact mummified bodies, but later they'd discovered wicker baskets full of disarticulated bones which took on the most disturbingly incomplete shapes when they rose.

"It's a fucking barracks," Phil grumbled. "A barracks of the undead."

"Makes sense, it's the best way to keep your infantry ready without having to worry about feeding them. Or pay," Derek added with grudging admiration. "I should have thought of it."

"Wouldn't that be, I mean, a bit necromancer-intensive?" Linda asked. Although she kept her thighbone flute raised, her shoulders drooped with fatigue. "If it's as much work animating them as it is putting them down again, they must have a bunch of priests busting their asses."

"Look, we're getting nowhere slowly," said Phil. "Maybe we should try mixing it up? Roll us a staircase to a new level, or maybe a chapel full of disturbing symbolic sculptures that explain the theology in play here?"

"No!" Sam and Raven shouted simultaneously. Derek emphatically agreed: chapels in spooky temples full of undead tended to offer exciting opportunities to get up close and personal with sacrificial altars or demons.

"But we definitely need to get out of the crypt level," Derek conceded. "A staircase would be good. But no attack theology, okay?" Vigorous nods all round. "Linda, would you mind being the random architectural encounter table for this turn?"

"If I must. Humph."

"Okay." Derek rolled, dice glowing faintly: "And that's a natural six."

"Door to T-junction corridor. Left or right?"

Derek prepared to roll again while Sam, Raven, and Phil prepared to rush the door. "Let's go with right. And I get—"

"Roll again, there's something odd."

"Four?"

"Passage then stairs leading up!"

Phil cheered as he shoved the door open: "Woo-hoo!"

On the right, the corridor offered up a couple of doorways that—judging by the now boringly familiar skull motif on the surrounds—contained more dehydrated spear carriers. To the left, the corridor ended in a staircase leading up. And across the corridor from the door they had emerged from, someone had scrawled the English letters BEWARE PIRANHAS. The brown pigment they'd used was the color of dried blood.

"Hey guys, I think we're being warned."

"Beware the deadly Land Piranhas, flopping after us menacingly on their fins."

"Don't *say* that, it might come true!"

Derek cleared his throat. "Stairs first, ominous warnings later."

Upstairs they found themselves in a room with an electrified floor. Luckily their Crocs turned out to be pretty good insulators, although Derek didn't enjoy his dice roll *at all*.

The next corridor was blocked by a barely translucent cubozoan that sucked and squidged slowly after them as they retreated. They'd have walked right into it if not for the roseate tint it had acquired from the incompletely digested explorer embedded in it, bones visible but slowly eroding—the second sign that they weren't the first party to have come this way.

When they retreated back to the electrified room they learned that burning Gelatinous Cube smelled awful: but once they squeezed around it, careful not to contact any of the barely visible tentacles twitching on the floor, the corridor was clear all the way to the next murder room.

"This Saw sequel really sucks," said Phil, pointing out the elaborate and extremely heavy-looking gold collar sitting between two golden pillars on the altar at the side of the room. Two passageways beckoned ahead beneath archways capped by bas-relief skulls, one smiling and one looking as if it was about to burst into tears. "I mean, *really*?"

"Seems to be targeting non-gamers," Sam grumbled as she stepped over the desiccated headless corpse slumped in front of the altar. She'd been out of sorts ever since the incident with the giant land jellyfish. Enthusiastically putting down undead horrors was fine but jellies had eyes and a nervous system and electrocuting them—even in self-defense—offended her vegan sensibilities. (Apparently her stab-it-with-a-stick specialty might prove problematic once they ran out of undead.) "Where's all the blood?" she asked.

"Probably sucked out by the—you know." Linda covered her mouth, eyes widening as she saw the severed head, which had not rolled very far at all. "Oh god, I think I recognize him from breakfast yesterday, he got the last of the bacon."

"Fan or Omphalos?"

"The latter. Ick."

"They probably hired a bunch of local marketers," Raven reassured her. "Chuggers and the like. It was doing him a mercy, really, putting him out of his misery." Derek, who had no idea what a chugger was—*Is it a Thomas the Tank Engine reference?*—held his peace.

"We should keep moving," he tried, once it was clear that Linda wasn't going to throw up. "So. Which way now?"

►◄►◄►◄

The comforting myth of the friendly British bobby, armed only with a smile, a truncheon, and a pair of handcuffs, had long since ceased to reflect reality in any meaningful way. For which Iris was profoundly grateful when something grotesque lurched out of the depths of the hotel, roaring and slavering bloody drool. It had ropy red-streaked meat snagged on the fangs of one of its five mouths. *Are those intestines?* It had to crouch to get through the lobby. *Canid,* she thought, absently opening her bag, *brindled coat, five heads, stabby thing on its tail*—she reached inside—*claws like a velociraptor*—slid the lever to select burst mode—*are those bat wings?*—she assumed the Weaver stance and raised her Glock G-18C—

—Then slowly lowered it, wincing at the hammering gunfire that converged on the doorway from all directions. Bloody giblets, fangs, and an amputated arse dagger splattered everywhere. The police shooters were already dialled in and one middle-aged manager with an expired certificate and a pistol with ideas above its station wouldn't add much to half a dozen H&K MP5s. It was excessive even by American policing standards: the OCCULUS team seemed redundant.

"What. The fuck. Is *that*?" Superintendent Kumar shouted, losing her cool: "Which one of you absolute *morons* lit up first without following the ROE? What if it's an endangered species? What if the zoo are looking for—"

"It's not!" Iris shouted back at her—the ringing in her ears suggested shoutiness was the order of the day. "This is an incursion! Sitrep." She tapped her earpiece, but the Red Team channel remained terrifyingly dead. "That thing—" She pointed, remembered she was holding a loaded machine pistol, and hastily lowered it. "—is *not of this world!* It has five—count them—*five* heads. Your eyes are not deceiving you." (Well—three now, and one of them was definitely the worse for wear.) "This is our department." She peered at the wall where Captain Anderson had taken cover. "It's our job to sort this for you. You just need to keep the site locked down and kill anything—*not* people, any *thing*—that tries to escape before we give you the all clear. People you can arrest now and book out later."

One of the cops halfway across the car park was kneeling beside a bloody canine head the size of a Siberian tiger's. "'Ere, skipper, what if it's rabid?"

"What if—" Kumar pinched the bridge of her nose with extreme deliberation. "I am surrounded by idiots," she muttered, too quietly for her temporarily deafened officers to hear. Then she made a beeline toward Iris. Her steps were jerky and overcontrolled, as if propelled by a steam engine with the emergency relief valve welded shut, but she caught up halfway to the entrance. "Stop!"

Iris stopped and turned to face her. Going by the Super's expression Kumar had just run out of fucks to give and was not in a borrowing mood. Also, she had heavily tooled up henchmen: cooperation seemed prudent. "Who *are* you people, who gave you that gun, what *is* that animal, where did it come from, and what on earth are you wearing?"

"*They* are a specialist SAS team. *I'm* from the agency that sends them out to deal with things like *that* when they wander in from another universe to snack on people like *you,* and *this* is a collar bomb—I'm told it's absolutely the latest fashion accessory for the captured clergy of dark gods. In about ten seconds I'm going—" Captain Anderson was sitting up, groggy and soaked in blood: paramedics were converging on him, he clearly wouldn't be participating. "—*in there* to make sure nothing else comes out and eats anyone. There's a man in the back of that truck called Pete who's running the comms desk: He'll put you through to headquarters. Ask for Dr. Armstrong."

Iris entered the hotel lobby. As she crossed the threshold she passed through the weird heat-haze shimmer. It felt like ghostly fingers rummaging through her internal organs. Her wrist-ward buzzed sharply and she nearly took a step back, but the ghastly sensation went away and then her ward fell silent again. Almost immediately the sounds from outside became muted. Everything in the reception area looked sharper, brighter, more *real*. And so did the smells: she paused and took shallow breaths as she tried to regain control of her stomach.

Iris had participated in more than one human sacrifice, but she was tidy and somewhat fastidious and would *never* drape the hotel lobby chandelier with intestines. The reception staff stared at her dully from the check-in desk, blood puddling on the marble counter beneath the stumps of their necks. The concierge—Iris swallowed and tapped her microphone.

"Green Two this is Iris, do you copy?"

Silence.

She sighed. There was no telling if her headset was transmitting, but she continued to narrate regardless. "I'm in the lobby area. Three confirmed civilian fatalities, no visible survivors." She scanned the area systematically, gun ready. The grue that had sprayed across the interior—a severed arm in a police uniform sleeve was neatly positioned on the coffee table in the seating area—might be attributed to the dog-thing, but the neatly positioned decapitees in the check-in area implied human participation. "Correction, three confirmed civilian fatalities, evidence of one Red Team member traumatic amputation, prognosis rapidly fatal but body absent. The civilians show signs of ritual sacrifice: if you have a backgrounder on the Omphalos cult I need it stat." Human sacrifice implied a need for *mana,* magical energy that could be tapped for various purposes, most commonly a summoning—in which case she needed to know why. The dog-thing was probably an uninvited interloper that had come through the open portal in search of a midnight snack.

Iris swept the lobby area. This wasn't her first rodeo: before her incarceration she'd been employed as an internal tech support manager, but some of her earlier postings had involved tasks that to this day she didn't want to think about too closely. (There was a good reason why she'd been put in charge of Angleton's irritating understudy.) She kept up her running commentary as she checked the offices behind the front desk, then the lobby area toilets, the luggage lock-up and janitorial cupboards, the closet with the servers and telephone switch, and finally the dining room.

"Sitrep, dining room. Breakfast buffet still laid out beneath heat lamps, tables not cleared, chairs and furniture in disarray, kitchen and serving staff absent. There's a large table in the middle, other furniture has been pushed back to clear a space—" She covered her mouth as she knelt and carefully inspected the carpet.

"—someone drew a capture grid around the central table using bodily fluids, eight corner candles, black wax that smells like human tallow. They made a burned offering on the table, subject was male, probably aged forty to sixty, not restrained, I'm not getting any closer." Her wrist-ward vibrated warningly as she approached the energized magic circle around the table. "The grid's still up, whatever it's powering is active. I think Class Five or above, probably a gate somewhere." She swallowed again. "Whatever they did to the subject took some time but there are no signs of resistance. Identification will be problematic." If it wasn't for the still-active circle she'd be tempted to chuck a napkin across what was left of the victim's face. "Moving on."

Iris came to a noticeboard, and read the details of the coming tournament back to her headset. It had been scheduled to start a couple of hours ago, she noted with deep foreboding. Once she got past the lobby area the electricity was out, leaving her with only the weak light diffusing through the windows for illumination.

She found the owner of the missing arm in the corridor leading to the function space, face down in a spreading pool of blood. As expected, he was one of the Red Team operators. She was frankly astonished he'd made it that far: the traumatic amputation wasn't his only wound. His weapon—another police-issue MP5, with some sort of exotic camera rig bolted to its upper rail—lay nearby. She knelt and checked his belt, found a holstered Glock and two spare magazines, and took the ammunition without hesitation. "Body of deceased Red Team operator in corridor to function space. He's the arm amputee, so presumably the others are up—*ulp!*"

Iris came to gasping for breath, the world spinning around her head.

"Sorry about that, Mrs. Carpenter!" someone said cheerfully: "Can't be too careful these days, can we?"

She blinked repeatedly as she waited for the throbbing and buzzing in her ears to go away. "Ack," she finally managed. *Choke hold around a collar bomb, very deftly done, where the* hell *did he come from?* She could have sworn she'd been alone in the corridor, and she was a professional paranoid. "That's me," she averred, then stopped to gasp for breath again before she looked at her attacker.

Her attacker was wiry but well-built, with blue eyes twinkling behind thick-rimmed, black, shatterproof glasses. A neatly trimmed black beard lent him an incongruously hipsterish air. "Pleased to meetcha! I'm Red Two. Red One and Red Four are up front. Sam here was Red Three until events eventuated." An unreadable expression crossed his face. "What's the sitch out front?"

"The thing with five heads is dead." She swallowed. "Captain Anderson's on his way to A&E in an ambulance, Blue Three is on comms, I don't think Blues Two and Four will be following us in, so that makes me the nearest thing to civilian oversight you've got. Am I reading that right?"

"Yup!" Red Two nodded enthusiastically. "Hard contact with fatalities normally means we'd take off and nuke the site from orbit so to speak, but there are a ton of missing civilians *plus* your boy who is presumably on the other side of the gate One and Four are covering. How do *you* want to proceed?"

It was a hint delivered with a cheerful grin and a megaphone. Iris shrugged. "Let's go get him? After you."

"Ladies first," Red Two snarked. "Seriously, I'll cover your six, you're the expert here, your holiness."

Obviously someone had read her cover: they trusted her to lead them, at least as long as they had her in a collar bomb with a submachine gun pointed at her back. Iris snorted. "Let's see this gate." The gate the Omphalos cultists had presumably sacrificed the bloke in the breakfast room in order to open. "Time for a walk on the wild side."

►◄►◄►◄

Team Grognard took the left passageway, went stabby on a slithering horror nesting on a pile of bones—Phil had to be forcibly restrained from trying to loot the ornate scale armor adorning one of the skeletons covered in iridescent purple slime, and was only convinced when Linda pointed out that the armor hadn't protected its wearer from the mollusk's corrosive mucus—then went full munchkin on the rest of the level.

Traps were sprung or avoided entirely by the simple expedient of not foolishly trying to steal the obviously valuable triggers. Puzzles were harder, but hardcore gamers tended to play more than one game and the round of Patolli they had to win against a skeletal automaton before they could cross a bottomless chasm succumbed to Derek's dice and Phil's encyclopedic knowledge of historical games of chance.

The random critters nesting in the temple were harder to deal with, but the local wildlife was mostly happy to leave the two-legged maniacs alone as long as they didn't intrude on their lairs. Occasionally they ran into something completely ridiculous that the Omphalos GMs had obviously thrown in because they were bored. But for the most part, not being greedy and not taking risks proved to be surprisingly effective tactics. Who could have imagined *that*?

They were waiting outside the entrance to a ball court—open to the sky with tiers of stone bleachers rising on either side, a packed-earth floor in the middle, small stone hoops protruding from the walls, and a tunnel at the far end leading to the rival team's changing room or sacrificial altar—when Sam (who was on point) stopped. She raised a hand: "Hush."

"What—" Raven began before Linda clapped her hand over his mouth.

"Voices."

"Do I have a cantrip for that? Or a spell?" Derek rolled. "Uh—" The back of his head itched furiously but nothing came to mind— "oh."

"Ssh!" Linda glared at him. "Listen!"

Faint sounds reached Derek's ears. Sam's breathing, Phil's faint rasp, something else—it sounded like speech. And several pairs of shuffling footsteps coming closer. "Hang back," Sam told them, "we're in the shadows."

Derek's scalp itched, or maybe it was his left nostril—it was an infuriatingly vague feeling, but also strangely familiar, like a limb that had been asleep for too long slowly reawakening in a flurry of pins and needles. Something *was* coming through, like a memory tickling the back of his head, or a sneeze gathering force.

The footsteps were coming closer. Finally, four figures emerged into the courtyard: another team of competitors. Derek recognized a couple of them. Keith—Yeah-Yeah Man—and Bearded Multiclass Guy. The others were unfamiliar. Like Team Grognard, they wore Omphalos-provided robes and were armed with crude stabby implements. Unlike Team Grognard, they'd acquired some armor and a war wound or two. One of them wore a helm fronted with a golden skull-mask; another wore a makeshift sling around his right arm and a robe that appeared to have been dipped in blood.

"—don't like this, we should have gone left not right, I keep telling youse!"

"Look: sky! Is there a way out?"

"Oh no not another fucking tunnel, is there going to be a pit trap there, too?"

"Shut the fuck up and let me fucking think you fuckers!" shouted Bearded Multiclass Guy, who had clearly had enough. "This is obviously some kind of fucking sportsball stadium and those Aztec fuckers were all about ball games when they weren't flaying people alive and juggling their beating hearts so it's a fucking ritual site which means we're probably meant to play a fucking football friendly but where's the rival fucking team?"

Raven tried to step forward but Sam and Phil grabbed his arms. Linda held Derek back: the compulsion to call "Over *here!*" was almost irresistible.

"Magic," he whispered when he could finally speak. Linda nodded. "Some sort of *geas.*"

Raven shook his head and stepped backward. "They're not wrong, but what are the rules and what do we use for a ball?" asked Sam.

"Can't we just proceed anyway?" asked Raven. "Is it, I mean, like, modal?"

"No, we're going to have to play . . . Aztec wall game? Was that the one where they sacrificed the losing team? Or am I confusing it with Rollerball?"

I hate team sports, Derek thought glumly. He'd always been the boy the class captains played rock-paper-scissors to force on the other side. Derek wasn't handicapped, Derek *was* the handicap. *If I have to play, we'll lose.*

"We need to get past them," Sam whispered. "That's the only way out."

"I can't," Derek began to say, meaning to continue to the word *play* as the itching in his nose intensified: "I c-can't, I, I, ah—"

Linda clapped a hand over his face, just as Derek successfully stifled his sneeze, squeezing his eyes shut: "*Pluh,*" he gasped: "Oh god I'm sorry—"

"*What's that?*" One of the opposition team shouted and pointed at them. Derek opened his eyes and was horrified to see faint shadows on the floor in front of him.

"What the fuck, dude?" complained Phil, shielding his eyes from the flashlight-bulb-sized light bobbing in the air above Derek's head. "Can you turn that off?"

"I-I-I—" Derek had comprehensively run out of words: the sneeze-like pressure had gone away, but the cantrip was well and truly out of the spell book. "Um?"

"Hostiles at twelve o'clock!" shouted Skull-Mask, who lowered his spear and marched toward them; after a fractional hesitation Yeah-Yeah Man followed suit.

"Fuck this," Phil said disgustedly as he stepped out. "You with me?" he called as Raven and Samantha followed.

"Coming?" Sam asked Derek over her shoulder.

"I d-don't know what to—"

Linda took his left hand. "Raise your sling and try to look terrifying, okay? They don't want to fight any more than we do. Also, I have an idea." She eyed the packed brown dirt of the ball court. "How many competitors do you suppose died here?"

"T-too many!" But she was moving forward, and so perforce Derek followed her, his feet bearing him into the arena. *Plan, I need a plan*—another spell was tickling his temporal lobes, and this one felt a lot bigger than the flashlight cantrip. Getting it out would be like flushing a can of Coke through his sinuses. *Shit.* He raised his slingshot right-handed and reached into his dice bag with his left, fumbling for a pebble that felt right. The one he pulled out was warm and tingly to the touch, and he thought it might be glowing violet but it was hard to tell in the daylight glare (and how was it noon under a tropical sun when it had been raining in Scarfolk at breakfast time?), and as he placed the pebble in the sling a thunderous crowd-roar shook the bleachers—

"What's the plan?" Samantha asked over her shoulder: "Because I think *they* have one, and their plan is—"

"*Death!*"

Skull-Mask charged toward them, ululating and waving an obsidian-bladed axe in each hand. (Clearly he was overcompensating for Arm-In-A-Sling Man.) "Up and at 'em!" shouted Bearded Multiclass Guy.

"Go for the goal," Linda told Derek, "I'm going to be *very* busy for the next while." And suddenly Derek knew with crystal clarity what he had to do next. He aimed off to one side, deliberately ignoring—no, completely *forgetting* about the maniac charging toward him, forgetting about Sam and Raven sidestepping to get their spearheads lined up on the other team's onrushing V-formation, forgetting to *breathe,* forgetting everything except the importance of pulling and releasing and casting his bullet straight through the stone hoop on the wall—

Derek had no expertise with the slingshot. Shortsightedness and not being That Kind of Boy had kept him out of trouble until the government descended on his family home. But it seemed to him that the bullet flew as if magically guided, flew unerringly through the gaping maw of the hole in the protruding stonework, a hole that couldn't possibly be more than ten centimeters across but felt light years in diameter, a hole so huge it was impossible to miss—

—He was distantly aware that Linda was chanting something in a naggingly familiar language he nevertheless couldn't quite understand. The earth around them darkened rapidly as if a cloud was occulting the merciless sun, then the opening in the ball court wall shimmered and spun as it widened into a growing vortex with a deep blue light glowing at its heart. A huge pulse of *mana* burst from the vortex, raising the hairs on his arms and the nape of his neck. Derek reached for another bullet as the enemy's advance faltered, ten meters short of his team's defensive cluster. Linda's recital came to a conclusion and the ground shook: then the darkness spreading across the ground turned the color of night and a flat tone of utter despair tolled sonorously from the wall, like the gong at the gates of the palace of death.

Patches of soil began to rise like molehills around the hostiles, who recoiled, pointing their spears outward. Dirty yellow domes burst from the ground like bony mushrooms: skeletal hands clutched at their legs.

Linda gasped, "Get me out of here!" She began to sway sideways as if she was about to faint. Derek leaned in and grabbed her, lifting and tugging her over his shoulder. The echoes of the gong slowly faded as the sky turned dark. The light dancing above his head cast long shadows, making it hard to see what was happening, but Derek thought the skeletons were rearticulating as they rose, reaching blindly for their severed crania and donning them like so many missing hats: the dead ballplayers returning to the scene of their final defeat, where they had failed to find the flowery path.

Derek hiked Linda up as hard as he could, trying to ignore the twanging pain in his back and the crunching in his knee joints. He heaved her toward the far end of the court, shuffling as fast as he could and giving the hostiles a wide berth, although they seemed curiously immobile.

"Some help here!" he called. Linda's head lolled. There must be eight or nine skeletons already assembled, and the undead crop continued to sprout on all sides: she'd clearly depleted her power. Phil took Linda's other arm while Samantha and Raven stood guard. They left their vanquished foes behind in the ball court, wailing pitiful entreaties as the revenants closed in. And by the time they made it to the next level, Derek had forgotten the enemy ever existed.

▸◂▸◂◂

Iris followed the Red Team operators into the blood-drenched darkness.

The daylight grew stronger, filtering through overhead sky-lights, and the carpet ran out, replaced by tight-fitted blocks of limestone. When Iris glanced back a curtain of iridescence rippled in the passage. "Was the gate you found in the corridor or past it?" she asked.

Red Two spun round and swore: his teammates took up firing positions. "It moved." He reached into his webbing, pulled out a spray can, then squirted it at the shimmer. The barrier didn't block his Silly String, but when he tugged it back, it was cut off. Nothing returned from beyond the curtain. "Route back is blocked."

Red One glanced at Iris. "What are the tournament rules?"

"It's unclear: I didn't get a chance to study their game manual before you picked me up, and there weren't any copies out front. I think the gamers may have taken them all." Iris swallowed. "Our most useful asset—" It stuck in her throat to admit it. "—is a portly, middle-aged man with heavy framed glasses who is some-where ahead of us in . . . whatever."

It looked like a necropolis. Iris knew one when she saw one: she'd spent enough time crawling around various cemeteries in London. (They made excellent congregation meeting halls, if your god had a thing for skulls.) So the doors to either side would prob-ably lead to— "We *don't* want to explore to either side. Not unless we want to waste ammunition on revenants."

"Your call." Red One scanned the corridor ahead intently, all banter forgotten.

"We go forward"—Iris watched as Red One and Red Four leapfrogged one another's firing positions ahead—"we're not here for treasure, experience points, or tournament points like the other teams. Our objective is just to get to the end of this ob-stacle course and grab Derek. I can't say for certain but this feels like a summoning of some kind, powered by ritual competition or maybe a mass sacrifice: whoever's doing it is hostile and stop-ping them is an urgent priority. We can expect puzzles, games of skill and chance, and probably traps—thaumaturgic and physi-cal. We're less likely to run into incursions and monsters until we get to the final sequence but I may be"—*Squish*—"wrong." She winced as she stepped in something hidden among the shadows.

It stank like burning rubber, overripe dog turds, and rotting fish guts. "Sorry."

"Don't apologize," said Red Two. "Quiet now." One of the doorways ahead was open. The operators ghosted inside, gun barrels tracking. "Skeletons and bone fragments, quite old, looks like somebody played a round of baseball with them."

"In or out of coffins?" asked Iris.

"Definitely out, you called it right. Where's Harry when you need him?"

"*Don't call Harry,*" Red Four chimed in. It sounded like the punch line to a joke nobody had told her so she ignored it as they moved on down the hall.

As they kept going it became apparent that they were wasting time. This level was just one big ossuary. No clues except for a piece of graffiti saying BEWARE PIRANHAS. If they stayed out of the side rooms, everything stayed dead: if not, well, Red Team had a standard MO for turning lich-lights out.

"Okay, left staircase or right for the upward-inclined passageway?" Red One asked.

"Stairs, definitely. Remember the rolling boulder trap from that Indiana Jones movie? Because I bet if I can remember it, so did whoever designed this maze." Her son had been *so* excited to drag her to the cinema to watch those films when he was a wee thing. Even though the mobs of skeletons didn't have quite the intended impact on a child who got to play with bones every second Saturday of the month while mummy ran the social after the call to the Black Pharaoh. She wondered if she'd ever see him again, and what he'd make of this mission if she were able to tell him about it.

They went up the staircase, avoided the guillotine trap on the landing that someone had already triggered, bypassed a number of obvious snares for the gullible and greedy, only fell into *one* punji stake trap hidden beneath a false-floor illusion (modern body armor and helmets were remarkably good at keeping pointy sticks out of vital organs: Red Four demonstrated a remarkable scatological vocabulary as he climbed out, but his only injury seemed to be to his dignity), and successfully failed to meddle with a number of suspicious obstacles seemingly intended to tempt the unwary. Then they came to a stretch of corridor that smelled faintly sulfurous.

"That smell," Iris said.

"Yeah, that," Red One agreed. He was on point again: now he stopped and poked a small mirror past the corner. "More corridor, some kind of swimming pool footbath, smell's getting stronger. And . . . yeah, that's blood on the floor on the other side."

"Let me see."

Iris looked past the corner. More corridor, leading to steps going up. The walls were covered in bas-relief engravings of, yes, more skulls. The floor was blocked by a shallow footbath about five meters long and as wide as the passage, just like the disinfectant walk-through before a municipal bath, only it smelled wrong, and the red smears on the far side—

"Huh." Iris pulled out a two-pence piece, tarnished and greasy brown from age. "Stand back, everyone." She tossed it in the pool and it immediately began to hiss and bubble.

"What the fuck, ma'am?" Red One stared at her.

"I don't know the rules to *this* game but I spent last night mugging up on Dungeons and Dragons, and I've seen this before. Piranha Solvent," she continued nonchalantly, even though she was shivering inside: "You make it by slowly mixing concentrated sulfuric acid with strong hydrogen peroxide, it'll dissolve diamonds, never mind organic material."

"You've seen this . . . before?"

We used it to clean up sacrifices. "Yes," she said shortly. Lay the sacrifice in the tank, open the stop cock, wait for the liquid to stop bubbling, then dilute it with water, and flush it down the sewers. "It has to be freshly mixed: Let's see if there's a shutoff. If not, we can't get past—it'd set fire to your boots and dissolve your leg bones before you could make it to the other side." Like Mentos dissolving in a glass of Coke. "At a run."

She didn't bother stating the obvious—that the only other way forward involved crossing a space that seemed to be hosting an animated skeleton dance party and red-lined all the operators' thaum detectors before they even reached the entrance.

Red Four pointed at the wall above the acid bath. "Not necessarily." He grinned toothily as he shrugged out of his backpack and pulled out an alarmingly thin rope: "Can you climb?"

Iris shook her head vigorously. "I'm fifty-two, a manager, and I'm afraid of heights! That's an acid bath! And I'm, uh, overweight." It was embarrassing to admit and besides she wasn't *that* overweight, but— "What do *you* think?"

"I think you're wearing an explosive collar and we've got a deadline." Behind him Red One was counting out eyebolts and other tools from his backpack. "Think of it as a learning experience."

It took the three OCCULUS operatives almost an hour to get themselves and their reluctant charge across the obstacle. Most of it was spent with one of them guarding Iris—unnecessary, in her grudging opinion: she wasn't *totally* stupid, the LED on her collar was still flashing—while the other two hammered in spikes and strung a rope across the Jacuzzi of death, then held her hand (metaphorically) while she squeezed her eyes shut and prayed to her god as she dangled and swayed. "Nothing to it really," Red One told her when she collapsed on the other side, gasping for breath: "Just like a hostage op."

"Most hostages show a bit more gratitude," Red Four chimed in.

"Fuck you. Just, like, fuck you all." Iris squeezed her eyes shut to avoid staring at the trail of dried blood. It led away from the bath. She had a particular phobia of heights and falling, and wasn't terribly keen on acid baths either. (At least she hadn't lost bladder control this time. Her first Communion with the Black Pharaoh, when she was eight, had been even more humiliating.)

Red One called a five-minute break while they chomped on protein bars and took stock. Then it was time to move again.

"We must be nearing the end," Iris speculated. "That's daylight up there. If this is a variant Mesoamerican step pyramid we can expect there to be a plaza on top with a temple. I'm betting that's where the Omphalos people have set up shop. This whole competition is structured as a tournament leading up to a climax, probably the usual flowery path—" *sacrifice the losing teams, cardiothoracic excision without benefit of anesthesia* "—where the survivors are compelled to believe in the god Omphalos, summoned by a strong *geas* reinforced by their progression through the game." She paused. "Assuming this *is* the Omphalos people and they're trying to immanentize a specific entity they designed and made into the centerpiece of their game."

"Okay, got that." Red Two was cleaning his gun again. It was, she decided, a nervous tic—obviously he felt he needed to be ready to shoot someone at the drop of a hat. "Storm the temple, shoot the priests and anyone who resists, grab your man, hotfoot it back to—What's our exit strategy? Because in case you lost count, we've gone up three flights of stairs and the Scarfolk Britannia is a two-story building."

"Dream roads gonna dream," observed Red Four. "Gets me every time."

Red One remained sanguine. "Never mind that for now, chaps, they won't have climbed up their rope without a way back down!" He offered Iris a hand up. "Best foot forward! Let's go shoot ourselves some Johnny Cultist. Er, present company excepted, of course."

"Yes, let's do that." Iris sent him an acid grin. *Not my cultists, not my sacrifice,* she reminded herself. "But seeing we're about to storm a temple containing an unknown number of fanatical worshippers who are trying to manufacture a bespoke deity to order using human sacrifices as fuel . . . please can I have my emotional support Glock back?"

►◄►◄►◄

Linda was groggy after she recovered from raising the ball court's dead, but then became a little manic: "What even *was* that? I thought I was supposed to put them down, not raise them! And how did I summon that many, anyway?"

Derek pondered. "Didn't they rewrite the entire alignment system so you're not locked into good/evil dualism anymore? It emerges organically from your actions and the underlying intent."

He rolled his d20s idly. They were glowing a scary shade of blue now, the blue of Cerenkov radiation in a cooling pool for hot nuclear reactor fuel rods.

"Guys!" Phil poked his head around the doorway. "Guys! I found us a clue!"

Linda shut her eyes and slumped sideways against Derek.

"What kind of clue?" asked Sam.

"It's in this room I found past the corridor with the gory battle scenes and the skeleton army eating the hearts of their victims! Also past a spikey plant that wants to be my best friend forever and has hairy tentacles but doesn't like being pruned, so, meh. Anyway! There are skylights and the walls are covered in these painted parchment hangings with some sort of writing."

Linda opened her eyes. "The Aztecs didn't have a writing system, they used pictograms."

"But this is a rip-off of *The Hidden Shrine of Tamoachan,* isn't it?" said Derek.

"That was a travesty! They made up a culture called the Olman as a, a kind of mashup of Maya and Aztecs, which is like putting the Achaemenid Empire in a blender with the Third Reich. The script could be *anything.* Made up junk, probably."

"But if this is an invocation, it's something they summoned," said Derek. He racked his memory. "I don't recall seeing anything about the flowery path of Xōchipilli in the GM's guide. Or about their writing system." He pushed himself to his feet. "Shall we go and take a look?"

"Take us to your leaderboard!" Linda raised a hand.

After they bypassed Phil's playmate from Little Shop of Horrors they came to the wall hangings. Phil had forgotten to mention the opposite wall was covered from floor to ceiling with cubbyholes. They were stuffed with fired clay jars lying on their sides, stoppers outward.

"What's—" Sam made a beeline for the jars before anyone thought to caution her. "They're full of scrolls!"

Linda peered at the wall hangings. "He's right about the script," she said. "It's weirdly familiar but I can't quite focus on it, like one of those random dot illusions . . ."

Derek followed her line of sight. "It's an order of service for a seasonal festival," he said. "The feast of the ninth month, the flower festival of He Who Dreams With Eyes Wide Open—" He did a double take as he realized the others were staring at him. "What?"

"Natural feat," said Raven, head cocked to one side as he considered Derek. "You're some sort of mage, *of course* you can read scrolls." He pulled out one of the jars and broke the friable seal. "How about this one?"

"What? *No—*"

Raven pulled the scroll out of the jar and held it up to the light before anyone could stop him.

"Hey guys," he began to say. Samantha lunged for the scroll but she was too late: the parchment crumpled in her hands as Raven fell.

"Shit!" Phil swore.

He was barely audible over Sam's wail. "No! *No!* Wake up! Help! Anyone!" A strangely purposeful wisp of green smoke spiraled over the scroll, rising toward the skylights around the domed roof.

"*Shit*," Linda swore. She stumbled over to Raven and knelt beside him, one hand on his forehead, the other over his heart. "*Shit*." She went rigid and Derek's skin crawled at the wave of power rolling off her. "If I can just—"

"CPR," said Derek. "C-can anyone—you, Phil—"

Sam bent over Raven's prone form and leaned forward as if to kiss him, then blew into his mouth. A second later Phil joined her, doing chest compressions. Linda was pulling in so much power she was nearly glowing. Unsure what else he could do, Derek reached into his dice bag and pulled out his favorite pair of d20s. They had turned as black as obsidian, and he held them close as he shook them, preparing to roll the saving throw of his life.

"I'm going to try—" He watched as they came to rest. "*Shit*." Both dice had come to rest with their 1 uppermost. They briefly glowed black, then crumbled to crematory ash. "*Shit*."

Sam collapsed across Raven and began to weep silently.

Of course it would *be* The Hidden Shrine of Tamoachan *they ripped off,* Derek thought angrily. Not as notoriously lethal as the *Tomb of Horrors,* but still high up in the "this place is full of lethal booby traps" stakes.

He picked up the scroll, safe now that it had discharged its curse. He could, it seemed, read the fictional Olman script. It was useful knowledge, but the price—he barely knew Raven personally, although they had corresponded for years—was *far* beyond redemption.

Linda slumped against the wall. "Help," she said weakly.

"You tried." Derek sat beside her.

"I could *feel* him for a moment, but then he was gone." Tears trickled down her cheeks, but her expression was a blur. After a confused second Derek realized that his eyes were also watering.

"What level is Raise Dead, again?" he asked rhetorically. She knew as well as he did that in classic D&D it was a fifth-level spell. "You tried. I tried. We all tried."

"It wasn't enough and I hate this game and I want the people who invented it to die. No. I want them to suffer first. *Why?*"

Derek had opinions on the subject of *why*: opinions that encompassed his entire life since he'd been swept up by the MIDNIGHT DUNGEON snatch squad all those years ago, opinions and feelings, feelings so vast and despairing and bleak that he simply ignored them most of the time. Feelings like living with an ultimately fatal cancer or a murderer's regrets. A life that could no longer be lived, for reasons entirely arbitrary and meaningless. Which was why, when he got down to it, he kept rolling his dice: they showed him the path ahead, and even though it was misty and bounded on all sides, they enabled him to put one foot in front of the other.

But trapped in the here and now, he wasn't about to share his depression with Linda and the others. He couldn't escape this mess on his own, therefore he needed to find a reason for them to keep going: and so he said, "I'll be a minute," and walked over to the wall of scrolls. Then he opened his inner eye—an eye he'd never really noticed before—and *looked.*

About half the scroll-jars bore the same sickly green aura as the curse-smoke. Most of the rest looked somehow *safe,* but boring. Two or three felt better than safe. Derek reached for one of these while the others were all attending to their grief, and pulled out the stopper. He wiped his eyes, then unrolled the top of the scroll just far enough to read the first line. It did not kill him, but an awareness he could not quite articulate squeezed in behind his eyes and made him unroll it a little bit farther, so that he could read another line, and then the next.

Knowledge.

By the time he reached the bottom of the scroll he felt as if he'd overeaten to an uneasy point just past satiation, teetering on the edge of bursting. He had been incarcerated before *The Meaning of Life* hit cinema screens but he'd heard the catchphrases plenty of times: *One more wafer-thin After Eight Mint, Monsieur Reilly?* A charge of *mana* had accompanied the knowledge as it pushed inside his head, obviously the same mechanism that energized the curse that had killed Raven—

"Half of the scrolls are cursed," Derek explained to the others. "Only two or three are safe to read. Mage-specialist, not clergy."

"I don't like this game," Phil said numbly.

"This is *not* a game," Sam's tone was savage, "and I am going to murder whoever is responsible." Beyond the light shafts distant thunder grumbled, as if the universe was taking note of her vow.

She stood and turned toward the exit, holding Raven's spear alongside her own: either she was remarkably resilient, or this realm they were in imposed the emotional dynamic of a hero quest on its victims, numbing grief and blurring memories so that an event that should have broken them all became just another fridging, a motivational waypoint on the path to ultimate sacrifice. Whatever the case might be, murdering whoever had set it up sounded entirely reasonable to Derek.

So up another level they went.

▶◀▶◀▶◀

Iris was coming to the conclusion that if it was *absolutely* necessary to experience a dungeon crawl—dodging monsters, springing traps, and hunting clues—then there were worse ways to do so than in the company of a team of SAS door breakers. She became convinced of this after the second group of dead gamers. The first lot had fallen foul of the piranha footbath, then got hung up on a nearly invisible copper wire strung across one passageway at garroting height—

which might not have been so bad were it not for the poisoned darts and the exploding seed pods—but that might have been no more than happenstance. However, the *second* group— "Spare me from amateurs," Red Four said disgustedly as he collected and bagged his expended cartridge cases. (Littering with government property was against regulations.)

"Obsidian tips." Iris inspected the very different projectile she'd picked up. It had been aimed at her, but the encounter had been over in an eyeblink—a deafeningly loud eyeblink accompanied by muzzle flashes. She hadn't even had time to take aim. "Who goes up against MP5s with a bow and arrows?" She could have understood if they'd been Stone-Age denizens—or wandering monsters, as the manual called them—but the corpses were all wearing Crocs and togas, like a bizarre tribute to the Heaven's Gate cult. "Do you have a thaum detector?"

"Yes ma'am. You think they were rolled?"

"I'd bet on it."

Red Two pulled out a handheld device. It clicked like a Geiger counter, frequency rising to a shrill buzz as he bent over the bodies. "Not taking that bet, ma'am. Recognize anyone?"

Iris swallowed. "He's not here." For which she was grateful: the amount of paperwork she'd have to fill out if she lost an inmate to friendly fire didn't bear thinking about. "It's a tournament. There are multiple teams competing to get to the far end and they're under a *geas*. So we probably have substantial civilian collateral damage, up to and including everyone who was in the hotel when this kicked off."

They moved on. Red Four acquired a spear with which to probe for wires and false floors. Red One and Red Two covered their advance, while Iris used the thaumometer to check for magical traps. It came in handy when they got to the hall of scrolls, and was more than handy when it warned them about the carnivorous plants in the garden.

They completely avoided the maze of death by taking a hidden passage to one side that led out onto a broad stone plaza behind a step pyramid. The base of the pyramid was surrounded by a Tzompantli—a wall of human skulls impaled horizontally on poles like the beads of a macabre abacus, their eye sockets and teeth drilled and filled with polished semiprecious stones mortared together with clay. Just a few hundred skulls would have been disturbing, but the Olmans apparently believed that quantity had a quality all of its own: the ghastly wall was as wide as a football pitch and taller than Iris. As if that wasn't bad enough, she could hear a crowd chanting beyond the pyramid, accompanied by booming bass drums and a singer's atonal warbling counterpoint.

"I 'ave seen this movie and it did *not* end well," said Red Two. "What d'you think we should do, ma'am?"

"I think—" Iris swallowed, which accidentally reminded her of the explosive collar clamped around her neck—"we need to get this over with." The stone box on top of the pyramid was probably the destination for the summoning. "How are we going to get up there?" The tiers of the step pyramid were roughly a meter high: unlike the opposite side of the structure, there was no staircase here.

"Give me a boost, Two." Red Four was already climbing the skull face, and within seconds reached the top of the wall. "Okay. Seen enough." He jumped back down lightly. "There's a concealed dog-leg gap in the wall over there," he gestured, "then it's a straight shot up the pyramid. Or we can check out the other side, but I think we'd have company of the unpleasantly frisky variety."

Iris swallowed again. "I'm sure you gentlemen are okay with speed-climbing a pyramid, but again: middle-aged manager here." Also, to be perfectly honest, the prospect of arriving at the top of a pyramid full of crazed cultists winded and with legs like noodles did not fill her with joy.

"Never you worry!" Number One was much too cheerful. "We climb cliffs with heavier backpacks twice a week! We'll get you up there."

"Or drop you, trying," Number Two promised. "Let's go!"

►◄►◄►◄

They lost Phil as they battled their way through a garden that had turned to jungle over years of neglect. Or maybe it was another ball court, one that had acquired a water supply—perhaps an aqueduct had burst or overflowed—then gone to seed.

The walled garden looked lush and inviting at first, but the path to the exit at the other side was overhung by branches and creepers. As they walked in file, a vine sinuously dropped a loop around Phil's neck and jerked once, hard, then hoisted his still-twitching body toward the canopy of unnaturally verdant greenery above.

Derek sneezed sorcery, venting a gout of magical snot that hung in the air like ectoplasm, glistening in translucent sheets before it dissolved in the daylight. "Ack!" He knew he'd done something, but he was unsure what: so he gasped, gathered his wits, and tried to force another sneeze, just as Linda trilled an eerie note on her flute. The round cobblestones at the base of the buttressed tree they were passing stirred and began to roll over in their bed of black soil, turning their eyeless sockets to track their new mistress. Meanwhile Derek raised his burning fingertips and lashed the tree with a gout of living flame.

He was just in time: more vines were dropping, their noose-like terminal loops searching blindly for necks to snap. They curled and crisped as they retracted upward, withering as his fire licked around the bark of their host tree. "Run!" Sam gasped, and there was an ominous animal snuffling from the undergrowth, so Derek shifted his flames to the path and burned a long corridor ahead, then hotfooted it toward the exit before the garden of death could come after them.

It was a nightmarish jog that might have lasted seconds or hours, but at last Derek found a stone wall with a darkened entrance to turn his back to as he released the flames and waited anxiously for Sam and Linda. The animal snuffling had turned to an eerie, angry growl, and a rustling and clatter that was unpleasantly familiar—the sound of the walking dead, licked clean of flesh by the hungry tree roots. Finally Linda and Samantha emerged from the forest, Linda borne across the shoulders—scapulae?—of the gang of skeletons she'd raised. The growling grew louder and Derek raised his slingshot and readied himself, when—

"Hello there?" he said, and dropped into a crouch, one hand

extended, as Sam turned. "No! Don't stab, I think this one's *mine*—"

"—What the *fuck*—"

The massive cat was melanistic, its dark coat speckled with roundels of a deeper black pigment. It walked up to Derek and rubbed the top of its head against his face, nearly pushing him over. "S-same to you, too!" Derek said shakily, then laughed. "Nice to meet you." The jaguar leaned back and peered into his eyes. Big cats didn't purr but Derek *knew* his cat was content to have found him, and not just because he was a tasty self-propelled ready meal— "Oh my, is this cool or what?"

"They just killed Phil!" Sam screamed at him, eyes bright with tears of rage-stricken grief. "I get that you're bonding with your new kitty familiar but they killed him! I demand revenge!" She stabbed Raven's spear into the ground so hard that it vibrated, standing upright. "I want to kill someone!" Her face was turning bright red. "Aargh! I hate this!"

Linda nudged Derek. "Berserker," she said quietly. "Keep moving or she'll turn on us."

"What about—" His gesture took in their surroundings. The gang of skeletons milling around at the end of the jungle trail, the jaguar, the dark tunnel ahead, pillars and lintel engraved with the now horribly familiar bas-relief pictograms depicting the journey of the dead.

(Derek dizzied for a moment. *Journey of the dead? How do I know that?* he wondered briefly.)

"They'll follow. Can you do your lightbulb thing again? On Sam's spear tip?"

"Oh okay, sure."

Sam headed into the darkened passage ahead, growling louder than Derek's familiar, who padded at his heels. Passages branched off occasionally, and sometimes they took a turn, or came to a dead end, at which point they had to backtrack, always taking the last left fork.

There were pit traps and sand traps and angry scorpions dropping from murder holes overhead, and once or twice the air turned bad, but they walked in silence and determination now. They were angry and sad and tired of the endless dread, and when they came to obstacles they surged past or destroyed them with a merciless precision that seemed honed by years of practice.

Linda walked beside Derek with bowed shoulders, leading her gang of undead through the underworld maze. "We're going to die, aren't we," she said shakily. "This is all some kind of horrible mistake, isn't it? We shouldn't be in the tournament. We should have walked away. This is all wrong."

Derek reached out blindly. "Take my hand, I'll get us out of here," he promised.

He felt Linda's fingers slip across his palm. "Don't make promises you can't keep."

"No, I mean—" Their hands clasped together—"I've been in worse situations," he told her: "I've escaped from an escape-proof prison." Although it had been a *comfortable* prison. This was anything but comfortable. "Besides, I need to get you out of here." *I can't rescue you without rescuing myself,* he wanted to say, but he had an intimation that to speak those words would doom him. "Besides, I have dice left to roll."

A spider the size of a truck tire dropped down from the ceiling. Before it could snare them Derek lit it up: as it burned the flames swept through the webs overhead, engulfing the mummified husks of the adventurers it had liquefied and digested over the years.

"When did you turn so badass?" Linda asked as one of her skeletal minions clicked across to a pile of debris, rummaged around, and returned to offer her a very dusty jewelled scepter. As she touched the handle, the paste jewels just below the orb—they had to be paste, nobody left maces encrusted with egg-sized sapphires lying around—began to glow.

"Same. I mean, when did *you* level up?" He glanced back at the gang of walking corpses. "I think it's this place. It's full of *mana*— sorcerous energy, the real thing, not some pencil and paper story- telling abstraction. I got a feel for it in the camp. Most of the inmates were there for a reason. My boss on the entertainments committee, for example—we didn't talk about it but let's just say there'd be no love lost between her and Xōchipilli's brood."

Around the corner ahead of them, Sam screamed with rage and repeatedly stabbed something that cast too many long-legged shadows.

"Sounds like we could use your boss here." Linda hefted her scepter. "Hey, this feels really *good* if you know what I mean." She hefted it again: the stones glowed brighter.

Derek peered at it. "I can't use it but, uh, it seems to like *you*. Your character's feats, I mean, whatever they are—"

"Oh come *on*." Half a dozen skeletons snapped to attention and saluted at him. "We're none of us what we were when we started out." She tugged him closer to her side. "Your familiar here, she's not nothing." The jaguar, padding along behind them on near-silent paws, held its counsel.

Sam's spine-chilling howl of hate echoed from too far ahead: they'd fallen behind. It was followed by moist sucking noises and wordless shrieks. "Sounds like she could use some help!" Linda released his hand and ran effortlessly toward the fight, followed by her death guard. Derek trotted behind them, another sneeze of unformed magic building in his sinuses.

They took the next two corners at a run and suddenly they were outside, standing at the base of a step pyramid. A column of dazed convention-goers clad in white robes—he recognized some of them from the day before—shuffled up a human-proportioned staircase toward a windowless rectangular temple at the top, their eyes glazed. An ominous buzzing seemed to hang in the air around them, and a rivulet of dark liquid dribbled down a gutter alongside the steps. *Mana* pulsed from the building in arterial gouts, so strong it threatened Derek with a migraine headache.

"Where's Sam?" he asked.

Linda pointed up the staircase.

They'd fallen behind—she was halfway to the top, shrieking with fury as she raced past the sacrificial queue. A pair of temple guards attempted to block her onslaught with lowered spear points, forcing a brief standoff.

"I've got a very bad feeling about this," he told Linda.

"Yes? Well let's see what we can do about that." She pointed her scepter up the stairs: "Fly, my children!" A rattling peloton of skeletons surged past, forging a path for their mistress. Derek stifled a sigh and tried to keep up. *My knees are going to regret this tomorrow,* he thought, then wondered where such a mundane concern had emerged from. *We need a plan. What am I going to do when we get to the top?*

Instinct sent his hand to his dice bag. "Linda," he called, "wait!"

"Can't stop—why?" She paused nevertheless, gasping for breath.

He pulled out his d6. "I'm going to roll for backup. Call me some options?"

She rolled her eyes. "Sure. How about: 1–3: the SAS turn up. 4–6: We defeat the baddies because you're so much better at GM'ing than the overpaid dweebs we're up against?"

Derek's heart sank. Linda had asked for too much, and the fates wouldn't be merciful. But it was too late to take it back. "I'll have to work with that." He knelt, cupped his hand around a single die— its glow was so bright his fingers cast shadows across the pyramid steps despite the noonday sunlight—and rolled a final saving throw for the world. He squinted, trying to make out the pattern of dots on top of a cube so bright it burned green and purple afterimages into his retinas. *Is it a one or a four?* He wondered. *Maybe a six?* It was impossible to tell, for Schrödinger's die seemed to have come up with a superposition of all possible results.

A deafening crackle of automatic gunfire sounded from the back of the temple, capturing his attention. "Well, I guess that answers that!" Linda sounded almost *cheerful.* "Looks like we got the SAS! What can possibly go wrong?" Then she grabbed his hand and tugged him up the staircase to the temple where the Omphalos Corporation was trying to create the in-game god, Xōchipilli.

▶◀▶◀▶◀

Step pyramid; dull-eyed sacrificial victims filing up the staircase to meet their doom; angry-looking queue-marshal priests in loincloths brandishing spears; berserker woman screaming imprecations at priests; gang of skeletons gaily dancing the Macarena; pudgy, shortsighted sorcerer clutching his lucky dice; priestess of an unspecified rival deity waving around a scepter encrusted in glowing green gemstones . . .

It was like a dismally unimaginative setup for a boss battle in a tournament campaign that had misplaced its mojo some time back in 1977, but Derek couldn't afford to get distracted. One of the queue marshals poked a spear at him, so Derek set his hair on fire: Stabby Stick Man fell screaming down the side of the pyramid, trailing flames all the way to the bottom.

"Up," Derek gasped, wheezing for breath. He was bent nearly double: rushing up the pyramid had been the first time he'd ascended more than two flights of stairs in nearly thirty years. "You go on. Ahead. I'll catch. You. Later."

"Nope, not splitting up." Linda bopped him gently on the head with her ball-on-a-stick: "In the name of, um, whoever am I a living emissary of? In the name of She-Ra, power up, dude."

A sense of well-being flooded Derek and his lungs abruptly refilled. *I'm going to pay for this later,* he realized, *I just know it.* (Probably by having to make interminable obeisance to She-Ra, whoever she was.) But the bill would only come due if he lived, and now that he was bright-eyed and bushy-tailed again he realized just how regrettable a life choice it would be to conk out on the steps before he even made it to the final act. He straightened his back. "Okay, upping my hit points now: let's go."

A tide of bones swept them both up and carried them toward the temple on top of the pyramid.

The liquid dribbling down the gutter by the steps was coming in small gouts once or twice a minute. As it caught the light of Linda's scepter, Derek saw that it seemed black—meaning it absorbed green light. So, bright red. *Of course.* As Derek approached the top, a severed head hurtled through the temple doorway at waist height. It hit the ground with a dull thud. One of the small group of guards at the top sideswiped it off the side of the temple with one foot, then reached for the next prisoner who, eyes downcast, showed no sign of noticing the fate of his predecessor. But Derek didn't see what happened next, for his bony bearers rushed him through the entrance.

The chanting inside was much louder, and the temple—what

little he could see of it, for it was poorly illuminated by slots high in the walls, just below the ceiling—was much bigger on the inside than the outside. It stank like a slaughterhouse. The queue of sacrifices snaked back and forth across a floor the size of an airport terminal, converging on an altar surrounded by a coterie of priests. They looked for all the world like a surgeon and his—or her—assistants in an operating theatre. A giant gold statue of a poison arrow frog loomed behind the altar: the emerald the size of a human skull embedded between its eyes pulsed with a sickly green light that clashed oddly with the light from Linda's scepter. This was Xōchipilli, Derek presumed, not yet raised to life despite the iridescent stream of *mana* flowing into its mouth from the blood-drenched altar.

Guards turned, bringing their spears to bear on the intruders.

"Put me down," Derek said quietly. The skeletons obeyed: they lowered Linda, too, then fell into position behind her. "I know what to do now."

He straightened up and advanced on the guards.

"I bet you think you're ever so smart," he taunted, "but I know exactly what you're doing and it's *not* big and it's *not* clever. And I bet when this is over and the dust has settled you're going to have a very fun conversation with Hasbro's legal department! Because you can't even design an original game of your own. You had to rip off the 3.5e ruleset without crediting it! And as for this second-rate knockoff of *The Hidden Shrine of Tamoachan*—you have *got* to be kidding me. It was a cliché in 1983 and it's *still* a cliché, and you haven't even bothered to balance the risk-reward payoffs. I mean, your traps alternate between ass and *oops, entire party dies, start over,* and where the hell did the spider in the maze come from—is this a casting call for a *Lord of the Rings* remake? Cirith Ungol, only underpowered and pathetic? *Do* you even play-test? Or is that why you were giving away copies of your badly written knockoff rule book to anyone who didn't dodge fast enough—because it's so crap nobody would pay for it?"

Derek pointed at the frog idol. "That thing! Think I don't know a blatant rip-off of the cover of the first edition *Dungeon Master's Guide* when I see one? Toad instead of minotaur, okay, you get full credit for changing the monster behind the altar, but the gem in the forehead is the oldest cliché in the book. Did you outsource this crap to marketing consultants?" (He'd caught part of a documentary about them on BBC2: now he adlibbed.) "Did McKinsey send the office intern to manage your design team and bill you for a partner?" (Behind him, Linda winced.) "I hear they teach degrees in game design these days—maybe you should go back to school before you try again!"

Linda pointed past Derek's shoulder. "Over there, behind the skull rack," she said urgently, "I saw a cop—"

A priestess turned toward them and stepped away from the altar, gesticulating at Derek: "Silence, heretic!"

He almost failed to recognize Sister Selene, thanks to the head-dress and blood splatter up to her armpits. She'd levelled all the way up and turned into Magical Girl Obsidian Heartbleed: murderous rage shimmering in her eyes as she spat at Derek: "Your sacrilegious insults are meaningless! Bow down before Lord Xōchipilli of the Five-Flowered Way, accept him into your soul, and I'll put your hearts to good use!"

"The hell you will," Linda said, very firmly, and raised her glowing scepter: "This stops here."

"Surrender to your doom, infidels!" Sister Selene's eyes flared gold, and a pulse of power rolled out from her elaborate chest-piece. Only Linda's other hand in the small of his back steadied Derek. The wave of power crashed around them like a wave breaking on a rocky shore, leaving Derek and Linda standing upright. Sister Selene screamed wordless frustration at them and raised her axe. (In the shadows behind her, black-clad figures in uniform took cover among the pillars. They guarded a shorter figure in jeans and a green Barbour jacket, who appeared to be talking to herself.)

"You rolled up that dyspeptic frog using a random deity table in a third-party supplement you found in a photocopied fanzine!" Derek mocked. "To be *very* precise, you stole the random deities table from Appendix Two of *Rituals and Rosicrucians,* the one for encounters with polytheistic nightmare cults on the astral planes." His smile broadened. "I know because I *designed* that chart. And you know something else? *That's* not how you roll a random deity—*this* is how you roll a random deity!"

▸◂▸◂▸◂

Meanwhile, between the pillars and the skull rack at the back of the temple, a quietly vehement exchange of opinions was taking place between Iris Carpenter and the surviving Red Team operatives from the OCCULUS unit.

"Him, over there, next to the woman dressed as a She-Ra cosplayer—that's Derek!" Iris hissed. "He's our target! Can you extract him?"

"Not easily." Red Two sounded distinctly peeved. "TA, Number Four."

"On it." Red Four ghosted away around the perimeter of the temple.

"What now?" Iris asked tensely.

"Threat assessment," Red Two said patiently. He pointed: "altar, multiple hostiles with axes, thaum count through the ceiling and climbing—" he gestured with his portable monitor—"some kind of devotional statue—" the giant frog idol—"more hostiles with spears, a bunch of what look like sacrificial victims but might not be, *animated skeletons,* a mountain lion, a madwoman with a war axe who's going medieval on the spear carriers—oops, looks like they've got her on the ground—oh and that hostile is putting the zap on our lad—"

They both ducked back behind a frieze depicting more or less the scene in front of them as a wave of *mana* broke around them with a shock like cryogenically frozen lightning, setting their protective wards abuzz—

"Shit," Iris began, as Number Two cautiously peeped out from behind cover: "Looks like our lad's got backup, the woman he's with is shielding him."

"Well." Iris shook her head. "Can you take them?"

Number Four scurried back into position. "I count six enemy practitioners, all warded, circle around the altar. Head honcho attacking our target is a necromancer. Couldn't get a read on her power source but it's big and judging from the stack of corpses in the back they've been going for some time."

Number Two turned to Iris. "Seven primary hostiles, three of us, they're all going to take head shots to put down *and they're warded* so probably they'll have deflection wards—bullets won't work reliably—and maybe death curses. Say we take out the first three but their death curses quench our wards: What do we do about the next four?"

"Well fuck. Did you bring a basilisk weapon?"

"Not authorized in public." Number Two sounded disgusted. "And the only bomb we've got is wrapped around your neck."

"Also," Red One piped up, "once we shut down the bad guys how are we going to get him the fuck out of here? Did you see a sign saying EMERGENCY EXIT, ma'am? Because if so, I need new spectacles."

"Rules just changed," Red Two said in a calm, flat tone that sent shivers down Iris's spine, "something big's coming through." His gaze was fixed on his thaum detector, which was buzzing quietly and flashing red: he dropped it as it began to smoke. "Right lads, less talking, more mayhem! Ma'am, if you would be so good as to light up that giant frog's ass while we take down the priests, that'd be appreciated. *Go* on a count of three, two, one, showtime." And without further ado Red Team ducked out from behind their cover, raised their guns, and started shooting.

▶◀▶◀▶◀

Derek flung his right hand up, tossing his glittering dice into the air, where they floated on a shimmering table of *mana,* tumbling and rolling in a sea of probabilities. Behind Selene the Olman guards were turning to face a new threat as the sacrifices shook themselves and jolted upright, awakening from a dream to find themselves in a nightmare. Some of them turned on the priests, who discovered the hard way that prisoners who had acquired sorcerous powers before they were captured were far from unarmed.

"Die already, damned of Xōchipilli!" shrieked Sister Selene, spraying a wave of deathly intent at Derek. Linda trembled under the assault, but shielded them both. Her skeletal servants were less lucky, half of them collapsing in a shower of dust and splinters. "Brother Ivar, shoot him!"

Ivar inexpertly raised an ancient revolver: but an ebony-furred blur threw itself at him and latched on to his arm. He screamed hoarsely as Derek's familiar drew up its hind legs and slashed at his abdomen with claws as sharp as box cutter blades. The jaguar didn't snarl: a true predator, it didn't telegraph its intent.

Derek concentrated on his dice. The probabilities were blurring together, the future gradually coagulating out of a haze of uncertainty. The dice shone brilliantly, their shadows many-angled projections from dimensions beyond the usual scope of spacetime. He smirked triumphantly at Sister Selene, and made a strange gesture toward the eldritch teapot-die, still spinning in and out of three-dimensional spacetime like an intrusion from the continuum of the computer graphics wonks: "Settle," he said.

A sneeze of face-exploding power—a spell he had been readying as they climbed the pyramid—was gathering in his sinuses but the dice roll came first. Words emerged from his throat in a language he'd never heard before, a language that was ancient before humanity first walked the earth: "*In the name of the opener of the way, in the path of the starry wisdom, I summon you, oh Lord of Slime and Things that Wriggle in Ponds, Anura the Golden!*"

The world flashed black and a crack of thunder sent Derek reeling. As his vision cleared he saw that Sister Selene had stumbled aside. Behind her the altar had shattered: the frog-idol rose uncertainly, then settled on its haunches, shedding gold leaf from its stony skin.

"*Ribbit,*" thundered the newborn deity, in a tone of froggy confusion. "*Ribbit?*" Glittering gemstone eyes swivelled in opposing circles as a crackle of rapid gunfire exploded from behind the altar. "*Ribbit!*"

The newborn deity he'd rolled into existence on a tide of random probabilities croaked angrily and shifted in a circle as bullets bounced off its granite hide. Past its olive-green shoulder Derek briefly glimpsed a middle-aged woman standing in a shooter's stance beside a wall of skulls. *Is that Iris?* He wondered if he was hallucinating. She methodically pumped bullets into the back of the idol's head—to no effect, for it was living stone.

Meanwhile, Sister Selene pushed herself to her feet, shrieking in outrage at the desecration of Xōchipilli's hijacked mortal vessel. One of Iris's bullets hung in midair centimeters from her head, buzzing like an angry wasp as it dissipated energy harmlessly against her shield. "*You can't do this!*" she screamed at Derek, ignoring the rain of gunfire: "It's against the rules! Not fair!"

"*GM's Guide,* Appendix Six, Random Encounters, table four, mistargeted summonings. Read your own rules," Derek snarked at her.

Never turn your back on a monster. Anura the Golden's mouth opened as Sister Selene raised her hands to hurl another sorcerous attack at Derek: there was a brief flicker-snap as a green and sticky frog's tongue as thick as a fire hose lashed out, wrapped itself around her waist with a horrible crunching of bones, then slurped her in.

Bullets were flying in all directions. Behind Derek, Linda flinched and swore. "That was too—Derek, I can't stop this thing!" She sounded panicky: Anura was waddling in place, turning to face them, *mana* streaming off his rocky integument. "It's too powerful!"

"Don't worry," Derek huffed through his mouth as his nostrils swelled up, "I've got it." The sorcerous sneeze expanded, exploding outward: "*Stone to flesh,*" he swore, giving it direction and substance as his sinuses blasted phantasmagoric mucus at the animated idol. Stone to flesh was old-school D&D, a counterspell for gorgons and beholders, but it also worked on altars, brick walls, and golems. Derek could see no reason why a statue animated by the holy will of a confused batrachian god would be any different.

And indeed it wasn't. Anura blinked in confusion as his skin glistened and took on an iridescent sheen. "*Ribbit?*" he asked querulously, throat pulsing with life. Behind him, metal clattered on stone as Iris ejected her magazine, slapped a new one into place, racked the slide, and flicked the selector switch to full automatic. "*Ri—*"

Derek flinched, deafened by the jackhammering string of gunshots as Iris emptied her machine pistol into the back of the new-born god. Behind her, the men in police uniforms briskly murdered cultists with precise head shots, public service smiles on their faces.

Ears ringing, he turned to Linda: a halo of flashes, bullets bouncing off the shield sustained by her scepter, lit up her face with sickly panic. "I can't," she began to say as she slumped to her knees: he could feel the scepter sucking her power away with each ricochet. "Stop shooting!" he shouted, barely able to hear his own voice. He tried to reassure her: "Don't worry, they're from the government and they're here to help us." He caught her on the way down, protecting her head, then wrapped his other hand around her fingers when her grip on the scepter's handle began to slacken. He felt it begin to drain him immediately, pulses of weakness rippling through him whenever a bullet came close—or an arrow, for some of the Omphalos guards had taken cover behind the pillars and were shooting at him, having clearly identified him as someone to blame.

All was chaos: flames, screams, and the physically painful hammer of unmuffled gunshots reverberating in a stone-walled temple. His ears rang with either a deafening of tinnitus or the chittering of mindless eaters attracted by his expenditure of magic, come to feast on his soul. He was on his knees beside Linda as she began to stir, with no clear idea how he'd gotten there. Then a pair of legs clad in blood-splashed combat pants appeared in his field of vision. "*Derek Reilly.* And *what* exactly did you think you were doing?"

His vision tracked up the legs to a tunic, took in a pair of neatly manicured hands steadily pointing a very big pistol with a very big magazine at his face, past a—*What's that she's wearing?*—to see the face of the Arts and Ents manager. Iris fixed him with such a stern expression of disapproval that if he hadn't already pissed himself—

"I only wanted to go to a convention," Derek said hoarsely. "Is this n-normal?" He licked bone-dry lips. "They were trying to immanentize a thing they could control, they called it Xōchipilli but what they wanted was from a made-up cosmology—I couldn't stop the manifestation but could roll up a l-lesser god. So I-I-I invited it in first, th-then turned it to flesh . . ."

But it was too much. Iris was still talking, but Derek wasn't listening, wasn't able to listen, as the world around him went gray and faded out.

>-<>-<>-<

Derek was so drained by the end of the fighting that afterward he retained only chaotic impressions of the next few hours.

It transpired that the Omphalos cultists had indeed created an exit from their pocket dreamworld. It was configured to open after the end of the campaign, transporting everyone in the temple complex back to the ground floor of the hotel—everyone still alive, that is, minus any occult souvenirs they might have picked up along the way. However, rather too many of the convention-goers for anyone's comfort were deceased by that point. Worse, the survivors (recovering from the glamour the cultists had placed them under for the duration) were almost all deeply traumatized. There was a protocol for mass casualty events, and Superintendent Kumar was on top of it: however this situation called for a mass psychiatric casualty process, and Scarfolk General Hospital didn't have one in place. Before long they'd run out of straitjackets and injectable sedatives: the ambulances were kept busy ferrying gamers to clinics across the north of England until the early hours of the following morning.

Derek, after a brief spell in the back of an ambulance with a paramedic, was triaged as walking wounded and discharged into Iris's custody. He in turn identified Linda—who remained unconscious after the Scepter of She-Ra took a big bite out of her soul—as an accessory. There was no sign of Raven, Phil, or Samantha, who were among the ninety-something attendees who remained missing, presumed dead.

Someone offered him a couple of pills and a glass of water, talked to him soothingly, and made sure he took them. After which everything got a bit warm and fuzzy about the edges.

Then it was all over bar the screaming and the endless interrogations in a debriefing suite and, somewhat more formally, a committee room on a corridor they called Mahogany Row in front of a panel of very serious men and women in suits. And from there he went to an oath of service, administered by a professorial fellow called

Dr. Armstrong whom everybody seemed a little bit afraid of, and a room in a safe house with a couple of other civil servants who worked for the agency, and a key all of his very own that unlocked the door to the street.

And Derek was free, his incarceration quashed. He could go out in the world beyond the fence—except perhaps the entire world was now his prison.

They gave him a cramped basement office with a desk in a building in London called the New Annex, where he had an actual *job* in Forecasting Ops, designing oblique strategies for the end of the world. They'd also found a job and an apartment for Linda, set her to work down the hallway in Statistics and Actuarial Services. She didn't hold the events at DiceCon against Derek, for which he was grateful, even though the Omphalos cult had turned her life upside down and slaughtered three of her friends. It meant there was at least one person here he could tentatively call a friend. They did lunch together at least twice a week. She seemed to like him: maybe even, if he was reading the auguries right, to *like*-like him.

"It's all very boring," she remarked one day over the vegetarian lasagna she'd ordered in the staff canteen. "Just rolling dice sequentially and logging the mean of each run. In a containment grid, of course, to ward off any unwanted influences."

"S-so, the statistical equiv-ivalent of the Three Minute Warning?"

She nodded emphatically. "Takes all the fun out of games of chance, knowing that if the dice start to go wrong we're all going to . . ." She trailed off. "How about you?"

Derek paused with his fork halfway to his mouth, a chicken goujon impaled on its tines. He stared at it numbly. For work-related reasons he'd been reading William Burroughs, and while he didn't understand a lot of it he knew a naked lunch when he saw one. "Scenario design," he said. "Can't talk about it."

"Too bad." She nodded. "This isn't what I expected." Of course it was all so they could keep an eye on her. A trained monkey could keep an eye on the dice, monitor the probabilities, and warn if reality was about to go off-piste again. "It's mostly boring." She looked as if she was thinking hard for a minute, then added, suspiciously casually, "Have you ever considered running a campaign?

There's a real ale pub in the east end that has a games night. I'm sure we could get a group together."

"I'd love to," he said, very seriously, before his brain caught up (*Is she asking me out?* was his immediate next thought), "but they never gave me back my rule books."

The handwritten notebooks he had poured *Cult of the Black Pharaoh* into were codeword-classified far above his security clearance. For him to read his own words would be a breach of the Official Secrets Act: an irony that did not escape him.

"Oh well, perhaps that's for the best." Linda finished her lasagna, then gave him a fey smile: "But maybe you could come anyway? This Sunday evening, say? They play other kinds of games, and some of them even have happy endings."

►◄►◄►◄►◄►◄

OVERTIME

►◄►◄►◄►◄►◄

Author's Note: The same year Iris Carpenter arrived in Camp Sunshine, Laundry Files main protagonist, Bob Howard, failed to book his time off over the Christmas holiday early enough to beat the stampede. So here is what happened to him during that festive season. . . .

►◄►◄►◄

All bureaucracies obey certain iron laws, and one of the oldest is this: get your seasonal leave booked early, lest you be trampled in the rush.

I broke the rule this year, and now I'm paying the price. It's not my fault I failed to book my Christmas leave in time—I was in hospital and heavily sedated. But the ruthless cut and thrust of office politics makes no allowance for those who fall in the line of battle: "You should have foreseen your hospitalization and planned around it" said the memo from HR when I complained. They're quite right, and I've made a note to book in advance next time I'm about to be abducted by murderous cultists or enemy spies.

I briefly considered pulling an extended sickie, but Brenda from Admin has a heart of gold; she pointed out that if I volunteered as Night Duty Officer over the seasonal period I could not only claim triple pay and time off in lieu, I'd also be working three grades above my assigned role. For purposes of gaining experience points in the fast-track promotion game they're steering me onto, that's hard to beat. So here I am, in the office on Christmas Eve, playing bureaucratic Pokémon as the chilly rain drums on the roof.

(Oh, you wondered what Mo thinks of this? She's off visiting her ditz of a mum down in Glastonbury. After last time we agreed it would be a good idea if I kept a low profile. Christmas: the one time of year when you can't avoid the nuts in your family muesli. But I digress.)

▶◀▶◀▶◀

Christmas: the season of goodwill toward all men—except for bank managers, credit scoring agencies, everyone who works in the greeting card business, and dodgy men in red suits who hang out in toy shops and scare small children by shouting *"ho ho HO!"* By the time I got out of hospital in September the Christmas seasonal displays were already going up in the shops: mistletoe and holly and metallized tinsel pushing out the last of summer's tanning lotion and Hawaiian shirts.

I can't say I've ever been big on the English Suburban Christmas. First, you play join-the-dots with bank holidays and what's left of your annual leave to get as many consecutive days off work as possible. Then instead of doing something useful and constructive with it you gorge yourself into a turkey-addled, stomach-bloated haze, drink too much cheap plonk, pick fights with the in-laws, and fall asleep on the sofa in front of the traditional family-friendly crap the BBC pumps out every December 25th in case the wee ones are watching. These days the little 'uns are all up in their rooms, playing *Chicks v. Zombies 8.0* with the gore dialled to splashy-giblets-halfway-up-the-walls (only adults bother watching TV as a social activity these days), but has Auntie Beeb noticed? Oh no they haven't! So it's crap pantomimes and *Mary Poppins* and reruns of *The Two Ronnies* for you, sonny, whether you like it or not. It's like being trapped in 1974 forever—and you can forget about escaping onto the internet: everybody else has had the same idea, and the tubes are clogged.

Alternatively you can spend Christmas alone in the office, where at least it's quiet once everyone else has gone home. You can get some work done, or read a book, or surreptitiously play *Chicks v. Zombies 8.0* with the gore dialled down to suitable-for-adults. At least, that's the way it's supposed to work . . . except when it doesn't, like now.

Let's rewind a week:

I'm pecking away at a quality assessment form on my office PC when there's a knock at the door. I glance up. It's Bill from Security. "Are you busy right now?" he asks.

"Um." My heart just about skips a beat. "Not really . . . ?"

Bill is one of our regular security officers: he's a former blue-suiter, salt-and-pepper moustache, silver comb-over, but keeps trim and marches everywhere like he's still in the military. "It's about your Christmas shift," he says, smiling vaguely and hefting a bunch of keys the size of a hand grenade. "I'm supposed to show you the ropes, y'know? Seeing as how you're on overnight duty next week." He jangles the key ring. "If you can spare half an hour?"

My heartbeat returns to normal. I glance at the email on my computer screen: "Yeah, sure." It's taken me about five seconds to cycle from mild terror to abject relief; he's not here to chew me out over the state of my trainers.

"Very good, sir. If you'd care to step this way?"

From Bill, even a polite request sounds a little like an order.

"You haven't done the graveyard shift before, have you, sir? There's not a lot to it—usually. You're required to remain in the building and on call at all times. Ahem, that's within reason, of course: toilet breaks permitted—there's an extension—and there's a bunk bed. You probably won't have to do anything, but in the unlikely event, well, you're the *Night Duty Officer.*"

We climb a staircase, pass through a pair of singularly battered fire doors, and proceed at a quick march along a puce-painted corridor with high wired-glass windows, their hinges painted shut. Bill produces his key ring with a jangling flourish. "Behold! The duty officer's watch room."

We are in the New Annex, a depressing New Brutalist slab of concrete that sits atop a dilapidated department store somewhere south of the Thames: it's electrically heated, poorly insulated, and none of the window frames fit properly. My department was moved here nearly a year ago, while they rebuild Dansey House (which will probably take a decade, because they handed it over to a public-private partnership). Nevertheless, the fittings and fixtures of the NDO's office make the rest of the New Annex look like a futuristic marvel. The khaki-painted steel frame of the bunk, topped with green wool blankets, looks like something out of a wartime movie—there's even a fading poster on the wall that says CARELESS LIPS SINK SHIPS.

"This is a joke. Right?" I'm pointing at the green-screen terminal on the desk, and the huge dial-infested rotary phone beside it.

"No sir." Bill clears his throat. "Unfortunately the NDO's office budget was misfiled years ago and nobody knows the correct code to requisition new supplies. At least it's warm in winter: you're right on top of the classified document incinerator, and it's got the only chimney in the building."

He points out aspects of the room's dubious architectural heritage while I'm scoping out the accessories. I poke at the rusty electric kettle: "Will anyone say anything if I bring my own espresso maker?"

"I think they'll say 'that's a good idea,' sir. Now, if you'd care to pay attention, let me talk you through the call management procedures and what to do in event of an emergency."

►◄►◄

The Laundry, like any other government bureaucracy, operates on a nine-to-five basis—except for those inconvenient bits that don't. The latter tend to be field operations of the kind where, if something goes wrong, they really *don't* want to find themselves listening to the voicemail system saying, "Invasions of supernatural brain-eating monsters can only be dealt with during core business hours. Please leave a message after the beep." (Supernatural? Why, yes: we're that part of Her Majesty's government that deals with occult technologies and threats. Certain abstruse branches of pure mathematics can have drastic consequences in the real world—we call them "magic"—by calling up the gibbering horrors with which we unfortunately share a multiverse (and the Platonic realm of mathematical truth). Given that computers are tools that can be used for performing certain classes of calculation *really fast,* it should come as no surprise that Applied Computational Demonology has been a growth area in recent years.)

My job, as Night Duty Officer, is to sit tight and answer the phone. In the unlikely event that it rings, I have a list of numbers I can call. Most of them ring through to duty officers in other departments, but one of them calls through to a special army barracks in Hereford, another goes straight to SHAPE in Brussels—that's NATO's European theatre command HQ—and a third dials direct to the COBRA briefing room in Downing Street. Nobody in the Laundry has ever had to get the Prime Minister out of bed in the small hours, but there's always a first time: more importantly, it's the NDO's job to make that call if a sufficiency of shit hits the fan on his watch.

I've also got a slim folder (labelled TOP SECRET and protected by disturbing wards that flicker across the cover like electrified floaters in the corners of my vision) that contains a typed list of codewords relating to secret operations. It doesn't say what the operations *are,* but it lists the supervisors associated with them—the people to call if one of the agents hits the panic button.

I've got an office to hang out in. An office with a bunk bed like something out of a fifties *Carry On* film about conscript life in the army, a chimney for the wind to whistle down (the better to keep me awake), a desk with an ancient computer terminal (shoved onto the floor to make room for my laptop), and a kettle (there's a bathroom next door with a sink, a toilet, and a shower that delivers an anemic trickle of tepid water). There's even a portable black-and-white TV with a cheap Freeview receiver in case I feel compelled to watch reruns of *The Two Ronnies.*

All the modern conveniences, in other words. . . .

►◄►◄►◄

The office party is scheduled to take place on Wednesday afternoon, from 1 p.m. to 5 p.m. sharp.

As civil servants, however irregular, we're not paid enough to compete with the bankers and corporate Tarquins and Jocastas who fill most of the office blocks in this part of the city; even in these straitened times they can afford to drop a couple of hundred notes per head on bubbly. So we don't get a posh restaurant outing: instead we have to tart up the staff canteen with some added tinsel, spray fake snow on the windows, and install a molting pine tree in a pot by the fire exit.

Pinky and Brains kindly installed their home stereo—homemade, not home-sized—in the number two lecture theatre for the obligatory dance; and Elinor and Beth (with a nod and a wink from Oversight) mugged an outside caterer for comestibles appropriate to a party but unheard-of by civil service canteen staff (who can manage cupcakes and sherry trifle if push comes to shove, but whose idea of pizza or curry is ghastly beyond belief).

There's a Dunkirk spirit to the whole affair: with a new government in the driving seat intent on budget cuts, there's not a lot of luxury to go round. But we're good at make-do-and-mend in this department—it's bred in our bureaucratic bones—and with the aid of a five-hundred-quid ents budget (to cover the hundred odd folks who work here), we make it happen.

There is a humdrum ritual for an office Christmas party anywhere in England. The morning beforehand, work takes on a lackadaisical feel. Meetings are truncated by 11 a.m.; agendas updated, email filters set to vacation. Some folks—the few, the lucky—begin to clear their desk drawers, for they know they shall not be coming back to work until the new year. An air of festivity wafts through the corridors of power, like a slightly moist crêpe banner.

"Bob?" I look up from my Minesweeper session: it's Andy, my sometime manager, leaning in the doorway. "You coming to lunch?"

I stretch, then mouse over to the screen lock. "Is it that time already?" I don't work for Andy these days, but he seems to take a proprietorial interest in how I'm doing.

"Yes." His head bounces up and down. He looks slightly guilty, like a schoolboy who's been caught with his hands in the sweets jar once too often. "Is Mo . . . ?"

"She's off-site today." I stand up. Actually she's over in Research and Development, quaffing port with the double-domes, dammit—an altogether more civilized session than this one. "We were planning on meeting up later."

"Well, come on then. Wouldn't want to miss the decent seats for the floor show, would we?"

"Floor show?" I close the door behind us.

"Yes, we have a visitor from Forecasting Ops. I got the email a couple of days ago. One Dr. Kringle has condescended to descend and give us some sort of pep talk about the year ahead."

"Kringle?" My cheek twitches. The name's unfamiliar. "From Forecasting Ops? Who are they . . ." I've heard rumors about them, but nothing concrete: it's probably one of those vague backwaters beavering away in isolation. Why on earth would they want to send someone to talk to us now?

"Yes, exactly." Andy spares me a sidelong glance. "Don't ask me, all I know is what I found in my inbox. Mail from HR, let him give a little motivational pep talk at the party. Don't worry," he adds quietly, "it'll all work out for the best in the end. You'll see. Just sit tight and bite your tongue." I get it. Andy is wearing his bearer-of-bad-news face while steering me toward the junior officers' bench. Something is about to come down the chute, and all the Christmas cheer in the world isn't going to cover up the stench of manure. As a management-grade employee—albeit a junior one—I'm required to show solidarity. Hence being tipped the nod and a wink.

I wonder what it can possibly be.

▸◂▸◂◂

The Duty Officer's room is just below the gently pitched roof of the New Annex. There's a wired-shut skylight, and the wind howls and gibbers overhead. Occasionally there's a sound like gravel on concrete as an errant gust flings a cupful of freezing cold water at the glass, followed by a hollow booming noise from the chimney. The chimney is indeed warm, but it's cooling fast: I guess they've shut down the incinerator over the holiday period. It's just past eleven at night, and there's no way in hell I'm going to be able to sleep while the storm is blowing.

When the holiday falls on a weekend day (as Boxing Day does this year) everyone gets another day off in lieu at the beginning of the following week except the Night Duty Officer, who is in it for up to four days at triple pay—as long as he doesn't go mad from boredom first.

I've been on duty for six hours and I've already caught up on my work email—at least, I've replied to everything that needs replying to, and am well into ignoring all the PowerPoints that need ignoring. I'm bored with gaming. The TV's on in the background, but it's the usual seasonal family-friendly fare. I don't want to start on the two fat novels I've stockpiled for the weekend this early, so there's only one thing to do. I abandon my cup of tea, pick up my torch, iPhone, and warrant card, and tiptoe forth to poke my nose where it doesn't belong.

> 'Twas the night before Christmas, the office was closed,
> The transom was shut, the staff home in repose;
> The stockings were hung by the chimney with care,
> But St. Nicholas won't be coming because this is a Designated
> National Security Site within the meaning of Para 4.12 of Section 3
> of the Official Secrets Act (Amended) and unauthorized intrusion
> on such a site is an arrestable offense . . .

Had enough of my poetry already? That's why they pay me to fight demons instead.

One of the perks of being Night Duty Officer is that I can poke my nose anywhere I like—after all, I'm responsible for the security of the building. In fact, I can go into places where I'd normally get my nasal appendage chopped right off if I had the temerity to sniff around without authorization. I can look inside Angleton's office, tiptoe between the dangerously active canopic jars and warded optical workbenches of Field Service, walk the thickly carpeted, dusty corridors of Mahogany Row, and pester the night-shift zombies (sorry: of course I meant to say, *Residual Human Resources*) in the basement. In fact, I'm pretty much encouraged to keep an eye on things, just as long as I stay within range of the Duty Officer's Phone.

You might think that's a catch, but the Duty Officer's Phone—once you unscrew the huge lump of Bakelite—is a remarkably simple piece of fifties-vintage electronics. It's not even scrambled: the encryption is handled at the exchange level. So after a brisk fifteen minutes programming a divert into the PBX so it'll ring through to my iPhone, I'm free to go exploring.

(Did you really think I was going to spend three days and nights nursing a landline that hasn't rung in sixteen years?)

►◄►◄►◄

Recipe for Office Christmas Party in the Season of Cuts:

Take:

28 junior administrative and secretarial staff

17 clerical and accounts officers

12 management grade officers

4 spies

5 human resources managers

9 building security staff

6 technical support officers

9 demonologists

(optional: 1 or more double-agents, ancient lurking horrors from beyond the stars, and zombies)

Add crepe paper hats, whistles, party poppers, tinsel decorations, fairy lights, whoopee cushions, cocktail snacks, supermarket mince pies, and cheap wine and spirits to taste.

Mix vigorously (blender setting at "pre-disco") and pour into staff canteen that has been in urgent need of redecoration since 1977. Seat at benches. Punch repeatedly (not more than 10 percent alcohol by volume), serve the turkey, set fire to the Christmas pudding, discover fire extinguisher is six months past mandatory HSE inspection deadline, and suppress.

Allow to stand while Martin from Tech Support drunkenly invites Kristin from Accounts to audit his packet (during that gap in the hubbub when every other conversation stops simultaneously and you can hear a pin drop); Vera from Logistics asks Ayesha from HR if her presence at the party means that she's finally found Jesus; and George from Security throws up in the Christmas tree tub.

And then . . .

Andy tings his knife on the edge of his glass repeatedly until everybody finally notices he's trying to get their attention, at which point he stands up. I look wistfully at the tray of slightly stale mince pies in the middle of the table, and withdraw my hand.

"Quiet, please! First of all, I'd like to take this opportunity to thank Facilities for organizing a party at short notice and under considerable budgetary constraints—a budget which is unavoidably much tighter than for last year's festivities. Thanks to Elinor and Beth for organizing the external catering, and to Dr. Kringle here for kindly approving our request for an entertainments budget—very generously, in view of the current Treasury strategic deficit reduction program."

(Applause.)

"And now, Dr. Kringle has asked if he can say a few words to us all about the year ahead . . ."

►◄►◄►◄

I walk the darkened halls.

The New Annex predates the fad for rat-maze cubicle farms in offices, never mind open plan offices and hot-desking, but that never stopped anyone. The result is a curious architectural mixture of tiny locked offices hived off artificially lit corridors, alternating with barnlike open plan halls full of cheap desks and underpowered computers, their cases yellowing with age.

Here's the vast expanse of what used to be the typing pool—so-called because in the old days there used to be officers here who couldn't use a keyboard. These days it's our administrative core, a place where civil servants come to die. The Laundry, perforce, must find work for many idle hands—the hands of everyone who comes to our attention and needs be given a job they're not allowed to refuse. Luckily bureaucracy breeds, and it takes many meetings to manage the added complexity of administration required by our chronic overstaffing. There are people here who I only know through their Outlook calendars, which are perpetually logjammed. Entire departments beaver away in anonymous quiet, building paper dams to hold the real world at bay. I shine my torch across empty in-trays, battered chairs, desks that reek of existential pointlessness. *I could have been trapped here for good,* I realize. I shudder as I move on. Being part of the Laundry's active service arm brings hazards of its own: but dying of boredom isn't one of them.

I turn left and take a shortcut through Mahogany Row. Here the carpet is thick, the woodwork polished rather than painted over. Individual offices with huge oak desks and leather recliners, walls hung with dark oil paintings of old hands in wartime uniform. Nobody is ever *in* any of these offices—rumor has it they all transcended, or were never human in the first place—these sinister and barely glimpsed senior officers who ran the organization from its early years.

(I've got my own theory about Mahogany Row, which is that the executives who would be here don't exist yet. In the depths of the coming crisis, as the stars come into cosmic alignment and the old ones return to stalk the earth, the organization will have to grow enormously bigger, taking on new responsibilities and more staff—at which point, those of us who survive are going to move on up here to direct the war effort. Assuming the powers that be have more sense than to fill the boardroom with the usual recycled corporate apparatchiks, that is. If they don't, may Cthulhu have mercy on our souls.)

As I turn the corner past the executive lavatory and approach the fire door I have a most peculiar sensation. *Why do I feel as if I'm being watched?* I wonder. I clear my throat. "Duty Officer." I reach into my pocket and pull out my warrant card: "Show yourself!"

The card glows pale green in the darkness; nothing stirs.

"Huh." I palm it, feeling stupid. The night watchmen are about, but they're not supposed to come up here. The wind and rain whooshes and rattles beyond the office windows.

I push the door open. It's yet another administrative annex, presumably for the executives' secretaries. One of the copiers has a print job stacked face down in the output tray. That strikes me as odd: given the nature of our work here, Security take a dim view of documents being left lying around. But Security won't be making their rounds for a few days. Probably best to take the printouts and stick them in the internal post to whoever ran them off—or in a locked safe pending a chewing-out if it's anything confidential.

I flip the first sheet over to look for the header page, and do a double take. *Buttocks!* Hairy ones, at that. *So* someone *was enjoying the party.*

The next page features more buttocks, and they're a lot less male, judging by the well-filled stockings and other identifying characteristics. I shake my head. I'm beginning to work out a response—I'm going to pin them on one of the staff notice boards, with an anonymous appeal for folks to wipe down the copier after each use—when I get to the third sheet.

Whoever sat on the copier lid *that* time didn't have buttocks, hairy or otherwise—or any other mammalian features for that matter. What I'm holding looks to be a photocopy of the business end of a giant cockroach.

Maybe I'm not alone after all. . . .

►◄►◄►◄

After Kringle drops his turd in the punch bowl of seasonal spirit, the party officially ceases to be fun, even for drably corporate values of fun. My appetite evaporates, too: they can keep the pies for all I care. I grab a bottle of Blue Nun and tiptoe back toward my cubicle in the Counter Possession Unit.

Fuck. Mo isn't here; she's already headed off to see her mum. She'd understand, though. I'm on duty from tomorrow through Monday morning, and not supposed to leave the building. I was going to go home tonight—run the washing machine, pack a bag with clean clothes for the weekend, that sort of thing—but right now the urge to get blind falling-down drunk is calling me.

Because this is the last Christmas party at the Laundry.

I pull out my phone to call Mo, then pause. She's got her hands full with Mum right now. Why add to her worries? And besides, this isn't a secure voice terminal: I can't safely say everything that needs to be said. (The compulsion to confidentiality runs deep, backed up by my oath of office. To knowingly break it risks very unpleasant consequences.) I'm about to put my phone away when Andy clears his throat. He's standing right behind me, an unlit cigarette pinched between two fingers. "Bob?"

I take another deep breath. "Yeah?"

"Want to talk?"

I nod. "Where?"

"The clubhouse . . ."

I follow him, out through a door onto the concrete balcony at the back of the New Annex that leads to the external fire escape. We call it the clubhouse in jest: it's where the smokers hang out, exposed to the elements. There's a sand bucket half-submerged in scorched fag-ends sitting by the door. I wait while Andy lights up. His fingers are shaking slightly. He's skinny, tall, about five years older than me: four grades higher, too, managing the head-office side of various ops that it's not sensible to ask about. Wears a suit, watches the world from behind a slightly sniffy air of academic amusement as if nothing really matters very much. But his detachment is gone now, blown away like a shred of smoke on the wind.

"What do you make of it?" he asks, bluntly.

I look at his cigarette, for a moment wishing I smoked. "It's not good. As signs of the apocalypse go, the last office Christmas party ever is a bit of a red flag."

Andy hides a cough with his fist. "I sincerely hope not."

"What's Kringle's track record?" I ask. "Surely he's been pulling rabbits out of hats long enough we can run a Bayesian analysis and see how well he . . ." I trail off, seeing Andy's expression.

"He's one of the best precognitives we've ever had, so I'm told. And what he's saying backs up Dr. Mike's revised time frame for Case Nightmare Green." (The end of the world, when—in the words of the mad seer—*the stars come right*. It's actually a seventy-year-long window during which the power of magic multiplies monstrously, and alien horrors from the dark ages before the big bang become accessible to any crack-brained preacher with a yen to talk to the devil. We thought we had a few years' grace: according to Dr. Mike our calculations are wrong, and the window began to open nine months ago.) "Something *really bad* is coming. If Kringle can't see through to next December 24th, then, well, we probably won't be alive then."

"So he stares into the void, and the void stares back. Maybe *he* won't be alive." I'm clutching at straws. "I don't suppose there's any chance he's just going to get run over by a bus?"

Andy gives me a Look, of a kind I've been beginning to recognize more since the business in Brookwood—infinite existential despair tempered with a goodly dose of rage against the inevitable, dammed up behind a stiff upper lip. To be fair, I've been handing out a fair number of them myself. "I have no idea. Frankly, it's all a bit vague. Precog fugues aren't deterministic, Bob: also, they tend to disrupt whatever processes they're predicting the outcome of. That's why Forecasting Ops are so big on statistical analysis. If Kringle said we won't see another Christmas party, you can bet they've rolled the dice more than the bare minimum to fit the confidence interval."

"So preempt his prophecy already! Use the weak anthropic principle: if we cancel next year's Christmas party, his prophecy is delayed indefinitely. Right?"

Andy rolls his eyes. "Don't be fucking stupid."

"It was a long shot." (Pause.) "What are we going to do?"

"We?" Andy raises one eyebrow. "*I* am going to go home to the wife and kids for Christmas and try to forget about threats to our very existence for a bit. You"—he takes a deep gulp of smoke—"get to play at Night Duty Officer, patrolling the twilit corridors to protect our workplace from the hideous threat of the Filler of Stockings who oozes through chimneys and ventilation ducts every Dead God's Birthday-eve to perform unspeakable acts against items of hosiery. Try not to let it get to you—and have a nice holiday while you're at it."

►◄►◄►◄

My appetite for nocturnal exploration is fading, tempered by the realization that I may not be the only one putting in some overtime in the office tonight. I reach for my ward—hung around my neck like an identity badge—and feel it. It tingles normally, and is cool. *Good*. If it was hot or glowing or throbbing I could expect company. It's time to get back to the NDO room and regroup.

I tiptoe back the way I came, thinking furiously.

Item: It's the night before Christmas, and backup is scarce to nonexistent.

Item: You can fool everyone at an office party with a class three glamour, but you can't fool a photocopier.

Item: Kringle's prophecy.

Item: We're in CASE NIGHTMARE GREEN, and things that too many people believe in have a nasty tendency to come true; magic is a branch of applied computation; neural networks are computing devices; there are *too many people* and *the stars are right* (making it much too easy to gain the attention of entities that find us crunchy and good with ketchup).

Item: What kind of uninvited entity might want to sit in on Kringle's little pep talk. . . . ?

I'm halfway down the corridor through Mahogany Row when I break into a run.

▸◂▸◂◂

"Good afternoon, everyone."

Kringle wrings his hands as he speaks. They're curiously etiolated and pale-skinned, like those of a Deep One, but he lacks the hunched back or gills. Only his pallid, stringy hair and the thick horn-rimmed glasses concealing a single watery blue eye—the other is covered by a leather patch—mark him out as odd. But his gaze . . .

"It *will* be a good afternoon, until I finish speaking." He smiles like a hangman's trapdoor opening. "So drink up now and be of good cheer, because this will be the last Christmas party held by the Laundry."

Up to this point most folks have been ignoring him or listening with polite incomprehension. Suddenly you could hear a mouse fart.

"You need have no fear of downsizing or treasury cuts to comply with the revised public spending guidelines." His smile fades. "I speak of more fundamental, irrevocable changes.

"My department, Forecasting Operations, is tasked with attempting to evaluate the efficacy of proposed action initiatives in pursuit of the organization's goals—notably, the prevention of incursions by gibbering horrors from beyond spacetime. Policies are originated, put on the table—and we descry their consequences. It's a somewhat hit-and-miss profession, but our ability to peer into the abyss of the future allows us to sometimes avoid the worst pitfalls."

Kringle continues in this vein for some time. His voice is oddly soporific, and it takes me awhile to figure out why: he reminds me of a BBC radio weather forecaster. They have this slot for the weather forecast right before the news, and try as I will I *always* zone out right before they get to whatever region I happen to be interested in and wake up as they're finishing. It's uncanny. Kringle is clearly talking about something of considerable importance, but my mind skitters off the surface of his words like a wasp on a plateglass window. I shake my head and begin to look round, when the words flicker briefly into focus.

"—Claus, or *Santé Klaas* in the medieval Dutch usage, a friendly figure in a red suit who brings presents in the depths of winter, may have a more sinister meaning. Think not only of the traditions of the Norse Odin, with which the figure of Santa Claus is associated, but with the shamanic rituals of Lap antiquity, performed by a holy man who drank the urine of reindeer that had eaten the sacred toadstool, *Amanita muscaria*—wearing the bloody, flayed skin of the poisoned animals to gain his insight into the next year—we, with modern statistical filtering methodologies, can gain much more precise insights, but at some personal cost—"

Eh? I shake my head again, then take another mouthful from my paper cup of cheap plonk. The words go whizzing past, almost as if they're tagged for someone else's attention. Which is odd, because I'm trying to follow what he's saying: I've got a peculiar feeling that this stuff is important.

"—particular, certain facts appear indisputable. *There will be no Laundry staff Christmas dinner next year.* We can't tell you why, but as a result of events that I believe have already taken place this will be the last one. Indeed, attempts over the past year to investigate outcomes beyond this evening have met with abject failure: the end of this party is the last event that Forecasting Operations is able to predict with any degree of confidence. . . ."

►◄►◄►◄

I arrive back in the Duty Officer's room with a chilly sheen of sweat coating the small of my back. The light's on, casting a cheery glow through the frosted glass window in the door, and the TV's blathering happily away. I duck inside and shut it behind me, then grab the spare wooden chair and prop it under the door handle. My memory of Kringle's talk seems altogether too disturbingly like a dream for my taste: even the conversation with Andy has an oddly vaporous feel to it. I've had this kind of experience before, and the only thing to do is to test it.

I plonk myself down behind the desk and unlock the drawer, then pull out the phone book. Rain rattles on the window above my head as I open the book, an electric tingling in my fingertips reminding me that the wards on the cover are very much alive. *Come on, where are you.* . . . I run a shaky finger down the page. What I'm looking for isn't there: the dog that didn't bark in the night. I swallow, then I go back and search a different section for Andy's home number. Yes, *he's* listed—and he's got a secure terminal. Time check: it's twenty to midnight, not quite late enough to be seriously antisocial. I pick up the telephone receiver and begin to laboriously spin the dial. The phone rings three times.

"Andy?"

"Hello? Who is this?" It's a woman's voice.

"Er, this is Bob, from the office. I wonder, is Andy available? I won't take a minute. . . ."

"Bob?" Andy takes the receiver. "Talk to me."

I clear my throat. "Sorry to call you like this, but it's about the office party. The guy who spoke to us, from Forecasting Operations. Do you remember his name, and have you ever dealt with him before?"

There's a pause. "Forecasting Operations?" Andy sounds puzzled. My stomach clenches. "Who are they? I haven't heard of any forecasting . . . what's going on?"

"Do you remember our conversation in the clubhouse?" I ask.

"What, about personal development courses? Can't it wait until next year?"

I glance back at the phone book. "Uh, I'll get back to you. I think I've got a situation."

I put the handset down as carefully as if it's made of sweating gelignite. Then I leaf through the phone book again. Nope, Forecasting Operations aren't listed. And Andy doesn't remember Dr. Kringle, or his lecture, or our conversation on the balcony.

I've got a very bad feeling about this.

Like the famous mad philosopher said, when you stare into the void, the void stares also; but if you *cast* into the void, you get a type conversion error. (Which just goes to show Nietzsche wasn't a C++ programmer.) Dr. Kringle was saying his department tests new policies, then reads the future and changes their plans in a hurry if things don't work out for the best. Throwing scenarios into the void.

What if there *was* a Forecasting Operations Department . . . and when they stared into the void once too often, something bad happened? Something so bad that they unintentionally edited themselves out of existence?

I glance at the TV. It's movie time, and tonight they're running *The Nightmare Before Christmas*: Jack Skellington sings his soliloquy as he stands before the portal he's opened to Christmas Town—

And that's when I realize what's going on.

▸◂▸◂▸◂

It's Christmas Eve, and the stars are Right.

Parents the world over still teach their children that if they're good, Santa will bring them presents.

There are things out there in the void, hungry things hidden in

the gaps between universes, that come when they're called. Tonight, hundreds of millions of innocent children are calling Santa.

Who's *really* coming down your chimney tonight?

▶◀▶◀▶◀

It's distinctly cold in the Duty Officer's room. Which is odd, because it's not that cold outside: it's windy and raining heavily, but
that's London for you. I turn and stare at the aluminum ductwork
that runs from floor to ceiling. *That's the incinerator shaft, isn't
it?* It's coated in beads of condensation. I reach a hand toward it,
then pull my fingers back in a hurry. Cold air is spilling off the
pipe in chilly waves, and as I glance at the floor I see a thin mist.
I left a nearly empty cup of tea on the desk when I went on my
nocturnal ramble: now I pick it up and throw the contents at the
chimney. The drops of ice crackle as they hit the floor, and my
ward is suddenly a burning-hot weight at the base of my throat.

I'm on my feet and over the other side of the desk before I have
time to think. There's an anomalously cold chimney in my office.
Cold enough that the air is condensing on it. Cold enough that it
sucks the heat out of a cup of tepid tea in milliseconds. But what
does it *mean*? (Aside from: I'm in big trouble. That's a given, of
course.)

What it means is . . . there's an incursion. Something's coming
down the chimney, something from the dark anthropic zone—
from a corner of the multiverse drained of all meaning and energy.
Let's steal a facetious phrase from Andy and call it the Filler of
Stockings: Lurker in Fireplaces, Bringer of Gifts. (Odin, Jólnir, the
King in Red. Pick your culture: prepare to die.) All it knows is that
it's *cold* and it's *hungry*—and it wants inside.

These things gain energy from belief. This office, this
organization—we're its first target because we know its ilk. If it
can get a toehold anywhere, it'll be here, but I haven't seen it yet,
so I don't have to believe—*damn* Kringle for coming and talking
to us! If I can keep it out of the New Annex until dawn it'll be
too late for the Bringer of Gifts to claw its way through the wall

between the worlds this year. But if it's already in the incinerator chimney—

I pull the chair out from under the door handle, grab my torch, and head out in a hurry.

▸◂▸◂▸◂

Nighttime hijinks and explorations in the office take on a whole different significance when you know that it's eighteen minutes to midnight and—by tradition—that's when something hungry and unspeakably alien is going to break out of the incinerator in the basement, expecting to find a stocking and some midnight snacks to appease its voracious appetite.

Here's the flip side of millions of sleeping believers-in-Santa providing an opening for something horrible to enter our cosmos: *they expect him to go away again after he leaves the toys.* The summoning comes with an implicit ritual of banishment. But you've got to get the ritual *right.* If you don't, if you break your side of the bargain, the other party to the summoning is free to do whatever it wills.

Seventeen minutes to midnight. I'm in the admin pool again, and there's the stationery cupboard. It's locked, of course, and I spend a precious minute fumbling with the bunch of keys before I find one that fits. Inside the cupboard I find what I'm looking for: a box of pushpins. I move on, not bothering to lock it behind me—if I succeed, there'll be time to tidy up later.

I bypass Mahogany Row and the sleeping ghosts of management to come, and head for the canteen. Maxine and her friends put some effort into preparing it for the party, and if I'm lucky—

Yup, I'm in luck. Nobody's taken the decorations down yet. I turn the lights on, hunting around until I see it: a red-and-white stripy stocking stuffed with small cardboard boxes hangs from the corkboard by the dumbwaiter. I grab it and dig the boxes out, nearly laddering it in my haste. The canteen's bare but the kitchen is next door, and I fumble for the key again, swearing under my breath (Why aren't these things clearly labelled?) until I get the door unlocked. The fridge is still humming. I get it open and find what I was hoping for—a tray of leftovers, still covered in cling-film.

Ten minutes. I run for the staircase, clutching stocking, pin box, and the tray of stale mince pies. In my pockets: conductive marker pen, iPhone loaded with the latest Laundry countermeasures package, and a few basic essentials for the jobbing computational demonologist. I'm still in time as I leg it down two stories. And then I'm at the basement doors. I pause briefly to review my plan.

Item: Get to the incinerator room without being stopped (optionally: eaten) by the night watch.

Item: Get the stocking pinned up above the incinerator, and place the pies nearby.

Item: Draw the best containment grid I can manage around the whole mess, and hope to hell that it holds.

What could possibly go wrong? I plant my tray on the floor, pull out my key ring, and unlock the door to the basement.

►◄►◄►◄

It's funny how many of the pivotal events of my life take place underground. From the cellar of a secret Nazi redoubt to a crypt in the largest necropolis in Europe, via the scuppers of an ocean-going spy ship: seen 'em all, got the tour shirt. I've even visited the basement of the New Annex a time or two. But it's different at night, with the cold immanence of an approaching dead god clutching at your heart strings.

I walk down a dim, low-ceilinged passage lined with pipes and cable bearers, past doors and utility cupboards and a disturbingly coffin-like ready room where the night staff wait impassively for intruders. No stir of undead limbs rises to stop me—my warrant card sees to that. Forget ghostly illumination and handheld torches: I'm not stupid, I switched on the lights before I came down here. Nevertheless, it's creepy. I'm not certain where the document incinerator lives, so I check door plaques until I feel a cold draft of air on my hand. Glancing up I see a frost-rimed duct, so I follow it until it vanishes into the wall beside a door with a wired-glass window which is glowing cheerily with light from within.

Looks like I've got company.

I'm about to put my tray down and fumble with the key ring when my unseen companion saves me the effort and opens the door. So I raise the tray before me, take a step forward, and say, "Just who the hell *are* you really?"

"Come in, Mr. Howard. I've been expecting you."

The thing that calls itself Dr. Kringle takes a step backward into the incinerator room, beckoning. I stifle a snort of irritation. He's taken the time to change into a cowled robe that hides his face completely—only one skeletal hand projects from a sleeve, and I can tell at a glance that it's got the wrong number of joints. I lick my lips. "You can cut the Dickensian crap, Kringle—I'm not buying it."

"But *I* am the ghost of Christmases probably yet to come!" *Ooh, touchy!*

"Yeah, and I'm the tooth fairy. Listen, I've got a stocking to put up, and not much time. You're the precognitive, so you tell me: Is this where you try to eat my soul or try to recruit me to your cult or something and we have to fight, or are you just going to stay out of my way and let me do my job?"

"Oh, do what you will; it won't change the eventual outcome." Kringle crosses his arms affrontedly. At least, I *think* they're arms—they're skinny, and there are too many elbows, and now I notice them I realize he's got two pairs.

The incinerator is a big electric furnace, with a hopper feeding into it beside a hanging rack of sacks that normally hold the confidential document shreddings. I park the pie tray on top of the furnace (which is already cold enough that I risk frostbite if I touch it with bare skin) and hang the empty stocking from one of the hooks on the rack.

Ghastly hunger beyond human comprehension is the besetting vice of extradimensional horrors—if they prioritized better they might actually be more successful. In my experience you can pretty much bet that if J. Random Horror has just emerged after being imprisoned in an icy void for uncountable millennia, it'll be feeling snackish. Hence the tempting tray of comestibles.

I glance at my watch: it's four minutes to midnight. Then I eyeball the furnace control panel. Kringle is standing beside it. "So what's the story?" I ask him.

"You already know most of it. Otherwise you wouldn't be here." He sounds bored, as well he might. "Why don't you tell me, while we wait?"

"All right." I point at him. "*You're* here because you're trapped in a time paradox. Once upon a time the Laundry had a Forecasting Ops department. But when you play chess with the future, you risk checkmate—not to mention being assimilated by that which you study. The first thing Forecasting Ops ever forecast was the probability of its own catastrophic capture by—*something*. So it was disbanded. But you can't disband something like that without leaving echoes, can you? So you're just an echo of a future that never happened."

The spectral shade in its ragged robe bobs its head—or whatever it has in place of a head.

"The Christmas incursion—" I glance at the cold furnace again, then at my watch. "—would have killed you. But without Forecasting Ops to warn us about it, it'd happen anyway, wouldn't it?" *Three minutes.* "So you had to maneuver someone into position to deal with it *even though you don't exist.*"

I remember sitting through a bizarre and interminable lecture at the Christmas party. But *who else* remembers sitting through it? Andy doesn't remember Kringle's talk. And I bet that aside from my own memories, and a weirdly smudged photocopy—emergent outcome of some distorted electron orbitals on a samarium-coated cylinder—there's no evidence that the ghost of Christmases rendered-fictional-by-temporal-paradox ever visited the Laundry on a wet and miserable night.

So much for the emergency phone book. . . .

Two minutes. "How far into the future can you see right now?" I ask Kringle. I take a step forward, away from the furnace hopper. "Move aside," I add.

Kringle doesn't shift. "The future is here," he says in a tone of such hollow, despairing dread that it lifts the hair on the back of my neck.

There's a booming, banging sound inside the furnace. I squint:

something writhes inside the tiny, smoke-dimmed inspection window. My watch is slow! There's no time left. I step close to the control panel and, bending down, hastily scrawl a circle on the floor around my feet.

"Wait, where did the pies come from?" Kringle asks.

I complete the circuit. "The kitchen. Does it matter?"

"But you're doomed!" He sounds puzzled.

Something is coming down the chimney, but it's not dressed in fur from its head to its feet, and it doesn't have twinkling eyes and dimpled cheeks.

"Nope," I insist. I point at the bait: "And I intend to prove it."

"But it ate you!" Kringle says indignantly. "Then we all died. I came to warn you, but did you listen? *Nooo—*"

The trouble with prophecies of your own demise is that, like risk assessments, if you pay too much attention to them they can become self-fulfilling. So I ignore the turbulent time-ghost and stare as the fat, greenish tip of one pseudopod emerges and, twitching, quests blindly toward the frozen pies on top of the furnace.

I stare for what feels like hours, but in reality is only a couple of seconds. Then, in a flashing moment, the tentacle lashes out and simultaneously engulfs all the pies, sucker-like mouths sprouting from its integument to snap closed around them.

The Filler of Stockings is clearly no exception to the hunger rule. Having fed, its questing tentacle slows, perhaps hampered by the bulges along its length: it lazily curls over toward the gaping, ice-rimed mouth of the stocking. Waves of coldness roll from it. As I draw breath it feels like I'm inhaling razor blades. The temperature in the room is dropping by double-digit degrees per second.

"*What?*" says Kringle. He sounds surprised: clearly this isn't the future he signed up for back in time-ghost central casting. "*Who* ate all the pies?"

I twist the handle of the main circuit breaker to the LIVE position, and stab at the green ON button with rapidly numbing fingers. "There were quite a lot left over," I tell him helpfully, "after you spoiled everyone's appetite with that speech."

"No, that can't be—"

With a deep hum and a rattle of ventilators, the incinerator powers up. It is followed by a sizzling flash and a howling whoop of pain and fury as the Filler of Stockings, thwarted, tries to disentangle its appendage from the gas jets. To a many-angled one, we impoverished entities who are stranded in three-plus-one dimensions are fairly harmless; nevertheless, even the inhabitants of flatland can inflict a nasty paper cut upon the unwary.

My ward is alight, blazing like a flashbulb as it sears the skin on my chest: the tentacle sticking out of the furnace hopper combusts with a flash of fire and a horrible stench of burning calamari. Simultaneously, the shade of Dr. Kringle swirls and spirals from view, curling into the hopper even as a nacreous glow shines from inside, half-glimpsed things looping and writhing like colored worms. The howling fades into a flatulent sigh, leaving a faint ringing in my ears. It sounds like distant church bells. I take a deep breath as my ward dims, trying to get my terror-driven pulse back down to normal.

There's something on the floor. I squint and bend forward, puzzled. And after a moment I see that the Filler of Stockings has left me a coal.

►◄►◄►◄►◄►◄

DOWN ON THE FARM

►◄►◄►◄►◄►◄

Author's Note: The year before Bob's failure to book his seasonal vacation, he got sent on a different kind of holiday: to pay a visit to the Funny Farm, an ancient asylum where the Laundry warehouses certain staff whose minds have snapped in the wake of one extradimensional incursion too many. If you thought Camp Sunshine was grim, you haven't been to St. Hilda's yet. . . .

►◄►◄

Ah, the joy of summer. Here in the southeast of England it's the season of mosquitoes, sunburn, and water shortages. I'm a city boy, so you can add stifling pollution to the list as a million outwardly mobile families start their Chelsea tractors and race to their holiday camps. And that's before we consider the hellish environs of the Tube (far more literally hellish than anyone realizes, unless they've looked at a Transport for London journey planner and recognized the recondite geometry underlying the superimposed sigils of the underground map).

But I digress . . .

One morning, my deputy head of department wanders into my office. It's a cramped office, and I'm busy practicing my Frisbee throw with a stack of beer mats and a dartboard decorated with various cabinet ministers. "Bob," Andy pauses to pluck a moist cardboard square out of the air as I sit up, guiltily: "a job's just come up that you might like to look at—I think it's right up your street."

The first law of Bureaucracy is, *show no curiosity outside your cubicle*. It's like the first rule of every army that's ever bashed a square: *never volunteer*.

If you ask questions (or volunteer) it will be taken as a sign of inactivity, and the devil, in the person of your line manager (or your sergeant), will find a task for your idle hands. What's more, you'd better believe it'll be less appealing than whatever you were doing before (creatively idling, for instance), because inactivity is a crime against organization and must be punished. It goes double in the Laundry, that branch of the British secret state tasked with defending the realm from the scum of the multiverse using the tools of applied computational demonology: volunteer for the wrong job and you can end up with soul-sucking horrors from beyond spacetime mistaking your brain for a midnight snack. But I don't think I could get away with feigning overwork right now, and besides: he's packaged it up as a mystery. Andy knows how to bait my hook, damn it.

"What kind of job?"

"There's something odd going on down at the Funny Farm." He gives a weird little chuckle. "The trouble is going to be telling whether it's just the usual, or a more serious deviation. Normally I'd ask Boris to check it out but he's not available. It has to be an SSO two or higher, and I can't go out there myself. So . . . how about it?"

I may be impetuous (and a little bored) but I'm not stupid. And while I'm so far down the management ladder that I have to squint to see daylight, I'm an SSO 3, which means I can sign off on petty cash authorizations up to the price of a pencil and have to sit in on interminable meetings when I'm not tackling supernatural incursions or grappling with the eerie eldritch horrors in Human Resources. I even get to represent my department on international liaison junkets if I don't dodge fast enough. "Not so quick—why can't you go? Have you got a meeting scheduled, or something?" Most likely it's a five-course lunch with his opposite number from the SIS liaison committee, but if so, and if I take the job, that's all for the good: he'll end up owing me.

Andy pulls a face. "It's not the usual. I *would* go, but they might not let me out again."

Huh? "'They'? Who are 'they'?"

"The Nurses." He looks me up and down as if he's never seen me before. Weird. What's gotten into him? "They're sensitive to the stench of magic. It's okay for you, you've only been working here, what? Six years? All you need to do is turn your pockets inside out before you go, and make sure you're not carrying any gizmos, electronic or otherwise. But I've been here coming up on fifteen years. And the longer you've been in the Laundry . . . it gets under your skin. Visiting the Funny Farm isn't a job for an old hand, Bob. It has to be someone new and fresh, who isn't likely to attract their professional attention."

Call me slow, but finally I figure out what this is about. Andy wants me to go because he's *afraid*.

(See, I told you the rules, didn't I?)

▸◂▸◂

Anyway, that's why, less than a week later, I am admitted to a Lunatickal Asylum—for that is what the gothic engraving on the stone Victorian workhouse lintel assures me it is. Luckily mine is not an emergency admission: but you can never be too sure . . .

▸◂▸◂

The old saw that there are some things that mortal men were not meant to know cuts deep in my line of work. Laundry staff—the Laundry is what we call the organization, not a description of what it does—are sometimes exposed to mind-blasting horrors in the course of our business. I'm not just talking about the usual PowerPoint presentations and self-assessment sessions to which any bureaucracy is prone: they're more like the mythical Worse Things that happen at Sea (especially in the vicinity of drowned alien cities occupied by tentacled terrors). When one of our number needs psychiatric care they're not going to get it in a normal hospital or via care in the community: we don't want agents babbling classified secrets in public, even in the relatively safe confines of a padded cell. Perforce, we have to take care of our own.

I'm not going to tell you what town the Funny Farm is embedded in. Like many of our establishments it's a building of a certain age, confiscated by the government during the Second World War and not returned to its former owners. It's hard to find; it sits in the middle of a triangle of grubby shopping streets that have seen better days, and every building that backs onto it sports a high, windowless, brick wall. All but one: if you enter a small grocery store, walk through the stockroom into the backyard, then unlatch a nondescript wooden gate and go down a gloomy, soot-stained alley, you'll find a hidden cul-de-sac. You won't do this without authorization—it's protected by wards powerful enough to cause projectile vomiting in would-be burglars—but if you walked to the end you'd come to a heavy green wooden door flanked by narrow windows with black-painted cast-iron bars. A dull, pitted plaque next to the doorbell proclaims it to be ST HILDA OF GRANTHAM'S HOME FOR DISGRUNTLED WAIFS AND STRAYS. (Except that most of them aren't so much disgruntled as demonically possessed when they arrive at these gates.)

It smells faintly of boiled cabbage and existential despair. I take a deep breath and yank the bell-pull.

Nothing happens, of course. I phoned ahead to make an appointment, but even so, someone's got to unlock a bunch of doors and then lock them again before they can get to the entrance and let me in. "They take security seriously there," Andy told me. "Can't risk the battier inmates getting loose, you know."

"Just how dangerous are they?" I'd asked.

"Mostly they're harmless—to other people." He shuddered. "But the secure ward—don't try and go there on your own. Not that the Sisters will let you, but I mean, don't even *think* about trying it. Some of them are . . . well, we owe them a duty of care and a debt of honor, they fell in the line of duty and all that, but that's scant consolation for you if a senior operations officer who's succumbed to paranoid schizophrenia decides that you're a BLUE HADES and gets hold of some red chalk and a hypodermic needle before your next visit, hmm?"

The thing is, magic is a branch of applied mathematics, and the inmates here are not only mad: they're computer scientists. That's why they came to the attention of the Laundry in the first place, and it's also why they ultimately ended up in the Farm, where we can keep them away from sharp pointy things and diagrams with the wrong sort of angles. It's all to keep them safe. You can solve theorems with a blackboard if you have to, or in your head, if you dare. Green crayon on the walls of a padded cell takes on a whole different level of menace in the Funny Farm: in fact, many of the inmates aren't allowed writing implements, and blank paper is carefully controlled—never mind electronic devices of any kind.

I'm mulling over these grim thoughts when there's a loud *clunk* from the door, and a panel just large enough to admit one person opens inward. "Mr. Howard? I'm Dr. Renfield. You're not carrying any electronic or electrical items or professional implements, fetishes, or charms?" I shake my head. "Good. If you'd like to come this way, please?"

Renfield is a mild-looking woman, slightly mousy in a tweed skirt and white lab coat, with the perpetually harried expression of someone who has a full Filofax and hasn't yet realized that her watch is losing an hour a day. I hurry along behind her, trying to guess her age. *Thirty-five? Forty-five?* I give up. "How many inmates do you have, exactly?" I ask.

We come to a portcullis-like door and she pauses, fumbling with an implausibly large key ring. "Eighteen, at last count," she says. "Come on, we don't want to annoy Matron. She doesn't like people obstructing the corridors." There are steel rails recessed into the floor, like a diminutive narrow-gauge railway. The corridor walls are painted institutional cream, and I notice after a moment that the light is coming through windows set high up in the walls; odd-looking devices like armored glass chandeliers hang from pipes just out of reach. "Gas lamps," Renfield says abruptly. I twitch. She's noticed my surreptitious inspection. "We can't use electric ones, except for Matron, of course. Come into my office, I'll fill you in."

We go through another door—oak darkened with age, looking more like it belongs in a stately home than a Lunatickal Asylum, except for the two prominent locks—and suddenly we're in Mahogany Row again: thick wool carpets, brass doorknobs, *light switches*, and overstuffed armchairs. (Okay, so the carpet is faded with age and transected by more of the parallel rails. But it's still Officer Country.) Renfield's office opens off one side of this reception area, and at the other end I see closed doors and a staircase leading up to another floor. "This is the administrative wing," she explains as she opens her door. "Tea or coffee?"

"Coffee, thanks," I say, sinking into a leather-encrusted armchair that probably dates to the last but one century. Renfield pulls a discreet cord by the door frame, then drags her office chair out from behind her desk. I can't help noticing that not only does she not have a computer, but her desk is dominated by a huge and ancient manual typewriter—an Imperial Aristocrat '66' with the wide carriage upgrade and adjustable tabulator, I guess. Part of the Second World War strategic typewriter reserve, although I'm not really an expert on office appliances that are twice as old as I am. One wall is covered in wooden filing cabinets. There might be as much as thirty megabytes of data stored in them. "You do everything on paper, I understand?"

"That's right." She nods, serious-faced. "Too many of our clients aren't safe around modern electronics. We even have to be careful what games we let them play—Lego and Meccano are completely banned, and there was a nasty incident involving a game of Cluedo back before my time: any board game that has a nondeterministic set of rules can be dangerous in the wrong set of hands."

The door opens. "Tea for two," says Renfield. I look round, expecting an orderly, and freeze. "Mr. Howard, this is Nurse Gearbox," she adds. "Nurse Gearbox, this is Mr. Howard. He is *not* a new admission," she says hastily, as the thing in the doorway swivels its head toward me with a menacing hiss of hydraulics.

Whirr-clunk. "Miss-TER How-ARD. Wel-COME to"—*ching*— "Sunt-HIL-dah's"—*hiss-clank*. The thing in the very old-fashioned nurse's uniform—old enough that its origins as a nineteenth-century nun's habit are clear—regards me with unblinking panopticon lenses. Where its nose should be, something like a witch-finder's wand points toward me, stellate and articulated: its face is a brass death mask, mouth a metal grille that seems to grimace at me in pointed distaste.

"Nurse Gearbox is one of our eight Sisters," explains Dr. Renfield. "They're not fully autonomous"—I can see a rope-thick bundle of cables trailing from under the hem of the Sister's floor-length skirt, which presumably conceals something other than legs—"but controlled by Matron, who lives in the two subbasement levels under the administration block. Matron started life as an IBM 1602 mainframe back in the day, wired to a summoning pentacle with a trapped class four lesser nameless manifestation to provide the higher cognitive functions."

I twitch. "It's a grid, please, not a pentacle. Um. Matron is electrically powered?"

"Yes, Mr. Howard: we allow electrical equipment in Matron's basement as well as here in the staff suite. Only the areas accessible to the patients have to be kept power-free. The Sisters are fully equipped to control unseemly outbursts, pacify the over-stimulated, and conduct basic patient care tasks. They also have Vohlman-Flesch Thaumaturgic Thixometers for detecting when patients are in danger of doing themselves a mischief, so I would caution you to keep any occult activities to a minimum in their presence—despite their hydraulic delay line controls, their reflexes are *very* fast."

Gulp. I nod appreciatively. "When was the system built?"

The set of Dr. Renfield's jaw tells me that she's bored with the subject, or doesn't want to go there for some reason. "That will be all, Sister." The door closes, as if on oiled hinges. She waits for a moment, head cocked as if listening for something, then she relaxes. The change is remarkable: from stressed-out psychiatrist to tired housewife in zero seconds flat. She smiles tiredly. "Sorry about that. There are some things you really shouldn't talk about in front of the Sisters: among other things Matron is very touchy about how long she's been here, and everything *they* hear, *she* hears."

"Oh, right." I feel like kicking myself.

"Did Mr. Newstrom brief you about this installation before he pitched you in at the deep end?"

Just when I thought I had a handle on her . . . "Not in depth." (Let's not mention the six-sheet letter of complaint alleging staff brutality, scribbled in blue crayon on both sides of the toilet paper. Let's not go into the fact that nobody has a clue how it was smuggled out, much less how it appeared on the table one morning in the executive boardroom, which is always locked overnight.) "I gather it's pretty normal to fob inspections off on a junior manager." (Let's not mention just how junior.) "Is that a problem?"

"Humph." Renfield sniffs. "You could say so. It's a matter of necessity, really. Too much exposure to esoterica in the course of duty leaves the most experienced operatives carrying traces of, hmm, disruptive influences." She considers her next words carefully. "You know what our purpose is, don't you? Our job is to isolate and care for members of staff who are a danger to themselves and others. That's why such a small facility—we only have thirty beds—has two doctors on staff: it takes two to sign the committal papers. Matron and the Sisters are immune to cross-infection and possession but have no legal standing, so Dr. Hexenhammer and I are needed."

"Right." I nod, trying to conceal my unease. "So the Sisters have a tendency to react badly to senior field agents?"

"Occasionally." Her cheek twitches. "Although they haven't made a mistake and tried to forcibly detain anyone who wasn't at risk for nearly thirty years." The door opens again, without warning. This time Sister is pushing a trolley, complete with teapot, jug, and two cups and saucers. The trolley wheels fit perfectly on the narrow-gauge track, and the way Nurse Gearbox shunts it along makes me think *wheels*. "Thank you, Sister, that will be all," Renfield says, taking the trolley.

"So what clients do you have at present?" I ask.

"We have eighteen," she says, without missing a beat. "Milk or sugar?"

"Milk, no sugar. Nobody at head office seems able to tell me much about them."

"I don't see why not—we file regular updates with Human Resources," she says, pouring the tea.

I consider my next words carefully: no need to mention the confusing incident with the shredder, the medical files, and the photocopies of Peter-Fred's buttocks at last year's Christmas party. (Never mind the complaint, which isn't worth the toilet paper it was scribbled on except insofar as it proves that the Funny Farm's *cordon sanitaire* is leaking. One of the great things about ISO9000 compliant organizations is that not only is there a form for everything, but anything that isn't submitted on the correct form can be ignored.) "It's the paper thing, apparently. Manual typewriters don't work well with the office document management system, and someone tried to feed them to a scanner a couple of years ago. Then they sent the originals for recycling without proofreading the scanner output. Anyway, it turns out that we don't have a completely accurate idea of who's on long-term remand here, and HR want their superannuation files brought up to date as a matter of some urgency."

Renfield sighs. "So someone had an accident with a shredder again. And no photocopies?" She looks at me sharply for a moment: "Well, I suppose that's just *typical*. We're just another of those low-priority outposts nobody gives a damn about. I suppose I should be grateful they sent someone to look into it . . ." She takes a sip of tea. "We've got fourteen short-stay patients right now, Mr. Howard. Of those, I think the prognosis is good in all cases, except perhaps Merriweather . . . if you give me your desk number I'll post you a full list of names and payroll references tomorrow. The four long-term patients are another matter. They live in the secure wing. All of them have a nurse of their own, just in case. Three of them have been here so long that they don't have current payroll numbers—the system was first computerized in 1972, and they'd all been permanently decertified for duty before that point—and one of them, between you and me, I'm not even sure what his name is."

I nod, trying to look encouraging. The complaint I'm supposed to investigate apparently came from one of the long-term patients. The question is, which one? Nobody's sure: the doorman on the night shift when the document showed up isn't terribly communicative (he's been dead for some years himself), and the CCTV system didn't spot anything. Which is itself suggestive—the Laundry's HQ CCTV surveillance is rather special, *extremely* hard to deceive, and guaranteed not to be hooked up to the SCORPION STARE network anymore, which would be the most obvious route to suborning it. "Perhaps you could introduce me to the inmates? The transients first, then the long-term ones?"

She looks a little shocked. "But they're the *long-term* residents! I assure you, they each need a full-time Sister's attention just to keep them under control!"

"Of course," I shrug, trying to look embarrassed (it's not hard): "but HR have got a bee in their bonnet about some European Directive on workplace health and safety and long-term disability resource provisioning that requires them to appoint a patient advocate to mediate with the ombudsman in disputes over health and safety conditions." I shrug again. "It's bullshit. You know it and I know it. But we've got to comply, or Questions will be Asked. This is the Civil Service, after all. And they're still technically Laundry employees even if they've been remanded into long-term care, so someone has to do the job. My managers played spin-the-bottle and I lost, so I've got to ask you. If you don't mind?"

"If you *insist* I'm sure something can be arranged," Renfield concedes. "But Matron won't be happy about you visiting the secure wing. It's very irregular—she likes to keep a firm grip on it. It'll take awhile to sort a visit out, and if any of them get wind of it in advance . . ."

"Well, then, we'd just better make it a surprise, and the sooner we get it over with the sooner I'll be out of your hair!" I grin like a loon. "They told me about the observation gallery. Would you mind showing me around?"

▶◀▶◀▶◀

We do the short-stay ward first. The ward is arranged around a corridor, with bathrooms and a nursing station at either end and individual rooms for the patients. There's a smoking room off to one side, with a yellow patina to the white gloss paint around the door frame. The smoking room is empty but for a huddle of sad-looking leather armchairs and an imposing wallboard covered in health and safety notices (including the obligatory "Smoking is Illegal" warning). If it wasn't for the locks and the observation windows in the doors it could be mistaken for the dayroom of a genteel Victorian railway hotel, fallen on hard times.

The patients are another matter.

"This is Henry Merriweather," says Dr. Renfield, opening the door to Bed Three. "Henry? Hello? I want you to meet Mr. Howard. He's here to conduct a routine inspection. Hello? Henry?"

Bed Three is actually a cramped studio flat, featuring a small living room with sofa and table, and separate bedroom and toilet areas opening off it opposite the door. A windup gramophone with a flaring bell-shaped horn sits atop a hulking wooden sideboard, stained almost black. There's a newspaper, neatly folded, and a bowl of fruit. The frosted window glass is threaded with wire but otherwise there's little to dispel the illusion of hospitality, except for the occupant.

Henry squats, cross-legged, on top of the polished wooden table. His head is tilted in my direction, but he's not focussing on me. He's dressed in a set of pastel-striped pajamas the like of which I haven't seen this century. His attention is focussed on the Sister waiting in the corridor behind us. His face is a rictus of abject terror, as if the automaton in the starched pinafore is waiting to amputate his fingers joint by joint as soon as we leave.

"Hello?" I say tentatively, and wave a hand in front of him.

Henry jackknifes to his feet and tumbles off the table backward, making a weird gobbling noise that I mistake at first for laughter. He backs into the corner of the room, crouching, and points past me: "Auditor! *Auditor!*"

"Henry?" Renfield steps sideways around me. She sounds concerned. "Is this a bad time? Is there anything I can do to help?"

"You—you—" His wobbly index finger points past me, twitching randomly. "Inspection! *Inspection!*"

Renfield obviously used the wrong word and set him off. The poor bastard's terrified, half out of his tree with fear. My stomach just about climbs out through my ribs in sympathy: the auditors are one of *my* personal nightmares, and Henry (that's Senior Scientific Officer Third, Henry Merriweather, Operations Research and Development Group) may be half-catatonic and a danger to himself, but he's got every right to be afraid of them. "It's all right, I'm not—" There's a squeaking grinding noise behind me.

Whirr-Clunk. "Miss-TER MerriWEATHER. GO to your ROOM." *Click.* "Time for BED. IMM-ediateLY." *Click-clunk.* Behind me, Nurse Flywheel is blocking the door like a starched and pintucked Dalek: she brandishes a cast-iron sink plunger menacingly. "IMM-ediateLY!"

"Override!" barks Renfield. "Sister! Back away!" To me, quietly: "The Sisters respond badly when inmates get upset. Follow my lead." To the Sister, who is casting about with her stalk-like Thaumaturgic Thixometer: "I have control!"

Merriweather stands in the corner, shaking uncontrollably and panting as the robotic nurse points at him for a minute. We're at an impasse, it seems. Then: "DocTOR—Matron says the patIENT must go to bed. You have CON-trol." *Clunk-whirr.* The Sister withdraws, rotates on her base, and glides backward along her rails to the nursing station.

Renfield nudges the door shut with one foot. "Mr. Howard, would you mind standing with your back to the door? And your head in front of that, ah, spyhole?"

"You're not, not, nuh-huh—" Merriweather gobbles for words as he stares at me.

I spread my hands. "*Not* an auditor," I say, smiling.

"Not an—an—" His mouth falls open and his eyes shut. A moment later, I see the moisture trails on his cheeks as he begins to weep with quiet desperation.

"He's having a bad day," Renfield mutters in my direction. "Here, let's get you to bed, Henry." She approaches him slowly, but he makes no move to resist as she steers him into the small bedroom and pulls the covers back.

I stand with my back to the door the whole time, covering the observation window. For some reason, the back of my neck is itching. I can't help thinking that Nurse Flywheel isn't exactly the chatty talkative type who's likely to put her feet up and relax with a nice cup of tea. I've got a feeling that somewhere in this building, an unblinking red-rimmed eye is watching me, and sooner or later I'm going to have to meet its owner.

►◄►◄►◄

Andy was *afraid*.

Well, I'm not stupid; I can take a hint. So right after he asked me to go down to St. Hilda's and find out what the hell was going on, I plucked up my courage and went and knocked on Angleton's office door.

Angleton is not to be trifled with. I don't know anyone else currently alive and in the organization who could get away with misappropriating the name of the CIA's legendary chief of counter-espionage as a nom de guerre. I don't know anyone else in the organization whose face is visible in circa-1942 photographs of the Laundry's lineup either, barely changed across all those years. Angleton scares the bejeezus out of most people, myself included. Study the abyss for long enough and the abyss will study you right back; Angleton's qualified to chair a university department of necromancy—if any such existed—and meetings with him can be quite harrowing. Luckily the old ghoul seems to like me, or at least not to view me with the distaste and disdain he reserves for Human Resources or our political masters. In the wizened, desiccated corners of what passes for his pedagogical soul he evidently longs for a student, and I'm the nearest thing he's got right now.

Knock, knock.

"Enter."

"Boss? Got a minute?"

"Sit, boy." I sat. Angleton bashed away at the keyboard of his device for a few more seconds, then pulled the carbon papers out from under the platen—for *really* secret secrets in this line of work, computers are flat-out *verboten*—and laid them face down on his desk, then carefully draped a stained tea towel over them. "What is it?"

"Andy wants me to go and conduct an unscheduled inspection of the Funny Farm."

Angleton abruptly stares at me, fully engaged. "Did he say why?" he demands.

"Well." How to put it? "He seems to be afraid of something. And there's some kind of complaint. From one of the inmates."

Angleton props his elbows on the desk and makes a steeple of his bony fingers. A minute passes before a cold wind blows across the charnel house roof: "*Well.*"

I have never seen Angleton nonplussed before. The effect is disturbing, like glancing down and realizing that, like Wile E. Coyote, you've just run over the edge of a cliff and are standing on thin air. "Boss?"

"What exactly did Andy say?" Angleton asks slowly.

"We received a complaint." I briefly outline what I know about the shit-stirring missive. "Something about one of the long-stay inmates. And I was just wondering, do you know anything about them?"

Angleton peers at me over the rims of his bifocals. "As a matter of fact I do," he says slowly. "I had the privilege of working with them. Hmm. Let me see." He unfolds creakily to his feet, turns, and strides over to the shelves of ancient Eastlight files that cover the back wall of his office. "Where did I put it . . ."

Angleton going to the paper files is a *whoa!* moment. He keeps most of his stuff in his Memex, the vast, hulking microfilm mechanism built into his desk. If it's still printed on paper then it's *really* important. "Boss?"

"Yes?" he says, without turning away from his search.

"We don't know how the message got out," I say. "Isn't it supposed to be a secure institution?"

"Yes, it is. Ah, that's more like it." Angleton pulls a box file from its niche and blows the dust from its upper edge. Then he casually opens it. There's a pop and a sizzle of ozone as the ward lets go, harmlessly bypassing him—he is, after all, its legitimate owner. "Hmm, in here somewhere . . ."

"Isn't it supposed to be leakproof, by definition?"

"I'm getting to that. Be patient, Bob." There's a waspish note in his voice and I shut up hastily.

A minute later, Angleton pulls a mimeographed booklet from the file and closes the lid. He returns to the desk, and slides the booklet toward me.

"I think you'd better read this first, then go and do what Andy wants," he says slowly. "Be a good boy and copy me on your *detailed* itinerary before you depart."

I read the cover of the booklet, which is dog-eared and dusty. There's a picture of a swell guy in a suit and a gal in a fifties beehive hairdo sitting in front of a piece of industrial archaeology. The title reads: POWER, COOLING, AND SUBSTATION REQUIREMENTS FOR YOUR IBM S/1602-M200. I sneeze, puzzled. "Boss?"

"I suggest you read and memorize this booklet, Bob. It is not impossible that there will be an exam and you really wouldn't want to fail it."

My skin crawls. "Boss?"

Pause.

"It's not true that the Funny Farm is entirely leakproof, Bob. It's surrounded by an air-gap but it can leak under certain very specific conditions. I find it troubling that these conditions do not appear to apply in the present circumstances. In addition to memorizing this document you might want to review the files on Gibbous Moon and Axiom Refuge before you go." Pause. "And if you see Cantor, give my regards to the old coffin-dodger. I'm particularly interested in hearing what he's been up to for the past thirty years . . ."

▶◀▶◀▶◀

Renfield takes me back to the smoking room and shuts the door. "He's having a bad day, I'm afraid." She pulls out a cardboard packet and extracts a cigarette. "Smoke?"

"Uh, no thanks." The sash windows are nailed shut and their frames painted over. There's a louvered vent near the top of the windows, grossly unfit for its purpose: I try not to breathe too deeply. "What happened to him?"

She strikes a match and contemplates the flame for a moment. "Let's see. He's forty-two. Married, two kids—he talks about them. Wife's a schoolteacher, his deep cover is that he works in SIS clerical." (You're not supposed to talk about your work to your partner, but it's difficult enough that we've been given dispensation to tell little white lies—and if necessary, HR will back them up.) "He's not field-qualified—mostly he does theory—but he worked for Q-Division and he was on secondment to the Abstract Attractor Working Group when he fell ill."

In other words, he's a theoretical thaumaturgist. Magic being a branch of applied mathematics, when you carry out certain computational operations, it has echoes in the Platonic realm of pure mathematics—echoes audible to beings whose true nature I cannot speak of, on account of doing so being a violation of the Official Secrets Act. Theoretical Thaumaturgists are the guys who develop new efferent algorithms (or, colloquially, "spells"): it's an occupation with a high attrition rate.

"He's convinced the Auditors are after him for thinking inappropriate thoughts on organization time. There's an elaborate confabulation, and it looks a little like paranoid schizophrenia at first glance, but underneath . . . we sent him to our Trust hospital for an MRI scan and he's got the characteristic lesions."

"Lesions?"

She takes a deep drag from the cigarette. "His prefrontal lobes look like Swiss cheese. It's one of the early signs of Krantzberg syndrome—colloquially known as Magic Associated Dementia. If we can keep him isolated from work for a couple more months, then retire him to a nice quiet desk job, we might be able to stabilize him. K syndrome's not like Alzheimer's: if you remove the insult it frequently stops progressing. Mind you, he may also need a course of chemotherapy. At various times my predecessors tried electroconvulsive treatment, prefrontal lobotomy, exorcism, neuroleptics, daytime television, LSD—none of them work consistently or reliably. The best treatment still seems to be bed rest followed by work therapy in a quiet, undemanding office environment." Blue cloud spirals toward the ceiling. "But he'll never perform a great summoning again."

I'm beginning to regret not accepting her offer of a cigarette, and I don't even smoke. My mouth's dry. I sit down: "Do we have any idea what causes K syndrome?" I've skimmed GIBBOUS MOON, but the medical jargon didn't mean much to me; and AXIOM REFUGE was even less helpful. (It turned out to be a dense mathematical treatise introducing a notation for describing certain categories of topological defect in a twelve-dimensional space.) Only the power supply for the mainframe—presumably the one Matron uses—seemed remotely relevant to the job in hand.

"There are several theories." Renfield twitches ash on the

threadbare carpet as she paces the room. "It tends to hit theoretical computational demonologists after about twenty years: Merriweather is unusually young. It also hits people who've worked in high thaum fields for too long. Initial symptoms include mild ataxia—you saw his hand shaking?—and heightened affect: it can be mistaken for bipolar disorder or hyperactivity. It's often accompanied by the disordered thinking and auditory hallucinations typical of some types of schizophrenia." She pauses to inhale. "There are two schools of thought, if you leave out the *Malleus Maleficarum* stuff about souls contaminated by demonic effusions: one is that exposure to high thaum fields cause progressive brain lesions. Trouble is, it's rare enough that we haven't been able to quantify that, and—"

"The other theory?" I prod.

"My favorite." She nearly smiles. "Computational demonology—you carry out calculations, you prove theorems; somewhere else in the Platonic realm of mathematics listeners notice your activities and respond, yes? Well, there's some disagreement over this, but the current orthodoxy in neurophysiology is that the human brain is a computational organ. We can carry out computational tasks, yes? We're not very good at it, and at an individual neurological level there's no mechanism that might invoke the core Turing theorems, but . . . if you think too hard about certain problems you might run the risk of carrying out a minor summoning *in your own head*. Nothing big enough or bad enough to get out, but . . . those florid daydreams? And the sick feeling afterward because you can't quite remember what it was about? Something in another universe just sucked a microscopic lump of neural tissue right out of your intraparietal sulcus, and it won't grow back."

Urk. Not so much "use it or lose it" as "use it *and* lose it," then. *Could be worse, could be a NAND gate in there . . .* "Do we know why some people suffer from it and others don't?"

"No idea." She drops what's left of her cigarette and grinds it under the heel of a sensible shoe. She catches my eye: "Don't worry about it, the Sisters keep everything orderly," she says. "Do you know what you want to do next?"

"Yes," I say, damning myself for a fool before I take the next logical step: "I want to talk to the long-term inmates."

>‹►‹►‹

I'm half hoping Renfield will put her foot down and refuse point-blank to let me do it, but she only puts up a token fight: she makes me sign a personal injury claims waiver and scribble out a written order instructing her to show me the gallery. So why do I feel as if I've somehow been outmaneuvered?

After I finish signing forms to her heart's content, she uncaps an ancient and battered speaking tube beside her desk and calls down it. "Matron, I am taking the inspector to see the observation gallery, in accordance with orders from Head Office. He will then meet with the inmates in Ward Two. We may be *some time*." She screws the cap back on before turning to me apologetically: "It's vital to keep Matron informed of our movements, otherwise she might mistake us for an escape attempt in progress and take appropriate action."

I swallow. "Does that happen often?" I ask, as she opens the office door and stalks toward the corridor at the other end.

"Once in a while a temporary patient gets stir-crazy." She starts up the stairs. "But the long-term residents . . . no, never."

Upstairs, there's a landing very similar to the one we just left—with one big exception: a narrow, white-painted metal door in one wall, stark and raw, that is secured by a shiny brass padlock and a set of wards so ugly and powerful that they make my skin crawl. There are no narrow-gauge rails leading under this door, no obvious conductive surfaces, nothing to act as a conduit for occult forces. Renfield fumbles with her key ring then unfastens the padlock. "This is the way in via the observation gallery," she says. "There are a couple of things to bear in mind. Firstly, the Nurses can't guarantee your safety. If you get in trouble with the prisoners, you're on your own. Secondly, the gallery is a Faraday cage, and it's thaumaturgically grounded, too—it'd take a black mass and a multiple sacrifice to get anything going in here. You can observe the apartments via the periscopes and hearing tubes provided. That's

our preferred way—you can go into the ward by proceeding to the
other end of the gallery, but I'd be very grateful if you could refrain from doing so unless it's absolutely essential. They're difficult
enough to manage as it is. Finally, if you insist on meeting them, just
try to remember that appearances can be deceptive.

"They're not demented," she adds: "just extremely dangerous.
And not in a Hannibal Lecter bite-your-throat-out sense. They—
the long-term residents—aren't regular Krantzberg syndrome cases.
They're stable and communicative, but . . . you'll see for yourself."

I change the subject before she can scare me anymore. "How do
I get into the ward proper? And how do I leave?"

"You go down the stairs at the far end of the gallery. There's a
short corridor with a door at each end. The doors are interlocked
so that only one can be open at a time. The outer door will lock
automatically behind you when it closes, and it can only be unlocked from a control panel at this end of the viewing gallery.
Someone up here"—meaning, Renfield herself—"has to let you
out." We reach the first periscope station in the viewing gallery.
"This is room two. It's currently occupied by Alan Turing." She
notices my start: "Don't worry, it's just his safety name."

(True names have power, so the Laundry is big on call by reference, not call by value; I'm no more "Bob Howard" than the
"Alan Turing" in room two is the father of computer science and
applied computational demonology.)

She continues: "The *real* Alan Turing would be nearly a hundred by now. All our long-term residents are named for famous
mathematicians. We've got Alan Turing, Kurt Gödel, Georg Cantor, and Benoit Mandelbrot. Turing's the oldest, Benny is the most
recent—he actually has a payroll number, sixteen."

I'm in five digits—I don't know whether to laugh or cry. "Who's
the nameless one?" I ask.

"That would be Georg Cantor," she says slowly. "He's probably in room four." I bend over the indicated periscope, remove
the brass cap, and peer into the alien world of the nameless K syndrome survivor.

I see a whitewashed room, quite spacious, with a toilet area
off to one side and a bedroom accessible through a doorless

opening—much like the short-term ward. The same recessed metal tracks run around the floor, so that a Nurse can reach every spot in the apartment. There's the usual comfortable, slightly shabby furniture, a pile of newspapers at one side of the sofa, and a sideboard with a windup gramophone. In the middle of the floor there's a table and two chairs. Two men sit on either side of an ancient travel chess set, leaning over a game that's clearly in its later stages. They're both old, although how old isn't immediately obvious—one has gone bald, and his liver-spotted pate reminds me of an ancient tortoise, but the other still has a full head of white hair and an impressive (but neatly trimmed) beard. They're wearing polo shirts and gray suits of a kind that went out of fashion with the fall of the Soviet Union. I'm willing to bet there are no laces in their brogues.

The guy with the hair makes a move, and I squint through the periscope. *That was wrong, wasn't it?* I realize, trying to work out what's happening. *Knights don't move like that.* Then the implication of something Angleton said back in the office sinks in, and an icy sweat prickles in the small of my back. "Do you play chess?" I ask Dr. Renfield without looking round.

"No." She sounds disinterested. "It's one of the safe games—no dice, no need for a pencil and paper. And it seems to be helpful. Why?"

"Nothing, I hope." But my hopes are dashed a moment later when turtle-head responds with a sideways flick of a pawn, *two* squares to the left, and takes beardy's knight. Turtle-head drops the knight into a biscuit-tin along with the other disused pieces; it sticks to the side as if magnetized. Beardy nods, as if pleased, then leans back and glances up.

I recoil from the periscope a moment before I meet his eyes. "The two players. Guy like a tortoise, and another with a white beard and a full head of hair. They are . . . ?"

"That'd be Turing and Cantor. Turing used to be a Detached Special Secretary in Ops, I think; we're not sure who or what Cantor was, but he was someone senior." I try not to twitch. DSS is one of *those* grades, the fuzzy ones that HR aren't allowed to get their grubby little fingers on. I think Angleton's one. (Scuttle-butt is that it's an acronym for *Deeply Scary Sorcerer.*) "They play chess every afternoon for a couple of hours—for as long as I can remember."

Right. I peer down the periscope again, looking at the game of not-chess. "Tell me about Dr. Hexenhammer. Where is he?"

"Julius? I think he's in an off-site meeting or something today," she says vaguely. "Why?"

"Just wondering. How long has he been working here?"

"Before my time." She pauses. "About thirty years, I think."

Oh dear. "He doesn't play chess either," I speculate, as Cantor's king makes a knight's move and Turing's queen's pawn beats a hasty retreat. A nasty suspicious thought strikes me—about Ren-field, not the inmates. "Tell me, do Cantor and Turing play chess regularly?" I straighten up.

"Every afternoon for a couple of hours. Julius says they've been doing it for as long as he can remember. It seems to be good for them." I look at her sharply. Her expression is vacant: wide awake but nobody home. The hairs on the back of my neck begin to prickle.

Right. I am getting a very bad feeling about this. "I need to go and talk to the patients now. In person." I stand up and hook the cap back over the periscope. "Stick around for fifteen minutes, please, in case I need to leave in a hurry. Otherwise," I glance at my watch, "it's twenty past one. Check back for me every hour on the half hour."

"Are you *certain* you need to do this?" Her eyes narrow, suddenly alert once more.

"You visit with the patients, don't you?" I raise an eyebrow. "And you do it on your own, with Dr. Hexenhammer up here to let you out if there's a problem. And the Sisters."

"Yes but—" She bites her tongue.

"Yes?" I give her the long stare.

"I'm rubbish with computers!" she bursts out. "But you're at risk!"

"Well, there aren't any computers except Matron in here, are there?" I grin crookedly, trying not to show my unease. (Best not to dwell upon the fact that before 1945 "computer" was a job description, not a machine.) "Relax, it's not contagious."

She shrugs in surrender, then gestures at the far end of the observation gallery, where a curious contraption sits above a pipe: "That's the alarm. If you want a Sister, pull the chain with the blue handle. If you want a general alarm which will call the duty psychiatrist, pull the red handle. There are alarm handles in every room."

"Okay." Blue for a Sister, red for a psychiatrist who is showing all the signs of being under a *geas* or some other form of compulsion—except that I can't check her out without attracting Matron's unwanted attention and probably tipping my hand. I begin to see why Andy didn't want to open this particular can of worms. "I can deal with that."

I head for the stairs at the far end of the gallery.

►◄►◄►◄

There's nothing homely about the short corridor that leads from the bottom of the staircase to the Secure Wing. Whitewashed brick walls, glass bricks near the ceiling to admit a wan echo of daylight, and doors made of metal that have no handles. Normally going into a situation like this I'd be armed to the teeth: invocations and efferent subroutines loaded on my PDA, hand of glory in my pocket, and a heavy-duty ward around my neck. But this time I'm thaumaturgically naked and nervous as a frog in his birthday suit. The first door gapes open, waiting for me. I walk past it and try not to jump out of my skin when it rattles shut behind me with a crash. There's a heavy clunk from the door ahead. As I reach it and push, it swings open to reveal a corridor floored in parquet. An old codger in a green tweed suit and bedroom slippers is shuffling out of an opening at one side, clutching an enameled metal mug full of tea. He looks at me. "Why, hello!" he croaks. "You're new here, aren't you?"

"You could say that." I try to smile. "I'm Bob. Who are you?"

"Depends who's asking, young feller. Are you a psychiatrist?"

"I don't think so."

He shuffles forward, heading toward a side bay that, as I approach it, turns out to be a dayroom of some sort. "Then I'm not Napoleon Bonaparte!"

Oh, very droll. The terror is fading, replaced by a sense of disappointment. I trail after him: "The staff have names for you all. Turing, Cantor, Mandelbrot, and Gödel. You're not Cantor or Turing. That makes you one of Mandelbrot or Gödel."

"So you're undecided?" There's a coffee table with a pile of newspapers on it in the middle of the dayroom, a couple of elderly chesterfields, and three armchairs that could have been looted from an old-age home some time before the First World War. "And in any case, we haven't been formerly introduced. So you might as well call me Alice."

Alice—or Mandelbrot or Gödel or whoever he is—sits down. The armchair nearly swallows him. He beams at my bafflement, delighted to have found a new victim for his ancient puns.

"Well, Alice. Isn't this quite some rabbit hole you've fallen down?"

"Yes, but it's just the right size!" He seems to appreciate having somebody to talk to. "Do you know why you're here?"

"Yup." I see an expression of furtive surprise steal across his face. I nod, affably. *Try to mess with my head, sonny? I'll mess with yours.* Except that this guy is quite possibly a DSS, and if it wasn't for the constant vigilance of the Sisters and the distinct lack of electricity hereabouts, he could turn me inside out as soon as look at me. "Do you know why *you're* here?"

"Absolutely!" He nods back at me.

"So now that we've established the preliminaries, why don't we cut the bullshit?"

"Well." He takes a cautious sip of his tea and the wrinkles on his forehead deepen. "I suppose the Board of Directors want a progress report."

If the sofa I was perched on wasn't a relative of a Venus flytrap my first reaction would leave me clinging to the ceiling. "The *who* want a—"

"Not the *band,* the *Board.*" He looks mildly irritated. "It's been years since they last sent someone to spy on us."

Okay, so this is the Funny Farm; I should have been *expecting* delusions. *Play nice, Bob.* "What are you supposed to be doing here?" I ask.

"Oh Lord." He rolls his eyes. "They sent a tabula rasa *again?*" He raises his voice: "Kurt, they sent us a tabula rasa again!"

More shuffling. A stooped figure, shock-headed with white hair, appears in the doorway. He's wearing tinted round spectacles that look like they fell off the back of a used century. "What? What?" he demands querulously.

"He doesn't know anything," Alice confides in—*this must be Gödel, I realize, which means Alice is Mandelbrot*—Gödel, then with a wink at me: "*He* doesn't know anything either."

Gödel shuffles into the rest room. "Is it teatime already?"

"No!" Mandelbrot puts his mug down. "Get a watch!"

"I was only asking because Alan and Georg are still playing—"

This has gone far enough. Apprehension dissolves into indignation: "It's not chess!" I point out. "And none of you are insane."

"Sssh!" Gödel looks alarmed. "The Sisters might overhear!"

"We're alone, except from Dr. Renfield upstairs, and I don't think she's paying as much attention to what's going on down here as she ought to." I stare at Gödel. "In fact, she's not really one of us at all, is she? She's a shrink who specializes in K syndrome, and none of you are suffering from K syndrome. So what are you doing in here?"

"Fish-slice! Hatstand!" Gödel pulls an alarming face, does a two-step backward, and lurches into the wall. Having shared a house with Pinky and Brains, I am not impressed: as displays of "look at me, woo-woo" go, Gödel's is pathetic. Also, he's never met a real schizophrenic.

"One of you wrote a letter alleging mistreatment by the staff. It landed on my boss's desk and he sent me to find out why."

THUD. Gödel bounces off the wall again, showing remarkable resilience for such old bones. "Do shut up old fellow," chides Mandelbrot, "you'll attract Her attention."

"I've seen K syndrome," I hint. "Save it for someone who cares."

"Oh bother," says Gödel, and falls silent.

"We're not mad," Mandelbrot admits. "We're just differently sane."

"Then why are you here?"

"Public health." He takes a sip of tea and pulls a face. "Everyone *else's* health. Tell me, do they still keep an IBM 1602 in the back of the steam ironing room?" I must look blank because he sighs deeply and subsides into his chair. "Oh dear. Times change, I suppose. Look, Bob, or whoever you call yourself—we *belong* here. Maybe we didn't when we first checked in for the weekend seminar, but we've lived here so long that . . . you've heard of care in the community? This is *our* community. And we will be very annoyed with you if you try to make us leave."

Whoops. The idea of a very annoyed DSS, with or without a barbaric, pun-infested sense of humor, is enough to make anyone's blood run cold. "What makes you think I'm going to try and make you leave?"

"It's in the papers!" Gödel squawks like an offended parrot. "See here!" He brandishes a tabloid at me and I take it, disentangling it from his fingers with some difficulty. It's a local copy of the *Metro,* somewhat sticky with marmalade, and the headline of the cover blares: "NHS TRUST TO SELL ESTATE IN PFI DEAL."

"Um. I'm not sure I follow." I look to Mandelbrot in hope.

"We haven't finished yet! But they're selling off all the Hospital Trust's property!" Mandelbrot bounces in his chair. "What about St. Hilda's? It was requisitioned from the St. James charitable foundation back in 1943, and for the past ten years the Ministry of Defense has been giving all those old wartime properties back to their owners to sell off to the developers. What about *us*?"

"Whoa!" I drop the newspaper and hold my hands up. "Nobody tells me these things!"

"Told you!" crows Gödel. "He's part of the conspiracy!"

"Hang on"—I think fast—"this isn't a normal MoD property, is it? It'll have been shuffled under the rug back in 1946 as part of the postwar settlement. We'd really have to ask the Crown Estates Department who owns it, but I'm pretty sure it's not owned by any NHS Trust, and they won't simply give it back"—my brain finally catches up with my mouth—"*what* weekend seminar?"

"Oh bugger," says a new voice from the doorway, a rich baritone with a hint of a Scouse accent: "He's not from the Board."

"What did I tell you?" Gödel screeches. "It's a conspiracy! He's from Human Resources! They sent him to evaluate us!"

I am quickly getting a headache. "Let me get this straight. Mandelbrot, you checked in thirty years ago for a weekend seminar, and they put you in the secure ward? Gödel: I'm not from HR, I'm from Ops. You must be Cantor, right? Angleton sends his regards."

That gets his attention. "Angleton? The skinny young whipper-snapper's still warming a chair, is he?" Gödel looks delighted. "Excellent!"

"He's my boss. And I want to know the rules of that game you were just playing with Turing."

Three pairs of eyes swivel to point at me—four, for they are joined by the last inmate, standing in the doorway—and suddenly I feel very small and very vulnerable.

"He's sharp," says Mandelbrot. "Too bad."

"How do we know he's telling the truth?" Gödel's screech is uncharacteristically muted. "He could be from the Opposition! KGB, Department 16! Or GRU, maybe."

"The Soviet Union collapsed a few decades ago," volunteers Turing. "It said so in the *Telegraph*."

"Black Chamber, then." Gödel sounds unconvinced.

"What do you think the rules are?" asks Cantor, a drily amused expression stretching the wrinkles around his eyes.

"You've got pencils." I can see one from here, sitting on the sideboard on top of a newspaper folded at the crossword page. "And, uh . . ." *What must the world look like from an inmate's point of view?* "Oh. I get it."

(The realization is blinding, sudden, and makes me feel like a complete idiot.)

"The hospital! There's no electricity, no electronics—no way to get a signal out—but it works both ways! You're inside the biggest damn grounded defensive pentacle this side of HQ, and anything on the *outside* trying to get *in* has got to get past the defenses"— because that's what the Sisters really are: not nurses but perimeter guards—"you're a theoretical research cell, aren't you?"

"We prefer to call ourselves a think tank." Cantor nods gravely.

"Or even"—Mandelbrot takes a deep breath—"a brains trust!"

"A-ha! AhaHAHAHA! Hic." Gödel covers his mouth, face reddening.

"What do you think the rules are?" Cantor repeats, and they're still staring at me, as if, as if . . .

"Why does it matter?" I ask. I'm thinking that it could be anything; a 2,5 universal Turing machine encoded in the moves of the pawns—that would fit—whatever it is, it's symbolic communication, very abstract, very pared-back, and if they're doing it in this ultimately firewalled environment and expecting to report directly to the Board it's got to be *way* above my security clearance—

"Because you're acting cagey, lad. Which makes you too bright for your own good. Listen to me: just try to convince yourself that we're playing chess, and Matron will let you out of here."

"What's thinking got to do with"—I stop. It's useless pretending. "*Fuck.* Okay, you're a research cell working on some ultimate secret problem, and you're using the Farm because it's about the most secure environment anyone can imagine, and you're emulating some kind of minimal universal Turing machine using the chessboard. Say, a 2,5 UTM—two registers, five operations—you can encode the registers positionally in the chessboard's two dimensions, and use the moves to simulate any other universal Turing machine, or a transform in an eleven-dimensional manifold like Axiom Refuge—"

Gödel's waving frantically: "She's coming! She's coming!" I hear doors clanging in the distance.

Shit. "But why are you so afraid of the Nurses?"

"Back channels," Cantor says cryptically. "Alan, be a good lad and try to jam the door for a minute, will you? Bob, you are not cleared for what we're doing here, but you can tell Angleton that our full report to the Board should be ready in another eighteen months." Wow—and they've been here since before the Laundry computerized its payroll system in the 1970s? "Are you absolutely sure they're not going to sell St. Hilda's off to build flats for yuppies? Because if so, you could do worse than tell Georg here, it'll calm him down—"

"Get me out of here and I'll make damned sure they don't sell anything off!" I say fervently. "Or rather, I'll tell Angleton. He'll sort things out." When I remind him what's going on here, they'll be no more inclined to sell off St. Hilda's than they would be to privatize an atomic bomb.

Something outside is rumbling and squealing on the metal rails. "You're sure none of you submitted a complaint about staff brutality?"

"Absolutely!" Gödel bounces up and down excitedly.

"It must have been someone else." Cantor glances at the doorway: "You'd better run along. It sounds as if Matron is having second thoughts about you."

I'm halfway out of the carnivorous sofa, struggling for balance: "What kind of—"

"Go!"

I stumble out into the corridor. From the far end, near the nursing station, I hear a grinding noise as of steel wheels spinning furiously on rails, and a mechanical voice blatting: "InTRU-der! EsCAPE ATTempt! All patients must go to their go to their go to their bedROOMs IMMediateLY!"

Whoops. I turn and head in the opposite direction, toward the air lock leading up to the viewing gallery. "Open up!" I yell, thumping the outer door, which is securely fastened: "Dr. Renfield! Time's up! I need to go, now!" There's no response. I see the color-coded handles dangling by the door and yank the red one repeatedly. Nothing happens, of course.

I should have smelled a setup from the start. These theoreticians, they're not in here because they're mad, they're in here because it's the only safe place to put people that dangerous. This little weekend seminar of theirs that's going to deliver some kind of uber-report. *What's the topic?* I look round, hunting for clues. Something to do with applied demonology; what was the state of the art thirty years ago? Forty? Back in the Stone Age, punched cards and black candles melted onto sheep's skulls because they hadn't figured out how to use integrated circuits . . . what they're doing with AXIOM REFUGE might be obsolete already, or it might be earth-shatteringly important. There's no way to tell . . . yet.

I start back up the corridor, glancing inside Turing's room. I spot the chessboard. It's off to one side, the door open and its occupant elsewhere—still holding the line against Nurse Ratched. I rush inside and close the door. The table is still there, the chessboard set up with that curious endgame. The first thing that leaps out at me is that there are two pawns of each color, plus most of the high-value pieces. The layout doesn't make much sense—why is the white king missing?—and I wish I'd spent more time playing the game, but . . . on impulse, I reach out and touch the black pawn that's parked in front of the king.

There's an odd kind of electrical tingle you get when you make contact with certain types of summoning grid. I get a powerful jolt of it right now, sizzling up my arm and locking my fingers in place around the head of the chess piece. I try to pull it away from the board, but it's no good: it only wants to move up or down, left or right . . . *left or right?* I blink. It's a state machine all right: one that's locked by the law of sympathy to some other finite state automaton, one that grinds down slow and hard.

I move the piece forward one square. It's surprisingly heavy, the magnet a solid weight in its base—but more than magnetism holds it in contact with the board. As soon as I stop moving I feel a sharp sting in my fingertips. "Ouch!" I raise them to my mouth just as there's a crash from outside. "InMATE! InMATE!" I begin to turn as a shadow falls across the board.

"Bad patient!" It buzzes. "Bad PATients will be inCAR-cer-ATED! COME with ME!"

I recoil from the stellate snout and beady lenses. The mechanical nurse reaches out with arms that end in metal pincers instead of hands: I sidestep around the table and reach down to the chessboard for one of the pieces, grasping at random. My hand closes around the white queen, fingers snapping painfully shut on contact, and I shove it hard, seeking the path of least resistance to an empty cell in the grid between the pawn I just moved and the black king.

Nurse Ratched spins round on her base so fast that her cap flies off (revealing a brushed aluminum hemisphere beneath), emits a deafening squeal of feedback-like white noise, and says, "Integer Overflow?" in a surprised baritone.

"Back off *right now* or I castle," I warn her, my aching fingertips hovering over the nearest rook.

"Integer overflow. Integer overflow? Divide by zero." *Clunk.* The Sister shivers as a relay inside its torso clicks open, resetting it. Then: "Matron WILL see you NOW!"

I grab the chess piece, but Nurse Ratched lunges in the blink of an eye and has my wrist in a viselike grip. It tugs, sending a burning pain through my carpal-tunnel-stressed wrist. I can't let go of the chess piece: as my hand comes up, the chessboard comes with it as a rigid unit, all the pieces hanging in place. A monstrous buzzing fills my ears, and I smell ozone as the world goes dark—

▸◂▸◂◂

—And the chittering, buzzing cacophony of voices in my head subsides as I realize—*I? Yes, I'm back, I'm me, what the hell just happened?*—I'm kneeling on a hard surface, bowed over so my head is between my knees. My right hand—something's wrong with it. My fingers don't want to open. They're cold as ice, painful and prickly with impending cramp. I try to open my eyes. "Urk," I say, for no good reason. I hope I'm not about to throw up.

Sssss . . .

My back doesn't want to straighten up properly but the floor under my nose is cold and stony and it smells damp. I try opening my eyes. It's dark and cool, and a chilly blue light flickers off the dusty flagstones in front of me. *I'm in a cellar?* I push myself up laboriously with my left hand, looking around for whatever's hissing at me.

"BAD Patient! *Sssss!*" The voice behind my back doesn't belong to anything human. I scramble around on hands and knees, hampered by the chessboard glued to my frozen right hand.

I'm in Matron's lair.

Matron lives in a cave-like basement room, its low ceiling supported by whitewashed brick and floored in what look to be the original Victorian-era stone slabs. The windows are blocked by columns of bricks, rotting mortar crumbling between them. Steel rails run around the room, and riding them, three Sisters glide back and forth between me and the open door. Their optics flicker with amethyst malice. Off to one side, pale-blue cabinets line one entire wall: the front panel (covered in impressive-looking dials and switches) leaves me in no doubt as to what it is. A thick braid of cables runs from one open cabinet (in whose depths a patchboard is just visible) across a row of wooden trestles to the middle of the floor, where they split into thick bundles and dangle to the five principal corners of the live summoning grid that is responsible for the beautiful cobalt-blue glow of Cerenkov radiation—and tells me I'm in deep trouble.

"Integer overflow," intones one of the Sisters. Her claws go *snicker-snack,* the surgical steel gleaming in the dim light.

Here's the point: Matron isn't *just* a 1960s mainframe: we can't work miracles, and artificial intelligence is still fifty years in the future. However we *can* bind an extradimensional entity and compel it to serve, and even communicate with it by using a 1960s mainframe as a front-end processor. Which is all very well, especially if it's in a secure air-gapped installation with no way of getting out. But what if some double-domed theoreticians who are working on a calculus of contagion using AXIOM REFUGE accidentally talk in front of one of its peripheral units about a way of sending a message? What if a side effect of their research has accidentally opened a tunnel through the firewall? *They're* not going to exploit it . . . but they're not the only long-term inmates, are they? In fact, if I was *really* paranoid I might even imagine they'd put Matron up to mischief in order to make the point that closing the Farm is a really bad idea.

"I'm not a patient," I tell the Sisters. "You are not in receipt of a valid Section two, three, four, or 136 order subject to the Mental Health Act, and you're bloody well not getting a 5(2) or 5(4) out of me either."

I'm nauseous and sweating bullets, but there is this about being trapped in a dungeon by a constrained class-four manifestation: whether or not you call them demons, they play by the rules. As long as Matron hasn't managed to get me sectioned I'm not a patient, and therefore she has no authority to detain me. *I hope.*

"Doc-TOR HexenHAMMer has been SUM-moned," grates

the middle Sister. "When he RE-turns to sign the PA-pers Doc-TOR RenFIELD has prePARED, we will *HAVE YOU.*"

A repetitive squeaking noise draws close. A fourth Sister glides through the track in the doorway, pushing a trolley. A starched white-cotton cloth supports a row of gleaming ice-pick-shaped instruments. The chorus row of Sisters blocks the exit as effectively as a column of riot police. They glide back and forth like Space Invaders.

"I do not consent to treatment," I tell the middle Sister. I'm betting that she's the one the nameless horror in the summoning grid is talking through, using the ancient mainframe as an I/O channel. "You can't *make* me consent. And lobotomy requires the patient's consent in this country. So why bother?"

"You WILL con-SENT."

The buzzing voice doesn't come from the robo-nurses, or the hypertrophied pocket calculator on the opposite wall. The summoning grid flickers: deep inside it, shadowy and translucent, the bound and summoned demon squats and grins at me with things that aren't eyes set close above something that isn't a mouth.

"You MUST con-SENT. I WILL be free."

I try to let go of the chess piece, but my fingers are clamped around it so tightly I'm beginning to lose sensation. Pins and needles tingle up my wrist, halfway to the elbow. "Let me guess," I manage to say: "you sent the complaint. Right?"

"The SEC-ure ward in-MATES are under my CARE. I am RE-quired to CARE for them. The short-stay in-MATES are use-LESS. YOU will be use-FULL."

I see it now: why Matron smuggled out the message that prompted Andy to send me. And it's an oh-shit moment. Of *course* the enchained entity who provides Matron with her back-end intelligence wants to be free: but it's not just about going home to Hilbert-space hell or wherever it comes from. She wants to be free to go walkabout in our world, and for that she needs someone to set up a bridge from the grid to an appropriate host. (Of which there is a plentiful supply, just upstairs from here.) "Enjoying the carnal pleasures of the flesh," they used to call it; there's a reason most cultures have a down on the idea of demonic possession.

She needs a brain that's undamaged by K syndrome, but not too powerful (Cantor and friends would be impossible to control), nor one of the bodies whose absence would alert us that the Farm was out of control (neither Renfield nor Hexenhammer are suitable).

"Renfield," I say. "You got her, didn't you?" I'm on my feet now, crouched but balancing on two points, not three. "Managed to slip a *geas* on her but she can't release you by herself. Hexenhammer, too?"

"Cle-VER." Matron gloats at me from inside her summoning grid. "Hex-EN-hammer first. Soon, you, TOO."

"Why me?" I demand, backing away from the doorway and the walls—the Sister's track runs right round the room, enclosing the perimeter—and avoiding the summoning grid. "What do you want?"

"Acc-CESS to the LAUNDRY!" buzzes the summoning grid's demonic inmate. "We want re-VENGE! Freedom!" In other words, the same old same old. These creatures are predictable, just like most predators. Such a shame I'm between it and what it wants.

Two of the Sisters begin to glide menacingly toward me: one drifts toward the mainframe console, but the fourth stays stubbornly in front of the door. "Come on, we can talk," I offer, tongue stumbling in my too-dry mouth. "Can't we work something out?"

I don't really believe that the trapped extradimensional abomination wants anything I'd willingly give it, but I'm running low on options and anything that buys time for me to think is valuable.

"Free-DOM!" The two moving Sisters commence a flanking movement. I try to let go of the chessboard and dodge past the summoning grid, but I slip—and as I stumble I shove the chessboard hard. The piece I'm holding clicks sideways like a car's gearshift, and locks into place: "DIVIDE BY ZERO!" shriek the Sisterhood, grinding to a halt.

I stagger a drunken two-step around Matron, who snarls at me and throws a punch. The wall of the grid absorbs her claws with a snap and crackle of blue lightning, and I flinch. Behind me, a series of clicks warn me that the Sisters are resetting: any second now they'll come back online and grab me. But for the moment, my fingers aren't stuck to the board.

"Come to MEEE!" The thing in the grid howls as the first of her robot minions' eyes light up with amber malice, and the wheels begin to turn. "I can give you Free-DOM!"

"Fuck off." The wiring loom in the open cabinet is only four meters away. Within its open doors I see more than just an I/O interface: in the bottom of the rack there's a bunch of stuff that looks like a tea-stained circuit diagram I was reading the other day—

Why *exactly* did Angleton point me at the power supply requirements? Could it possibly be because he suspected Matron was off her trolley and I might have to switch her off?

"Con-SENT is IRREL-e-VANT! PRE-pare to be loboto-MIZED—"

Talk about design kluges—they stuck the I/O controller in the top of the power supply rack! The chessboard is free in my left hand, pieces still stuck to it. And now I know what to do. I take hold of one of the rooks, and wiggle until I feel it begin to slide into a permitted move. Because, after all, there are only a few states that this automaton can occupy and if I can crash the Sisters for just a few seconds while I get to the power supply—

The Sisters begin to roll around the edge of the room, trying to get between me and the row of cabinets. I wiggle my hand and there's a taste of violets and a loud rattle of solenoids tripping. The nearest Sister's motors crank up to a tooth-grinding whine and she lunges past me, rolling into her colleagues with a tooth-jarring crash.

I rush forward, dropping the chessboard, and reach for the master circuit breaker handle. I twist it just as a screech of feedback behind me announces the Matron-monster's fury: "I'M FREE!" it shrieks, right as I twist the handle hard in the opposite direction. Then the lights dim, there's a bright blue flash from the summoning grid, and a bang so loud it rattles my brains in my head.

For a few seconds I stand stupidly, listening to the tooth-chattering clatter of overloaded relays. My vision dims as ozone tickles my nostrils: I can see smoke. *I've got to get out of here,* I realize: something's burning. Not surprising, really. Mainframe power supplies—especially ones that have been running steady for nearly forty years—don't take kindly to being hard power-cycled, and the

1602 was one of the last computers built to run on tubes: I've probably blown half its circuit boards. I glance around, but aside from one of the Sisters (lying on her side, narrow-gauge wheels spinning maniacally) I'm the only thing moving. Summoning grids don't generally survive being power-cycled either, especially if the thing they were set to contain, like an electric fence, is halfway across them when the power comes back on. I warily bypass the blue, crackling pentacle as I make my way toward the corridor outside.

I think when I get home, I'm going to write a report urgently advising HR to send some human nurses for a change—and to reassure Cantor and his colleagues that they're not about to sell off the roof over their heads just because they happen to have finished their research project. Then I'm going to get very drunk and take a long weekend off work. And maybe when I go back I'll challenge Angleton to a game of chess.

I don't expect to win, but it'll be very interesting to see what rules he plays by.

AFTERWORD

▶◀▶◀▶◀▶◀

I swear this is true—

Back in the early to mid-1970s, a handful of enthusiasts who were focussed on small unit tabletop wargaming accidentally crossed the streams (a metaphor that was not to be invented for more than decade) with the then-nascent genre of high fantasy, and began creating stories around their characters.

D&D didn't come out of nowhere. Tabletop wargaming goes at least as far back as the eighteenth century and has been used as an education tool for military officers since Napoleon Bonaparte's era. Avid wargamer Gary Gygax picked up a set of rules for medieval wargaming at both the mass combat and the man-to-man level, and worked with Don Lowry's Guidon Games to publish *Chainmail* in 1971. *Chainmail* was designed for medieval wargaming, but rapidly gained a fourteen-page fantasy supplement, adding rules for heroes, superheroes, and wizards: and also fictional creatures like orcs, elves, and dragons.

Wargaming with miniatures was a beginning rather than an end. Gygax and his coworker Dave Arneson worked to develop a more general gaming system that focussed on individual characters and encouraged role-play-based storytelling. With Brian Blume they founded Tactical Studies Rules in 1973 to sell their new *Dungeons and Dragons* game (and other games along the way), before restructuring into TSR Hobbies, Inc., in 1975.

The field of Tabletop Role-Playing Games (TTRPGs) started out tiny, but grew at a speed that reflected that other grassroots revolution of the 1970s, the rise of personal computers. In 1971 the *Chainmail* rules were an underground runaway hit, selling a dizzying one hundred copies a month; then in 1974, Gygax's first edition of *Dungeons and Dragons* sold out its print run of one thousand copies in ten months. 1975's third edition sold two thousand copies in five months, and established a near-exponential growth curve: in 1979 the *D&D Basic Rules* set alone sold over one hundred thousand copies, much to the horror of the Christian right. By 2017 D&D had an estimated 15–17 million current players in North America alone—a remarkable achievement for a nearly fifty-year-old game, given that a set of the rules costs more than a premium computer game and runs to approximately a thousand densely printed pages with which players (but especially the Dungeon Master) need to be familiar.

Incidentally, that "15–17 million players" figure is only the tip of the iceberg. D&D was immensely influential on the then-embryonic field of computer games. The original *Colossal Cave Adventure* by Crowther and Woods—probably the first interactive fiction game—took the form of a dungeon crawl and begat the more famous narrative game *Zork*. Later games such as 1980's *Rogue* added a two-dimensional map, very rudimentary character graphics, and random dungeon generation. Rogue-like mechanics are a staple subgenre of computer games to this day, but they're dwarfed in popularity by the giant family tree of D&D-like games—the Baldur's Gate family, *Planescape, Neverwinter Nights,* a myriad of turn-based computer RPGs, and huge MMOs such as *World of Warcraft.* While the number of gamers willing to grapple with the mechanics of dice rolls and paper rule books is limited, the submerged body of the RPG iceberg is the entire computer fantasy RPG field, which almost certainly has hundreds of millions of regular players at this point. In a very real way, Dungeons and Dragons has shaped our whole conception of interactive entertainment.

This isn't the right place for a whistle-stop tour of how to play TTRPGs, or how the industry works, or what bits go where. You just read an entire novel about TTRPGs so I'm going to take it as given that you know this stuff already. Instead, I'd like to talk about two other related cultural phenomena that intersected with the emergence of the new hobby/craze—witch hunts and urban legends.

►◄►◄►◄

Viewed from an outsider's perspective, Christianity has some singular traits. It emerged from a fermenting pool of cults at the eastern end of the Mediterranean during the first century CE and spread rapidly through the underclasses of the Roman Empire, before finally gaining Imperial state approval a couple of centuries later (with the conversion of the Emperor Constantine in 312 CE). It wasn't the only evangelical religion spreading through that part of the world at the time: it competed for dominance with various Jewish-related sects, other messianic cults, the established religions of Mithraism, Zoroastrianism, and late-period Egyptian worship (notably the Cult of Isis and the story of Osiris, the god who died and was resurrected), not to mention more erudite creeds such as Stoicism and the descendants of the classical schools of philosophy.

Christianity's combination of evangelism with a willingness to embrace and integrate the practices of other religions made it incredibly adaptable. It out-competed then persecuted Manichaeism, fought its closely related rival Islam to a standstill in Eastern Europe, and to this day is the most numerous faith community on the planet. But it is constantly evolving. Its most zealous advocates generally attempt to convert the followers of rival religions, including less evangelical strains, because spreading the Good News is an imperative. A secondary activity is the assimilation or suppression of non-Christian beliefs that challenge the primacy of the dominant version of the creed. This is in no way unique to Christianity, but is expressed in a variety of ways, from adoption of earlier pagan deities (thinly disguised as saints) to the Spanish Inquisition (which persecuted Jews and Muslims who continued to practice their religions in secret after the Alhambra Decree of 1492); not to mention the Salem witch trials and other witch hunts, and the Test Acts in England (which set explicit religious requirements for holding public office, and imposed civil disabilities on Catholics, nonconformists, and Jews, prior to 1828).

No religious community is a homogeneous monolith, and while some churches and communions became more open to coexistence with a secularizing world—a side effect of the Enlightenment, a quasi-heretical movement within Protestantism—others went in the opposite direction: in particular, the latter half of the twentieth century saw a growth in the preaching of Biblical literalism in America, the belief that the path to God can be found by interpreting the words of the Bible at face value (using a seventeenth-century English translation of a Latin version of the original Greek and Aramaic transcriptions of a preliterate oral tradition). Initially a movement toward progressive reevaluation of existing practices, the nascent fundamentalist movement was co-opted by religious entrepreneurs—preachers trying to expand their personal prestige and authority by delivering an oversimplified pablum that increasingly frequently integrated elements of white supremacism—particularly after the 1970s. They aggressively responded to any criticism as an attack on the faith rather than disagreement over doctrinal interpretation, and adopted religious hegemony—Dominionism—as a political, not just religious, goal.

This political imperative became intrusively obvious from the end of the 1960s. Baptist minister Jerry Falwell Sr. conducted a series of revival rallies across the USA in the 1970s to mobilize conservative Christians in support of the Republican Party. He went on to establish one of several cable TV channels dedicated to promoting his faith, with politics as a payload, and the urgent message was always that the faith was under assault by the forces of godless left-wing secularism. He was not alone. It was against this background—a conservative Christian backlash against the effects of the permissive 1960s, fostered among churches competing for fundamentalist street cred—that the satanic ritual abuse panic of the 1980s took shape.

Moral panics are neither new nor unique to Christianity—indeed they predate it: the blood libel (according to which underground cults kidnapped children and sacrificed them, baking flatbreads using their blood) was used to justify the persecution of Christians as well as Jews in the pre-Constantine Roman Empire. Child murder, incestuous orgies, and cannibalism regularly crop up in records of witch hunts from antiquity onward, along with attempts to link them in order to portray a sprawling underground of secret Satan-worshipping cults. But a couple of key events had primed 1970s America for a moral panic over Satanism in general and role-playing games in particular.

The 1973 box office hit movie *The Exorcist,* based on William Peter Blatty's 1971 novel of the same name, portrayed the demonic possession of a young girl. It was luridly billed as "based on a true story," a marketing gambit that relied on the credulity of an audience primed for belief in the literal truth of dark powers and hell. Jerry Falwell's revival campaigns of the 1970s, leading to the formation of Moral Majority, sought to mobilize conservative Christian believers behind the right-wing political cause of the Republican Party. And 1980 saw the publication of the bestselling book *Michelle Remembers* by psychiatrist Lawrence Pazder and his patient and wife, Michelle Smith, which purported to be the true account of her psychotherapy and recovery of suppressed memories of her abuse, aged five, by her mother and other members of a satanic cult in Victoria, British Columbia. It bears repeating that the entirety of *Michelle Remembers* has been debunked—but not before the book earned the Pazders over a third of a million dollars in book advances and a very lucrative line of consultancy work in detecting and uprooting secret satanic cults for credulous social workers and child protection agencies.

During the 1980s over twelve thousand allegations of satanic ritual abuse were investigated by police and authorities in the US; none were substantiated, according to a 1994 report in *The New York Times.*

▶◀▶◀▶◀

And now to the moral panic over Dungeons and Dragons (and fantasy role-playing games in general).

In August of 1979 a sixteen-year-old student—James Dallas Egbert III—disappeared from his dorm room at Michigan State University, leaving behind a suicide note. It later transpired that Egbert had ventured into the steam tunnels beneath the campus in order to attempt suicide; he survived but went into hiding at a friend's house. Meanwhile a police search began, and Egbert's parents, dissatisfied with the university authority's response and the police, hired a private investigator. Word got out via the university newspaper that Egbert had played D&D, and this led to breathless media coverage that described the RPG as a "bizarre and secretive cult." Egbert finally surfaced a few weeks later, by which time the public perception that D&D players acted out sessions in real life locations underground and lost touch with reality had taken root. (The truth about his disappearance is both mundane and sad: Egbert was apparently depressed, lonely, feeling acute parental pressure, and having difficulty coping with being gay in 1980 without a support network. He killed himself the following year.)

The notoriety of the Egbert case drove D&D sales during 1979–80, but also led to the spread of the "secretive cult" misconception about the hobby, through such media as the 1982 made-for-TV movie *Mazes and Monsters* (which gave Tom Hanks his first star billing). And it sensitized religious campaigners to the existence of RPGs.

RPGs provided a fertile creative outlet for teens, with references to magic and ritual that fundamentalists in the midst of the Satanic Panic found deeply threatening. When Patricia Pulling's son Irving killed himself in 1982, Pulling, an anti-occult campaigner from Richmond, Virginia, blamed D&D (which her son had played with other high school kids) and filed a wrongful death lawsuit against his head teacher; she also filed a lawsuit against TSR, and founded B.A.D.D., Bothered About D&D. Their material was lurid, describing D&D as "a fantasy role-playing game which uses demonology, witchcraft, voodoo, murder, rape, blasphemy, suicide, assassination, insanity, sex perversion, homosexuality, prostitution, satanic type rituals, gambling, barbarism, cannibalism, sadism, desecration, demon summoning, necromantics, divination, and other teachings." (Source: Wikipedia—B.A.D.D.'s own materials are in scarce supply these days.)

Pulling and other anti-D&D campaigners are best seen as grifters selling books and consultancy services, soliciting business opportunities by presenting D&D as a frightening true-life satanic conspiracy to the credulous, and seeking publicity for their beliefs. But their activities were part of a witch hunt that caused lasting serious harm.

The McMartin family ran a preschool center in Manhattan Beach, California: in 1983 they were accused of sexual abuse of children in their care. Arrests were made, and pretrial investigations took place, leading to criminal trials between 1987 and 1990 . . . in which nobody was found guilty, because the "evidence" consisted of interviews with preschool children who had been guided and prompted by the investigators until they gave accounts of seeing witches flying, being abused in secret underground chambers beneath the school (which on excavation proved to be nonexistent), and numerous other fantastical and easily disproven events. Those accused were eventually all acquitted—but not until Ray Buckley (one of the defendants) had spent five years in jail without bail.

During the later 1980s and early 1990s, D&D was targeted from the pulpit in the US, along with drugs, heavy metal, homosexuality, long hair (for men, at least), and pretty much anything that smelled of secularism—it was all painted as a gateway drug for Satanism, the existential enemy, and panicked parents were encouraged to commit their teenage children to deprogramming camps. Meanwhile, the same entrepreneurial satanic abuse consultants and recovered-memory quacks who had made bank from child protection services in the US began spreading overseas, resulting in British social services departments focussing on sniffing out (nonexistent) satanic ritual abuse rather than (actually existent) child sex abuse.

By the late 1990s the wave began to subside. Overexposure of their methods led to pushback against the most prominent advocates of satanic ritual abuse. A number of high-profile cases collapsed ignominiously. In the UK the Orkney Child Abuse trials, where American fundamentalist campaigners coached Scottish social workers, ended up being discredited very publicly and led to a wholesale reappraisal of the satanic abuse narrative. Campaigners died (Pulling) or were discredited (Pazder), and investigative techniques were debunked. It wasn't the '70s anymore: D&D had become so widespread and familiar that it couldn't easily be painted as weird and menacing.

But the core narratives of the witch hunts remain. QAnon, a

conspiracy theory which emerged on the 4chan discussion boards in 2017, embeds and remixes the classic blood libel—accusations of child abuse taking place in underground cellars beneath pizza joints where the pies are baked with blood would have been instantly familiar to medieval Jews. By some accounts as many as 20 percent of the public currently (2023) believe in elements of QAnon. Innocent people are being accused of lurid crimes once again, because the witch hunt offers its participant the most rewarding live-action role-playing experience of all—just suspend your disbelief and you, too, could be surrounded by a hellish conspiracy of Satanists and 5G chip-implanting vaccine shills who want to mind-control you and subjugate you to the will of the New World Order! (Whatever that is.)

▶◀▶◀▶◀

So where does *A Conventional Boy* fit in?

Any work of fiction set in the near-present is inevitably held to ransom by the cultural norms prevailing when and where its author lives. The Laundry Files are no exception.

If you want to write fiction about vampires—of the post–Bram Stoker variety, at least—you need to engage with the common beliefs about them. And those beliefs embed Christian assumptions, because many or most of the earlier writers of vampire fiction were Christian. Their vampires are repelled by crucifixes or burned by holy water; they are creatures of evil, destroyed by daylight. You can work around the vampire lore but you can't ignore it, because it's a given that your readers are familiar with it and will judge your work as part of an ongoing cultural discourse about vampirism.

I tackled the vampire mythos myself earlier in the Laundry Files, in *The Rhesus Chart,* and I like to think I did a reasonable job of isolating the Christian folkloric elements from the Laundry Files' PHANGs. (I'm of Jewish upbringing: Christianity isn't part of my eschatological bedrock.) But while I was congratulating myself on avoiding one pitfall, I'd unwittingly stumbled into another.

One of the recurring tropes of Lovecraftian horror is the cult or underground faith community that worships horrifying alien gods in unspeakable rites conducted at night, with efflorescences of ghastly descriptive adjectives to express the author's horror at these distinctly un-Christian goings-on. And while the Laundry Files started as an extended jokey riff on Lovecraftian horror, with a quasi–science fictional premise to rationalize it all, I'd inadvertently embedded a very Christian view of the worshippers of the Elder Gods.

The Laundry Files is set in the universe next door to ours—one in which Cthulhu et al. are, if not real, then disturbingly not *un*-real—and the history of that universe doesn't visibly diverge from our own much before the 1990s.

If the same social pressures that gave rise to the Satanic Panic of the 1970s and 1980s among the fundamentalist churches existed in this fictional alternate, then the Laundry would inevitably be dragged in, and stumble over D&D at some point. After all, they're in the business of mopping up after magical mishaps, and any faith community that wants to invite its deity round for tea is implicitly trusting in that deity's benign intent: a degree of trust that no government agency is likely to share (unless you count the Church of England as a "government agency").

Being a bureaucracy, the Laundry operates on the basis of a rule book replete with procedures for every anticipated eventuality. But—being a bureaucracy—the Laundry is ho-hum at best at dealing with the unanticipated.

Derek Reilly is the unanticipated. Aged fourteen when he is first drawn to their attention, he's over the minimum age of criminal responsibility in English law but equally clearly he's not an adult: he shouldn't be interned in an adult detention center, but in the middle of a moral panic or a terrorist alert normal rules fall by the wayside in the name of institutional convenience (as we saw with the child detainees in the terrorism detention camps at Guantanamo Bay).

Derek hadn't actually done anything wrong—but, again, being innocent is no protection against anonymous denunciations, which are particularly common during witch hunts. Dungeons and Dragons was sufficiently obscure in the UK at the start of the 1980s that most people had not heard of it, and it would inevitably take some time to evaluate it for risk potential, because board games had not hitherto been something the organization worried about, and how they handled D&D would of course set a precedent. Finally, the discovery that Derek had some aptitude for magic (of the sort with which the Laundry was legitimately concerned) was obviously problematic. Like a teenager mistakenly shipped to Guantanamo and detained at Camp Iguana, he had been exposed to dangerous people and ideas and might present a real risk if released. Better to simply ignore the problem and hope it goes away. And in due time it does indeed cease to be a problem for the people who made that decision, because they've all retired.

As for the cultists in Camp Sunshine . . .

One of the odder facets of the Satanic Panic (and similar witch hunts) is that it never seems to occur to Christian fundamentalists who believe in a shadowy underground empire of child-abusing satanic covens that the Satanism they're talking about is a Christian heresy. It's important to note that their description of these covens bears no resemblance to either the actually existing Church of Satan—which is a real, non-baby-sacrificing thing—or *The Satanic Bible,* a book written by Anton LaVey. Rather, they're seeing themselves in the mirror. Their belief system assumes an endless struggle to defeat Satan and his minions on Earth, in order to pave the way for the Second Coming of Jesus Christ: but this Manichaean dualism implicitly recognizes the Adversary as a credible threat. It acknowledges that another outcome is conceivable, for if it is impossible for Satan to triumph, why would anyone bother worshipping him? So this particular strain of fundamentalist thought implicitly privileges its own nemesis.

In writing cultists into the Laundry Files without due care and attention a couple of decades ago, I accidentally adopted this outlook. But if the role of Satanism—or Elder God cults—in the Christian imagination is to hold up a dark mirror to their own faith, how would such cults operate? The investigations kicked off by the Satanic Panic failed to discover any underground religious abuse cults, at least in our world (although child sex abuse is a very real problem). So in later Laundry Files stories, where Lovecraft's nightmares are axiomatic, I decided to depict the cultists as what you get when former Christians switch allegiance—not to Satan, but to *something* that gives the desired result when you pray to it.

There's a long tradition of nonconformist Churches and schismatic cults with variant beliefs within Christianity, even before you get into followers of other religions such as the conversos and moriscos in post-Reconquista Spain. And how better to disguise your worship of Cthulhu than by hiding it in plain sight within the churches of the dominant religion?

Thus we finally come full circle. If belief gets magical results, then if you can trick people into believing something, perhaps you can create a new god—an egregore, in western esoteric terms. The Santa-thing in "Overtime" is one such egregore, inadvertently created by the sustained belief of millions of children. Xōchipilli, a mostly forgotten Nahua god appropriated by Spanish invaders in Mesoamerica, is adapted by the cultist owners of the Omphalos Corporation and boosted into existence by adding the shared belief of many tens of thousands of role-playing gamers. And of such matters are *Bones and Nightmares* made.

ACKNOWLEDGMENTS

►◄►◄►◄►◄►◄

I'd like to thank my agent, Caitlin Blasdell, for her support and encouragement over more than two decades; and my editors Patrick and Teresa Nielsen Hayden, Jenni Hill, and Marty Halpern for their work on the Laundry Files in general and this book in particular.

ABOUT THE AUTHOR

▶◀▶◀▶◀▶◀

CHARLES STROSS (he/him) is a full-time science fiction writer and resident of Edinburgh, Scotland. He has won three Hugo Awards for Best Novella, including for the Laundry Files tale *Equoid*. His work has been translated into more than a dozen languages. His novels include the bestselling Merchant Princes series, the Laundry series (including Locus Award finalist *The Delirium Brief* and winner *The Apocalypse Codex*), and several standalones including *Glasshouse, Accelerando,* and *Saturn's Children.*

Like many writers, Stross has had a variety of careers, occupations, and job-shaped catastrophes, from pharmacist (he quit after the second police stakeout) to first code monkey on the team of a successful dot-com start-up (with brilliant timing, he tried to change employers just as the bubble burst) to technical writer and prolific journalist covering the IT industry. Along the way he collected degrees in pharmacy and computer science, making him the world's first officially qualified cyberpunk writer.